The Devil's Tree

The Hunter Series
Book One

Ali Spooner

The Devil's Tree

The Hunter Series
Book One

Ali Spooner

Affinity
eBook Press
NZ
2016

The Devil's Tree
© Ali Spooner 2016

Affinity E-Book Press NZ LTD
Canterbury, New Zealand

1st Edition

ISBN: 978-0-908351-42-8

Editor: Ruth Stanley
Proof Editor: Alexis Smith
Cover Design: Irish Dragon Designs

Acknowledgments

I would like to thank my fans for following my stories, providing great feedback and encouragement. Writing wouldn't be so much fun without you. Thanks to Affinity, Irish Dragon for the cover art, and the team of editors, readers, and publishers who continue to help me grow as a writer.

Dedication

Rhonda, thanks for your patience and faith in me.

Table of Contents

Also by Ali Spooner

Line of Sight
The Settlement
Terminal Event
Love's Playlist
Cowgirl Up
Twisted Lives
The Epitaph
Bailey's Run
Sugarland
Bayou Justice

Prologue

Droplets fell soundlessly to the ground, tainting the once pristine snow, turning it to a deep red as pools began to form. The heat from the droplets sent splashes of steam into the air as it soaked into the frigid ground. The young were-child looked up from the pooling blood at the tree and cocked her head as a bloody handprint glowed on the trunk of the tree.

Devin bolted upright in her bed, the remnants of the dream fleeing away quickly, but the bright red glowing handprint remained fixed in her vision. She knew that tree and the legend of what had just occurred in the dream. With a restless spirit, she lay back on the bed to attempt to recapture sleep.

†

Deep in the forest south of Baton Rouge, a woman with wild blond hair stood before a large man.

"Are you sure there is no other way, Cedra?" he implored.

"Not if you want your own pack," she sneered. "Your father is too powerful for you to challenge, and you're too impatient to wait for his retirement and the planned succession to his position as Alpha of the Monroe pack."

"Yes, that will be many years before that happens," he admitted.

"Then we have no other choice than to proceed with the plan."

"It just seems so dishonorable to do it this way," he pleaded.

Exasperated with the man, she placed her hands on her hips. "Laurent, do you want to be the Alpha of the Baton Rouge pack or not?"

"Yes, you know I do."

"Then be quiet and stand back while I begin," she warned and spun away from him and the small group behind him.

Cedra grinned as she approached the tree. She had Laurent exactly where she wanted him, safely tucked under her thumb. He would do anything she asked of him. Ironically, she hadn't needed her magic to induce this behavior from him. She had seduced him months ago, and he willingly complied to her every whim.

She had dreamed of this day for years, when she would advance to a position of power among the were-folk. The profitable businesses of the Baton Rouge pack would provide her riches she had only begun to comprehend. She took a knife from beneath her belt and sliced open her palm, and as her blood began to flow, she began reciting the spell. She stopped in front of the gnarled tree, feeling the power well deep within the trunk as she lifted her bloodied hand out toward the bark.

A swirling wind arose as her hand touched the weathered bark, and Cedra moved closer to the tree, drawn by a current of power. She tossed her head back, reveling in the power surging into her.

When the power of the tree released her, she stepped back and turned toward her audience, the newly achieved power glowing in her eyes. "It is time," she said, and her voice echoed in the clearing.

Chapter One

Two years later…

The night was beautiful for a run. The full moon reflected on the slow-moving water of the bayou as Devin ran through the night with her parents, Darwin and Darla, the Alpha leaders of the Baton Rouge pack. A soft breeze drifted through the air bringing the scents of the bayou to her nose as they ran down a familiar path. She could also smell a storm gathering in the distance, which would move in soon to refresh the bayou and replenish the life that depended on the rainfall. The clouds racing in front of the moon were pregnant with the promise of rain.

Her father guided Devin through the forest and her mother ran behind her, placing her in a safety zone of protection. She looked forward to this monthly treat of spending time with her parents away from the rigors and pressure of leading a pack. She cherished every moment of their time together.

Their path brought them to a crossroad that was marked with an ancient oak tree, its gnarled branches looking like arms reaching upward in the night sky.

The sight of the tree always made Devin's heart race faster. She increased her speed as she approached the tree, eager to race past the wicked monument and flee the dreadful energy that emanated from its core. However tonight, as they approached, she felt her father's speed drop to a trot and then he came to a halt, his teeth bared as he scented an evil presence. Devin watched in confusion as her mother pushed by her and joined him at the base of the tree. Together they stared at the bloody handprint that burned a crimson red against the dark bark of the tree. She knew then that someone had recently made a pact with the devil, the afterglow of the dark energy still vibrating through the trunk.

Her mind raced back to the story her parents had shared with her when she was still just a pup. The tree she was standing in front of was known as the Devil's Tree, a place where humans and other creatures made a pact with the devil. When they placed a bloodied hand on the tree, the bark coated with blood sealed their fiendish bargain.

She watched as her father looked at her mother, their amber eyes glowing. Devin felt a thought pass between them. This was a bad omen and they would cut their run short to return to the pack then come back with others to investigate the evil that had invaded the bayou. Devin witnessed the brilliant glow of her parents' amber eyes and knew they were afraid of the encounter at hand.

†

Darwin turned them to make their run back to the compound, and once more stopped in his tracks. He realized an unknown group was stalking them, and felt the imminent danger for his family. He lifted his nose to the air to scent the strangers as the skies opened up and large raindrops began to fall to the earth.

Darwin, known outside the pack as the Dark One, turned to his mate. "This is bad," he projected to her. "Take Devin and go," he commanded. There were members of his pack who dared to defy his orders, but his mate refused to leave his side.

"I will not abandon you," she answered. "We have always lived and fought side by side and that hasn't changed." She turned to Devin. "Run with the wind, Devin, and bring back help."

Devin took off at a full run.

"The rain will hopefully disguise her scent," Darwin said to his mate as a woman and a pack of six wolves stepped out of a clearing to face them. "At least she will survive."

Darwin grimaced as he watched one of the wolves peel off from the main group to pursue Devin as the remainder of the group advanced. "Run faster, Devin, you are being chased," he projected and then a strange burst of energy surrounded the clearing, locking the combatants inside and cutting off all chance of escape and further communications.

"Magic," Darwin snarled as he realized what the strange energy was. There had not been any active local witches in his lifetime, but he recognized the woman too late for him and his mate to flee.

†

Devin ran faster than she ever had, spurred on by fear as she heard the clash of conflict raging behind her. She feared for her parents and the encounter that had brought danger upon them and the pack.

As she ran away from the clearing, Devin caught the scent of the other werewolves and something even stranger that she did not recognize. She received her father's warning and called on the last burst of speed she could muster. She called out to her brother as she ran, hoping he would be in range to sense her distress and bring assistance to her parents. She ran with the speed of the wind as she heard a much larger wolf crashing through the forest behind her.

†

"Well, isn't this a nice surprise, Dark One," the woman said with a sneer.

"I wouldn't have chosen the word nice," he snarled as he watched the remaining wolves begin to fan out to prepare for an attack. "Have we met?"

"No, but the pleasure is all mine. My name is Cedra of Monroe." She smiled at Darwin. "Lucas, the Alpha of the Monroe pack, has told me much about you," she said. "How you have become such a strong leader and how your pack has grown. He even suggested it would make a nice pack for his oldest son to take over," she taunted.

"Over my dead body," he snarled.

"We figured you would say that," she said and motioned for the wolves to attack.

†

Darwin was an intense fighter, as was his mate, but the magic the witch cast sucked the energy from their bodies and fed it to the attacking wolves. They had managed to kill two of the attackers when Darwin heard Darla cry out in pain. One look over his shoulder and he knew she had taken a fatal blow as a large black wolf ripped a gaping hole in her throat. His momentary lack of focus allowed the two remaining wolves to gain advantage over him and he faltered to the ground. A broken left shoulder prevented him from regaining his feet and he awaited the delivery of the killing blow.

"You can give up now." The witch had a high-pitched laugh.

Darwin looked over at his dead mate. "Go to hell," he said as the black wolf lunged for his throat.

"I've already been there," the witch yelled as her maniacal laughter filled the air.

✝

The energy force left the clearing, opening the line of communication to Devin for one brief moment. "Cedra from Monroe," filled her head in her father's voice and then a deathly silence returned.

Devin was less than a quarter of a mile from the compound when she heard the other wolf gaining on her. She had sent out several distress calls to Damien, her brother, crying out for help but had gotten no response. Devin made the decision to turn and fight when a large black figure sailed over her head and crashed into her assailant.

Several other members of the pack arrived and Devin cried out, "The Devil's Tree," and they fled to assist her parents.

✝

Damien easily killed the smaller, less skilled wolf and returned to his sister. "Are you okay?"

"Yes," Devin said. "Go help Mother and Father."

One of the pack females stayed with Devin as Damien rushed after the pack.

"I need to go back and help." Devin began to leave.

"No, Damien and the rest will handle the situation. We need to get you home."

The beta female insisted she return with her and Devin had no choice but to follow her instruction, though her heart yearned to return to the clearing. Devin hung her head as she followed the wolf back to the compound and then changed back to human form.

She heard a mournful howl come from the direction of the clearing and the beta held her by the shoulders to prevent Devin from reentering the bayou. She collapsed into a chair by a bonfire the others had been sharing and burst into tears, fully comprehending the fate of her parents.

✝

The first of the pack arrived to find Darwin and his mate Darla lying side by side in death, their blood mixing together with the rain to form a large pool. They had transformed back to human form prior to their deaths and the injuries that caused their deaths were apparent for all to see. Both of their leaders had their throats ripped open. The trail of blood showed Darwin had managed to crawl to his mate and collapse next to her as they made their journey together into death.

By the time Damien skidded to a halt at his parents' bodies, the pack was full of snarls and hatred. He lifted his muzzle to the air and caught a faint scent. "Track them," he said to the members of his pack. "I will tend to my parents."

9

One other wolf stayed behind with Damien as the rest barreled after the murderous lot that had killed his parents. Two of the attackers were killed, their bodies left behind as the others left in a great hurry. Damien walked over to one of the bodies and searched it for any signs of identification. As he expected, there was no information to identify the location or identity of the attackers. He fully expected them to be an assassination squad from a competing pack.

He too scented the strange smell still lingering in the clearing and he looked at the other wolf in surprise.

"Magic," he growled. Damien nodded his head.

Several more members of the pack arrived to help move the bodies back to the compound. When they arrived, Damien rushed over to Devin and placed a protective arm around his younger sister. "Are you okay? Any injuries?" he asked.

"No, I'm okay. They're dead aren't they?"

"Yes, I'm afraid so. Can you tell me what happened?"

Devin told Damien and the others what they had seen at the tree. She also told him the last projection her father had sent her.

"Cedra of Monroe," he repeated, "I wonder who she could be?"

"I don't know, Damien, but I smelled something other than Were at the clearing, something strange I've never smelled before."

"It was magic," he said. "I think our parents were attacked by an assassination squad and a witch."

"A witch?" Devin asked, still in shock.

"Yes, there hasn't been one of those in the swamps for years, but I'd bet that's who Cedra is." He looked at his little sister with absolute love in his eyes. "Will you be okay with Tara for a while? I need to get the pack set on alert for a possible invasion."

"Yes, brother, go do what you need to protect the pack."

Devin allowed Tara, her sister-in-law, to take her by the hand and walk her back to her parents' home. Devin's body shook with tears and the knowledge that she would never again see her parents alive. She collapsed on the couch as Tara attempted to console her to no avail.

†

The pack members that had pursued the attackers returned to the compound and located Damien. A man near his age approached him. "We caught up with the attackers and killed the remaining three wolves, but the witch escaped. I recognized one of them from the pack in Monroe."

"So it was her magic I smelled at the scene?"

"Yes. When we finally caught up with them, she cast a spell to enclose us inside a shield with her wolves to allow herself to escape with one other wolf. The shield failed only after we killed the last of the wolves."

"Thank you and the team for your efforts. Do you think we should prepare for a potential attack?"

"We should be on alert. The pack from Monroe may sense we are caught off guard by the death of your parents and weakened."

"I'm sure they will have some form of challenge for us, if not outright war," Damien said. "I would think too many lives would be lost in war, so the smart move would be to challenge for the Alpha role."

"You would make our best Alpha, Damien, and you've trained long and hard with your father for years."

"Thanks for your vote of confidence, Jonathon, but I have to uphold the honor of a challenge if there are others who wish to lead."

"It's a shame the council won't take measures against the Monroe pack for the murder of your parents."

"If we had irrefutable evidence against them, they would. None of the wolves had any identification on them so we can't prove what pack they were from."

"Still we know it," he said.

Damien looked at his friend. "Yes, we do, and we will have our revenge." His amber eyes glowing in the moonlight. "But, we will make our plan and execute it properly and not fly off the handle."

"That is a wise decision," Jonathon said. "We have an eternity to exact revenge."

"Have the pack set up a perimeter and change shifts every four hours to keep everyone alert. I'll go check on Devin and return for my shift."

"You leave the detail to us. You need your rest, especially if you will be challenged for the Alpha position."

Reluctantly, Damien agreed with his friend's assessment. "Let me know if anything happens tonight then." He left the small group.

†

The sentry left on duty sent word to Damien just after sunrise the next morning that there was a small contingent of Weres approaching the compound.

Damien and several of the local council met the group on the border of the compound. The leader carried a white handkerchief displaying the sign of peace as he approached. Damien recognized them as the Monroe pack.

"Ballsy motherfuckers," one of Damien's men growled.

"Yeah they are."

As the small group approached, Damien recognized the leader as Lucas, the Alpha from the Monroe pack. His jaw muscles clenched tightly as he watched them approach. He could feel the hair on the nape of his neck stand on end as the rage began to boil in his blood. "That's close enough," he snarled. "What do you want?"

"I am Lucas from Monroe," the man began.

"I know who you are, now tell me what it is you want."

"First and foremost, to offer my sincere condolences about the murder of your parents," he boldly stated.

"You have them murdered and then come to offer condolences?" Damien raged. "How fucking dare you?"

"I know you won't believe me, but I had nothing to do with their murders," Lucas said.

"You're right, I don't believe you, especially since your witch was accompanied by six of your pack," Damien snarled.

"My witch?" Lucas was truly confused.

"Cedra from Monroe. Are you going to deny now she wasn't working for you?"

"I have heard of her, but no, she nor any other witch works for my pack."

Damien believed the older Alpha's words, but noticed several of the younger Weres that accompanied him were fidgeting around nervously. The largest of the group was a blond-haired man, well over six feet tall, with broad shoulders and forearms that looked like bands of steel. He eyed Damien, assessing his physical appearance closely.

He wondered if the younger Weres had made an alliance with the witch in an effort to take over the Baton Rouge pack and expand their control across the state.

"I do have a request to make of you," Lucas stated.

"What would that be?"

"Your pack is without an Alpha, so I want our packs to merge," Lucas said.

Damien chuckled. "There is no way in hell that we are going to be swallowed up by your pack," he growled.

"If that is your final answer I invoke the right to challenge whoever in your pack for the right to become the new Alpha."

Damien knew pack law well and knew that Lucas was within his rights to make this request. "Consider your challenge accepted."

"My son Laurent will take on your challenger." Lucas motioned to the large blond man standing next to him.

"Be here tonight an hour after the sun goes down," Damien said. He spun on his heel and returned to the compound followed by his men. The group from Monroe stared as they walked away and then turned and disappeared into the forest.

†

"That's a big son of a bitch," Jonathon said.

"You noticed that too, huh?"

"You know what they say, the bigger they are…"

"I have a very strong suspicion that Lucas had no idea about the hit placed on my parents."

"I believed him too."

"I think Junior and some of the young pack may be up to no good," Damien said. "Lucas is probably too strongly

14

embedded for him to take over the pack, so he's decided on ours."

"I wouldn't put it past him at all."

"I swear on the ground I'm standing on, I will make him admit to the murders before I kill him tonight," Damien promised.

✝

"Are you sure a challenge is the correct thing to do right now?" Devin asked her brother.

Damien smiled at his younger sister. "I have no choice according to pack law. A challenge has been made and accepted."

"Our parents haven't even been buried yet."

"That will happen today at sunset. We will honor our parents tonight so they can move on to the next world."

"Do you know anything about this Laurent?"

"Just that he's huge."

"I worry for you Damien. You're all the family I have left." Devin was on the verge of tears.

"That's not true, you have the entire pack as family," he reminded her.

Devin smiled at him. "You know what I mean."

He flexed his muscles for her and smiled. "Have a little faith in your brother," he teased.

"I have all the faith in you I could possibly have."

Damien pulled her into a tight hug. "That's much better. Let's get some rest and then have a late lunch before the ceremony."

"Okay Damien," she said and went to her room as Tara joined Damien.

✝

15

Devin lay down on her bed and was surprised how easily she drifted off to sleep. However, her dreams were filled by the recollection of the murder of her parents, and the strange scent of magic that she feared would never be removed from her memory. When she woke with a start, she found she was soaked in sweat from the dream of running from the wolf through the forest. She could still see the burning of his red eyes as they glowed in her dreams. She walked to her bathroom for a shower to rinse the residue from her skin and then went to her closet to find something presentable to wear to the ceremony.

✝

Damien made love to Tara and then settled next to her. He was relaxed from their lovemaking, but his mind whirled with the events of the last twenty-four hours and sleep eluded him.

"You need to get some rest." Tara snuggled deeper into him.

"I'm trying." He pulled her closer and let the rhythmic sound of her breathing lull him to sleep.

When he woke, Damien heard the sounds of activity in the compound. He looked out the window to see members of the pack building a large bonfire that would serve two purposes tonight. First, it would burn as a sign of respect as Darwin and Darla were laid to rest. Then later, it would be the site of the battle for the right to become the new Alpha of the pack. There were no other challengers so it would be between Damien and Laurent. If Damien died in the battle, Laurent would take over as Alpha and the packs would merge.

16

Damien knew he could not let that happen. His pack had developed a great business and had amassed a small fortune that would be lost to them if Laurent won the fight. He and his pack had worked too hard for too many years to let anyone assume their assets. His confidence was a bit shaken by the sheer size of Laurent, but he would also be avenging his parents' murders and the rage would bolster his strength.

✝

When they disappeared back into the forest, Lucas turned to his son. "What do you know about the murders?"

Laurent knew he could not admit to his father his involvement in the deaths of the Baton Rouge alphas. "I'm as much at a loss as you are, Father," he lied.

"After this challenge we'll need to investigate who was involved and hunt down this witch that has tainted our name," he growled.

Laurent hid a smile. He knew that Cedra was long gone after fulfilling her part of the bargain last night. He had paid dearly for her services, but after he won the challenge, the price would be well worth the cost. He rested his head against a large oak and dreamed of the young, soon-to-be Alpha female, Devin, who he would take as his mate once he won the challenge. She was young, but he was certain she would grow to love him, besides, after tonight she would be an orphan, all alone.

17

Chapter Two

Damien escorted Devin and Tara to the bonfire when it was time for the service for their parents. The fire burned with a rage as one of the pack elders spoke briefly. The pack followed in procession as the men carried the coffins to the small cemetery for interment. Devin reached up to hold Damien's hand as they watched the coffins lifted into the crypt, the seals bolted to secure the door. Damien would go into Baton Rouge and purchase a plate to place on the outer surface of the crypt to memorialize their passing. First, he must prove his worth to lead his pack as an Alpha by defeating the challenger from Monroe. His thoughts remained heavy as he walked with Tara and Devin back to the compound. They returned to the bonfire and listened to the pack singing a song of passing to honor their parents.

Devin sat next to Damien at the bonfire as they awaited the arrival of the group from Monroe. He remained quiet while he prepared his mind for the battle ahead. Darwin had been the Alpha for as long as he and Devin were alive, so they had never witnessed a challenge for the role of Alpha.

†

Jonathon and one of the pack elders approached Damien. The elder, whom Devin knew as Thomas, knelt in front of Damien. "You know you do not have to meet this challenge tonight. You have the right to mourn your parents' death, if you so choose," he suggested.

Damien looked up to the elder, his rage burning in his golden eyes. "Waiting won't bring them back."

"No it won't, but are you mentally prepared for this challenge? Have you taken into consideration your sister will be orphaned if you lose the challenge?"

Damien's eyes flickered over to Devin. She was in her mid-teens, but he knew she was not prepared to challenge the world on her own yet. His gaze turned back to the elder. "I have even more to prove to her. I need to show her that I am strong enough to guide her to adulthood."

"Very well." The elder had a pleased expression on his face. "The challenger is waiting at the edge of the woods. When you are ready, I will signal them to approach."

"I'm ready." He stood to face Devin. "I love you, baby sister."

"I love you too, Damien. Make our parents proud."

"I will." He kissed Tara before he stepped to the edge of the bonfire.

†

The elder gave the signal to the small group from Monroe to enter the compound, and hundreds of amber eyes locked on them as they approached. Laurent separated from the group and approached the elder.

The elder spoke in a strong voice. "Laurent from Monroe challenges Damien Benoit for the role of Alpha of the Baton Rouge pack." He paused as he looked around the crowd. "The challenge will be won when one of the combatants is dead or submits defeat to the other challenger. Are there any questions?"

Damien shook his head no, as did Laurent.

"Very well then, the challenge may begin."

The air quivered as the two men transformed into their wolf forms and began to slowly circle, gauging the other's strength and quickness. Laurent, the golden wolf, was slightly larger than Damien's dark wolf.

Laurent obviously felt he could use his size to an advantage as he made the first move and rushed Damien.

Damien easily moved away from Laurent's attack and used his quickness to sink his teeth into his opponent's left shoulder, drawing first blood as he felt the bones crunch between his powerful jaws. Laurent howled his rage as Damien shredded the muscles in his shoulder. He would heal from the wound, but since it was made from another Were, it would heal much slower than if he had taken a wound from a human.

Damien shook his head as the salty sweet taste of the wolf's blood flooded his senses and his rage poured through him, energizing his body. He feigned several moves, forcing Laurent to move painfully away on his injured shoulder. They circled each other slowly, snarls and guttural growls filling the night as saliva dripped from the muzzles of the combatants. Laurent shifted too much of his weight on his back legs leaving him off balance. Damien saw the weakness and aggressively attacked, driving his opponent to the ground where they rolled in a giant mass of fur and fury. The two wolves struggled for what seemed an eternity to Devin. Neither was able to establish control over the other until a stumble allowed Damien to grip his opponent's neck between his powerful jaws, ripping open a gash in Laurent's throat, but not a killing blow. His teeth wrapped tightly around Laurent's throat, Damien felt his challenger changing back to human form. Laurent was in a position of defeat and if he wished to save his life, he had to submit to Damien's dominance by changing forms and immediately admitting defeat.

Damien changed back to human form, his hand wrapped tightly around Laurent's throat ready to crush his windpipe at a moment's notice. He used the advantage of his weight and position, leaning forward to place more pressure on Laurent's throat, stopping six inches away from his face as his eyes glared his rage at Laurent.

"Tell your father what you did," Damien demanded.

Laurent shook his head.

"I will rip the rest of your throat out if you refuse," he warned.

Laurent's eyes grew wide as he considered his options. Death during a challenge would be honorable, unlike admitting to his father what he had done and then living out his life as a traitor to his pack. "Kill me," he growled.

"That would be letting you off too easily. Tell him," he roared.

Lucas stepped forward to look down upon his defeated son. "Tell me what?"

Laurent saw the shame in his father's gaze at his defeat. Not raised to lose at anything, Laurent knew if he remained alive, he would always be a failure to his father. "No," he growled and then twisted in Damien's grasp and crushing his windpipe to ensure his death.

Damien released his grasp on Laurent's throat as Lucas rushed forward and knelt next to his son. Blood filled Laurent's lungs and Lucas was forced to watch him drown, unable to do anything to save his son. When Laurent's eyes closed in death, Damien stood over his challenger.

Lucas looked up to him. "What was it you wanted him to tell me?"

Damien's eyes still glowed with rage as he looked down at Lucas. "That he and several of your pack were the ones who bargained with the witch to have my parents murdered."

"What are you talking about?"

"Laurent bargained with the witch to kill my parents thinking he could take over our pack," he explained. "We killed the rest of the group that helped him ambush my parents."

Lucas's face contorted with the horror of his son's dishonorable behavior. "I'm sorry for my son's stupidity." Lucas stood. He turned to the members of his pack and motioned to his son's body. "Take him away," he ordered and turned to face Damien.

"Your father was an honorable man and your mother a good woman. I am truly sorry for the involvement of my family and my pack in their deaths." He reached out with his hand, his head bowed in sorrow. "Good fortune to you and your pack. We will bother you no more."

"Good fortune to you." Damien shook the offered hand.

Four members of Lucas's pack approached and carried Laurent's corpse into the forest. Lucas turned to follow as the wolves of Damien's pack lifted their voices to the night to honor their new Alpha.

A short while later the pack joined Damien in the lodge to celebrate his victory and the passing of Darwin and Darla. Food and drink were plenty as the pack reveled deep into the night.

Chapter Three

For the next eight years, Devin lived with Tara and Damien in the Alpha house, where she watched her nieces and nephews as they grew. Under his leadership, the pack continued to grow and flourish, but Devin found she was becoming increasingly restless living in the compound until one day she finally approached Damien.

"I feel like something is missing from my life, brother."

"Could it be a mate?" he teased. "I know Jonathon and several other young males who would love to take you for a companion"

"I have no interest in any of them," Devin admitted. "They are all fine men, but none of them brings the slightest spark of desire to me."

"What do you wish to do, little sister?"

"I wish your blessing to leave the compound," Devin said. "I have to find what it is my soul is seeking."

Damien looked into his sister's eyes and saw the longing and sincerity in them. He could sense her loneliness. "You realize how dangerous it will be as a rogue with no pack for protection?"

"Yes, Damien, I have considered that, but I feel I am withering here."

"Where do you wish to go?"

"I thought I would start my search in New Orleans."

"I have a contact with the pack down there and its close enough for you to come home if you need to," he said. "When do you wish to leave?"

"I will take my leave tomorrow, if I have your blessing."

Damien smiled at his only sibling. "No matter how much I hate to see you leave, I cannot deny my baby sister anything."

"Thank you, Damien. I may be back in a week, but my heart is yearning for something I have not found here amongst the pack."

"You will always be welcomed with open arms, but I must insist you break the news to my children. They absolutely adore their aunt and will miss you greatly, as will I."

"I will tell them tonight at dinner."

"I will withdraw some cash from the account for you."

Devin attempted to interrupt, but Damien insisted. "You will need some start-up money wherever you end up. I will not see my baby sister living in some flophouse or out on the streets."

She knew it was pointless to argue with her brother and her Alpha. "Very well, Damien." She left to pack a small bag of essential belongings. Devin's prize possession was her Harley Davidson Fat Boy; its only drawback was the lack of space for carrying items. She would be limited to her saddlebags and a small duffel, so she made her selections carefully. Devin would shop for other items once she decided where she would live; until then she would travel light.

†

Later that evening, eight-year-old Elizabeth took the news the hardest and fled the dinner table in tears when Devin broke the news. The relationship they had shared was special and always would be. She was the firstborn and had stolen Devin's heart on that day. It broke her heart to leave Elizabeth and the others behind, but she could no longer deny the aching of her soul.

Elizabeth's reaction caused Devin to lose what little appetite she had left and she pushed back from the table to follow the young pup up the stairs. When she reached the door to the bedroom Elizabeth shared with her two younger sisters, Devin knocked softly. She did not hear an answer so she slowly opened the door. Elizabeth was facedown on her bed, her body quaking with the tears she was shedding. Devin approached and sat down on the edge on her bed.

Devin placed a hand on the young girl's shoulder. "Elizabeth Benoit, you need to sit up and talk to me," she said in her most stern voice.

"Why, why do you have to go now?" Elizabeth brushed her bangs out of her swollen eyes.

"I wish I knew how to explain it to you, heck I wish I understood it myself, but my heart is being drawn away from the pack."

"Are you not happy with us?" the young child asked between shudders.

"Since the day you were born, you have made me happy and proud," Devin said. "There is something missing in my life and I have realized I won't find it here. I won't be gone forever." She made the promise even though she knew not what lay ahead for her future.

"Will I be able to call you and come to visit?"

"You can call anytime your parents say it is okay, and once I get settled where I am going, we can discuss a visit." Devin placed a large hand under Elizabeth's chin and lifted her face to look into her amber eyes. "There is one thing you can do for me."

"What is it, Devin?"

"You can move into my room and keep it clean for me."

"Really Devin?" she squealed.

Devin knew Elizabeth longed to have a room of her own, and as the firstborn, she should have some privacy. "If it is okay with your father, I would really appreciate your help."

"I promise to keep it clean and keep your things in order for when you return," Elizabeth vowed.

Devin couldn't help but chuckle at the instant change of emotion. "Thank you, Lizard," she teased; using the nickname she had given her niece when she was still an infant.

Elizabeth crawled into Devin's lap and wrapped her arms around her neck. "I am really going to miss you." Tears threatened to fall again.

"I will miss you too, but this is something I have to do for me. Can you understand that?"

"I think so." Elizabeth was struggling with her torn emotions.

"You will have to step up and help your mom out with your brothers and sisters now."

"I will, Devin. I will make you proud of me."

"I already am, but someone will have to read bedtime stories to little Lily and teach baby Edward how to walk."

"I can do that." Elizabeth sat up straighter in Devin's lap.

"Now, I do believe your mom has made strawberry shortcake for dessert. I don't know about you, but I would hate to miss out on it."

"Let's go then." Elizabeth stood and took Devin's hand, leading her back down to the dinner table just as Tara brought out the sumptuous dessert.

†

The next morning, just before sunrise, Devin walked out to the garage hoping to slip away as quietly as she could.

"I thought you might try to sneak out before sunrise," a deep voice said.

Devin turned toward the sound and found her brother leaning against a black Hummer. "I didn't want to wake up the kids."

"Well, don't think you are getting away without giving your big brother a hug."

She dropped her bag and walked over to Damien. Devin wrapped her arms around her brother. "I wouldn't think of it," she whispered as he pulled her close.

"Good, I have no desire to track your ass all the way to New Orleans."

"You make it sound like it's across the planet."

"Planet no, but it is a much different world than here. You can't trust everyone you meet like you can here at the compound."

"I promise I will be careful," she said as she pulled away.

Damien reached into his back pocket, pulled out an envelope, and handed it to her. "Here's some start-up money, and I have already tucked a cell phone and charger into your saddlebags. I programmed my numbers in for you in case you forget where you're from," he teased.

"I will never forget," she answered. "Thanks for all your support."

"There is something else I need to give you before you go." He opened a small box. "I just got this yesterday and it seems fate is taking a twisted turn." Damien reached inside the box and pulled out a gold chain with a round charm attached to it. "This box was delivered from Lucas yesterday morning with a letter."

"Lucas from Monroe?"

"Yes, it seems his clan has been tracking Cedra the witch, who was in league with his son in the murder of our parents."

"Were they able to kill the bitch?"

"No, they were not that successful. Her magic prevented them from killing her, but they were able to get something very valuable from her."

"What would that be?"

"This." Damien lifted the amulet in front of her eyes.

Devin's eyes came to rest on the moon-shaped amulet that dangled from the end of a gold chain. She reached for it and found it filled with black liquid.

"His pack bled the witch and escaped with several pints of her blood. One of his pack members used the vile liquid to create protection amulets and a protective barrier along the borders of their compound."

"What does this mean and why did he send them to you?"

"According to his letter, anyone wearing this amulet is protected from the witch's magic. He sent six for my family as an apology for the murders of our parents. I want you to promise you will never take it off," he said as he secured the chain around her neck.

Devin felt the warmth of the amulet against her skin as its protection activated. "Will you and Tara wear these as well?"

"Yes, and the kids," Damien answered.

"Then I will wear mine." Devin tucked the amulet beneath her shirt.

"I don't know the exact extent of its powers, but I feel confident that Lucas would not lead us astray."

"Doesn't it seem strange to you that after all these years, these arrive now?"

Damien chuckled softly. "Like I said, fate is taking a few strange twists. I wouldn't be surprised if our parents knew you were about to leave the safety of the compound."

"I hope one day I will cross paths with the witch and I can claim revenge for our parents," Devin said, catching her brother off guard.

"Please don't do anything foolish, baby sister. If you get information on Cedra let me know, the pack will take care of that nasty business."

She nodded her agreement and stepped forward to hug Damien one last time.

He hugged her close and when he released her, he looked deep into her eyes.

"You need to find whatever is tugging at your heart. I know if I were in your shoes, I'd want to do the same. Just come home as soon as you can and give me a call to let me know how things are going for you."

"I will call you once a week and once I get settled somewhere I will give you an address."

"The name and contact information for the New Orleans pack is also in the phone and envelope. Be sure to check in with them so they know you are a friendly in their territory."

Devin tucked the envelope inside the deep interior pocket of her jacket and climbed onto her bike. "I will give them a call today or tomorrow."

Damien handed Devin her helmet. "Stay safe, baby sister."

Devin looked up to find tears welling in Damien's eyes and felt hers growing wet. "I love you, Damien."

"I love you too, Devin. I will tell the kids goodbye for you, but don't forget to call soon."

"I won't." Devin placed the helmet on her head.

"I'll get the door for you," Damien said as she turned on the ignition and started the bike.

Devin traveled quickly down the drive before she could stop and change her mind.

The sun was just cresting over the bayou as she pulled onto a state road and headed south toward New Orleans.

Damien had taken her to New Orleans once to see a Mardi Gras parade. Devin remembered how she had pulsated with the buzz of vibrant life that seeped into her pores as she watched the masked participants dance through the streets. She had no idea if she would stay in New Orleans, but she would begin her search there.

She drove at a leisurely pace, enjoying the views of the bayous that she crossed, inhaling the fresh, clean air of the country. She was certain the air in New Orleans would not be so pure so she filled her lungs with its sweetness. She took a route that paralleled the Big Muddy and watched the early morning river traffic flowing slowly south. Tankers and barges passed in the deeper sections of the river creating small wakes as the heavy-laden ships cruised within feet of one another.

When Devin made a turn and the shining white exterior of the Superdome came into view she pulled her bike off the side of the road. This was really it. She was out on her own for the first time in her life, which both excited and terrified her. She took a moment to look across the sprawling city, one she may soon call home. A blast from one of the southbound barges brought her back to reality and she climbed back onto the bike and rode into New Orleans.

Damien had suggested she find a hotel in Kenner, which was close enough to New Orleans but far enough away to be relatively safe for a single female. When she reached Interstate 10 and saw the exit to Kenner, she took the turnoff and began looking for hotels. She quickly found what she was looking for, and despite the early morning hour, she checked in. She dumped her pack in the room and then walked back to her bike intent on exploring New Orleans in the daylight.

Her stomach reminded her that it was empty so her first stop was Café Du Monde for coffee and beignets. While she ingested the sugarcoated pastries, she surveyed the crowd of tourists and all-night revelers stumbling in for strong coffee and a sweet breakfast treat. She sipped her coffee and watched the local artists flock to Jackson Square to set up their wares in hopes of good sales to the tourists who wanted to take a piece of N'awlins home with them.

Devin left her bike parked at the Square and walked down to the French Market to stroll through the aisles. She bought a few pieces of fresh fruit and walked back to her bike, tucking them into her saddlebags. Climbing on to her bike, she merged into the slow-moving traffic to resume her tour of New Orleans. The odor of urine and stale beer let her know she had reached the Bourbon Street district. The street cleaners had not made it through yet that morning and the smell grew stronger with each climbing degree of heat. Not a pleasant aroma for someone who had a heightened sense of smell. Devin dodged drunks and early tourists in the street as she sought fresh air. When she found herself in the Garden District, she slowed her pace and marveled at the large antebellum homes with meticulously kept lawns that lined the streets. She drove by the zoo and then back into town to cross over the river and explore southward. She drove through small towns and bayous until she reached Houma where she stopped for lunch.

Devin found a small diner and ordered a shrimp po'boy with fries. The server kept her tea glass filled to the brim and entertained Devin with her endless chatter. Even the language seemed strange here and she found herself chuckling at some of the words and phrases the server hurled at her.

By midafternoon, she decided to return to her hotel for a nap and a shower before she hit the town to explore some of the nightlife of New Orleans. Devin parked her bike and dropped the thermostat to its lowest setting as she shucked her riding clothes and climbed into bed.

Chapter Four

Devin was drawn to a dimly lit bar by the driving beat of the music, or so she thought. The minute she walked through the door she scented her. The warm smell of cinnamon and apples stirred her blood as she sought out the owner of the scent. Her eyes wandered to the DJ booth where a young woman in her early twenties cranked out the tunes. Her shoulder-length light brown hair held a slight curl and her blue eyes twinkled in the dim lighting.

Devin paid the entrance fee to a large bouncer sitting at the door. The man sneered at her as she stamped her hand. She smiled at him then turned back to the club her eyes never leaving the DJ.

She walked over and took a seat at the end of the bar where she could observe the woman and watch the dancers working up a sweat on the dance floor. "What can I get you?" the lovely bartender asked.

"Do you have Single Barrel Jack?"

"I sure do. You are a woman of good taste."

It took all of her restraint to keep from saying, "and one that tastes good too," but Devin swallowed back her smart-assed response. "With Coke please," she added.

"Coming right up then, love." The bartender winked at her.

Devin felt a large paw plop down on her shoulder and a gravelly voice say, "We don't like your kind here."

"And what kind would that be?" she asked without moving. Devin could feel her amber eyes beginning to glow and her gums ached as her canines wanted to extend and tear out the man's throat.

"You leather dyke bitches," he snarled.

Dressed in her best leather pants, tight black T-shirt and leather vest Devin thought she looked rather presentable. She had even polished the black engineer boots she wore, for Christ sakes.

The bartender placed the drink in front of her and waited to see how Devin would respond to the man's aggression.

"If you plan on using that hand the next time you jack off, I suggest you move it now and go on your way. I'm thirsty and I plan to throw back a few."

Devin could see the heat rising to his cheeks as the customers within earshot had heard her comment and laughed.

"Not in this bar," he said.

She spun around on the barstool so quickly the room seemed to spin and stood to her six-foot height. He gave her a once-over and grinned then drew back his fist to throw a punch. Devin caught his fisted hand a good foot from her face and stopped his forward motion completely. She used his energy to drive him to his knees. She felt the bones in his hand grind together and begin to shatter as he cried out in pain.

"Let me go, you bitch," he growled.

She squeezed his fist tighter. "You do not have permission to call me that."

"I'd suggest you change your tune quickly, George," the bartender said. "The lady appears to be a bit more than you can handle."

George looked up at her glowing amber eyes and his eyes widened in fear. "I'm sorry for insulting you. Will you please let me go now?" he begged.

"Since you asked so nicely," Devin let go of his fist. He fell to the floor cradling his broken hand.

"You broke my fucking hand," he whined.

"I asked you to leave me be, but you insisted," she reminded him.

"Yeah, you did." He made it to his knees and two customers that she assumed were regulars helped him to his feet.

"You need to go get that hand tended to, George," the bartender said as he stalked toward the door and entered the night.

"I'm sorry about George, he gets a little possessive at times, but he's been a good bouncer." The bartender turned back to Devin.

"Ya think?" Devin shot back a smart-assed comment. "Nothing I'm not used to. Egomaniacs see my size and decide they have to prove themselves better than me all the time."

"Any of them ever win?"

"Not yet." With an impish grin, she reached for the drink as she slid a ten across the bar.

"That one's on me," the bartender said. "My name is Kaitlin and this is my place."

"I'm Devin and it's a pleasure to meet you, ma'am. Sorry for hurting your employee."

Kaitlin chuckled from behind the bar and Devin cocked her head with curiosity. "What's so funny?"

"Devin, only one letter off from the devil."

"No resemblance though, I'm much better looking than he is."

"Aye, and the arrogance to go with it."

"Not really," Devin said. "I'm confident, but generally not a cocky person, except when I need to be."

"You sure put a hurting on George. He has been the best bouncer I've had in quite some time."

"So there's a vacancy?"

"Well, I do believe I heard the bones in his hand breaking, so he won't be much good with his hand in a cast for several weeks."

"Sorry to put you in a bind." Devin took a sip of the drink. The cool liquid burned like fire down her throat, but she knew there wasn't enough liquor in the building to give her a buzz. Her increased metabolism burned through alcohol like gas to a flame but my word, did the Jack have a smooth taste.

"Do you pay a decent wage?"

"I think I'm pretty fair with the staff. Why, you interested?"

"I might be. I just hit town and need a job and a place to live."

Kaitlin eyed her closely. The woman could be pure trouble, but she sure handled a much larger man in George, and she was sure she could have done much more damage if she had desired. She thought about the small apartment

35

attached to her house. It had been vacant for several months and would need a good cleaning, but it was available.

Devin sensed the woman sizing her up as she sipped her drink. Soon she would make an offer too good to refuse she thought as she glanced across the dance floor.

"I have a small apartment attached to my house that has been vacant for several months. It needs a good cleaning and maybe some fixing up. Parking is a bitch too," she added. "If you're interested, I could do free rent and two fifty a week. Free drinks, but not Single Barrel."

I could drink her into the poor house with the expensive liquor. Devin grinned.

"What would the rent be when George makes it back?"

Kaitlin returned her smile. "We'll see when that time comes."

"You have yourself a deal." Devin offered her a handshake. "Do I need to start tonight?"

"Why don't you stick around for a bit and survey the crowd. They seem to be pretty tame so far."

"Yes, boss." Devin smirked. "If anything gets heated while I'm here, I will handle the situation."

Devin turned in her seat to get a better view of the crowd and the DJ booth. The young woman in the booth had her head down as she adjusted some of the equipment and when she lifted her head, she found Devin watching her. She returned Devin's smile and then turned her attention back to the music. Devin left her seat to tour the bar, surveying exits, and the restroom locations before going back to her seat at the bar.

"Nice place you have here," she said to Kaitlin who brought her a fresh drink.

"Thanks, it took some damage in Katrina but we were able to bounce back quickly."

"You have a pretty diverse crowd."

Kaitlin chuckled at her comment. "This is New Orleans, honey, we get all types in here. Mostly a heterosexual crowd, but the gay boys love the dance music and we get our share of lesbian customers too, mostly tourists."

"The local lesbians don't like to party?"

"They tend to stick primarily to the exclusively lesbian clubs."

"I see." Devin sipped her drink.

"Something tells me you aren't from here," Kaitlin said.

Devin gave her one of her warmest smiles. "No, ma'am, I'm from Baton Rouge."

"So what brings you down to N'awlins?"

"I'm searching for something."

"What?"

"I don't know what, but I think I'll know when I find it," she said.

"I wish you well with your search then." Kaitlin left to serve another customer.

Even though she could feel the air conditioner on full blast, the packed dance floor generated plenty of heat, which made the customers very thirsty. The DJ kept the tempo cranked and Kaitlin kept the alcohol flowing. Devin noticed that the server barely kept pace with the orders in the club and Kaitlin had her hands full behind the bar filling table orders and bar orders. When there was a customer at every inch of the bar and at least one behind, Devin stepped behind the bar.

"Mind if I help?"

"Not at all." Kaitlin wiped the sweat from her brow. "Everything is listed on the register and it's a pretty easy system."

"You work on the table orders then and I'll take the bar."

"Thanks." She handed the server another tray of drinks.

Devin fell into place filling beer and simple drink orders and after an hour, she learned how to mix several new drinks. She found she was actually having fun tending the bar and Kaitlin more than welcomed her help.

When they had finally caught up with the orders, Kaitlin made her a fresh drink. "Thanks for the help."

"No problem. It looks like you get a rush whenever the DJ slows the tempo for a song or two."

"You pick up on things quickly don't you?"

"Yeah, I guess I do. Have you considered adding a bartender?"

"I have, but I'm not sure I can afford another staff."

Devin nodded and considered Kaitlin's comments as they served several other customers. In the short time she had been helping Kaitlin, she had amassed a small stack of bills from tips. She picked them up and started to add them to the tip jar behind the bar.

"Hang on a second, you earned those, so keep them," Kaitlin instructed her.

Devin pocketed the tips and an idea came to mind. When the crowd rushed back to the dance floor and Kaitlin slowed for a moment, Devin approached her with an idea.

"I really feel bad about taking away George's job. I know he will probably be casted, but it doesn't look like you have many hard-to-handle customers."

"As a general rule we don't," Kaitlin agreed. "Are you turning down my job offer?"

"No, but I would like to offer a suggestion."

"I'm all ears then."

"Let George stay on the door as a bouncer and I will help you tend bar. If things get rough I will help him out."

"That's not a bad idea."

"If these tips are the norm then I would accept the apartment and a hundred dollars a week plus tips," Devin said.

"That's almost too good to be true," Kaitlin replied.

"Well, if I turn into a decent bartender I figure I can make up the difference in tips."

Kaitlin broke into laughter and Devin cocked her head at her response.

"What's so funny?"

"Once the locals get a whiff of you tending bar here I think the local lesbians may be visiting more often, and they are generally very good tippers."

"Oh." Devin's cheeks flushed.

"We open at three and close at three. The afternoons are pretty mild so you could come in around eight and work until closing if that's good for you."

The front door opened and George strolled in sporting a cast up his right wrist. He walked up to the bar and sat down in front of Kaitlin. "I guess I'm out of work for a couple of weeks."

"Actually, no, you're not. Devin has agreed to help me tend bar and help you out if anyone wants to get feisty. So, I think you owe her a sincere apology for saving your job and not breaking anything other than your hand."

George bobbed his head as he gathered his thoughts. When he looked up at Devin, he saw her watching him closely. "I am very sorry for acting like a jerk," he said. "Thanks for helping me keep my job."

"Apology accepted." Devin held out her hand.

George placed his uninjured left hand in her right. "Thanks."

"I'm really glad we will be on the same team. I don't know what I'd do if you really got angry."

"That rarely ever happens, but we could work on your approach some," she said. "I think you should do more talking to a rowdy customer to see if you can defuse the situation instead of trying to manhandle everyone."

He held up his broken hand. "I think now would be a good time to learn that lesson." He grinned and it quickly turned into a grimace.

"I think you're right." Devin chuckled and slapped him on the back.

"Go handle the door and keep your eyes open, but I think we are in for a quiet night," Kaitlin said.

George took his leave and returned to the front door post wearing a huge smile.

Kaitlin turned back to Devin. "When did you want to move in?"

"I have a hotel room booked for tonight and the next few days if needed."

"I usually get up by nine and I think if we worked together we could get the place livable by late afternoon."

"Will that give you enough rest?"

"Yeah, I don't sleep that well anymore anyhow." Kaitlin wrote down the address and her phone number.

Devin tucked the note in her pocket as a new wave of customers rushed the bar.

†

Tia kept a close eye on the dark stranger during the evening from her DJ booth. The exchange with George was impressive. She had witnessed many men who either had cowered to George's intimidation or that he had physically removed. It was something to see someone, especially a woman, give him a dose of his own medicine.

She had felt the stranger's eyes on her several times during the evening and when she looked up to find glowing golden amber eyes watching her she felt a warm rush through her veins. She knew what that rush meant, but she had promised herself that she would be not swept off her feet again by a smooth-talking stranger and especially not a woman. Tia was very open to the different lifestyles in New Orleans, but had never felt an attraction to any of the female customers that had visited their establishment—until now. She couldn't help but see how easily she had worked her way behind the bar to help Kaitlin or how she interacted so well with the customers she served. She was a powerhouse of a woman, but was quick to smile or laugh with a customer. Tia found her eyes drifting over to the bar more frequently during the night and was eager for her midnight break to come so she could meet the alluring stranger. She quickly set up a string of tracks that should keep the dance floor hopping for at least fifteen minutes and made her way toward the bar.

Tia slid onto the barstool the dark stranger had sat on earlier in the evening. She turned away from the cash register, saw her sitting at the bar, and graced her with a beautiful sexy smile. As she walked toward her, Tia suddenly, felt like she was prey and the stranger was a predator of the worst kind.

"Hello," she said as the woman approached.

"Hello to you. My name is Devin."

"I'm Tia, the DJ." She nervously pointed at her sound booth.

"Yes, I know. It's a pleasure to meet you."

Tia felt her cheeks blush with the silliness of her statement. The woman had been in the bar for hours and certainly knew she was the club's DJ. Thankfully, Kaitlin came to her rescue as she walked up and cut the silence that had enveloped them.

"Tia, I want you to meet Devin, our new bartender/bouncer and soon to be your new neighbor."

Both women's heads flashed around to look at Kaitlin. She smiled at Devin. "She rents an apartment next door to where you will be living, so that makes you neighbors." Kaitlin smiled at the two young women and felt the electricity flowing between them. "Maybe you will be a kind neighbor and come help us clean up the old place tomorrow," she suggested.

Tia tried to slow the racing of her heart. "Sure, I'd like that."

"I would welcome any help." It was Devin's turn to blush.

"Fine then, that's settled. We will meet at my place at nine for coffee and beignets then start on Devin's apartment." Kaitlin turned away.

"May I get you a drink?"

"Two fingers of Gentleman Jack." Tia was hoping the smooth drink would calm her shivering.

"May I suggest you try something else?"

"Sure, I'm game," Tia said.

Devin turned and reached for the Single Barrel, pouring half a cocktail glass. She turned back to the bar and settled the glass in front of Tia.

Tia took a tentative sip and then a longer one. She sat the glass back on the bar and asked, "That's smooth, what is it?"

"Single Barrel Jack, a step up from Gentleman Jack." Devin smiled.

"That's very good, thank you."

"My pleasure." Devin moved away to serve thirsty customers.

Tia watched her serve the rowdy customers with the ease of a seasoned server. Devin's tip jar overflowed with bills as she served each customer with a sexy smile. She had to tear her eyes away from Devin and get back to her booth. The last song in her set had just begun and would be ending shortly and she needed to keep the music rolling strong for at least another hour before the night would start to wind down.

After a moderate rush of customers, Kaitlin found Devin wiping down the bar. "It's almost one. Why don't you head out and get some rest and we will see you tomorrow at nine."

"If you don't need my help."

"I can handle it from here. Don't forget those." Kaitlin pointed to the overflowing tip jar.

"Yes, ma'am." Devin tucked the wad of bills into her pocket. She glanced toward the sound booth and when Tia looked up from her mixer, Devin smiled and nodded to her. She walked to the front door. "Goodnight George," she said and stepped into the humid New Orleans night.

Not quite ready for sleep, Devin mounted her bike and drove back toward her hotel and then beyond into the night. The cool breeze near the water blew through her hair and soothed her heated skin. The scent of Tia's soul had a fire burning through her veins and Devin felt that maybe she had found what she was looking for in Tia. She had always known she was different, but never dreamed that her mate would turn out to be female. Devin twisted the bike's grip and it kicked into a higher gear, sending her flying down a relatively empty boulevard into the night.

†

Tia shut down her equipment and wiped down her booth as George and Kaitlin cleared the bar. The cleaning service would arrive in the morning to clean the bar in preparation for the next evening's business.

She and Kaitlin said goodnight to George and then walked the short distance to their homes.

"I really liked Devin," Kaitlin said unexpectedly.

"I guess so, if you hired her and offered her a place to live in a matter of a few hours," Tia teased.

"There is something unique about her. I noticed you couldn't keep your eyes off her tonight either."

Even in the moonlight, Kaitlin could see the blush on Tia's cheeks. Tia felt them burning as she turned to her boss and friend.

"I've fallen for my fair share of bad boy biker types, but never for a female," she said, a bit perplexed. "There is something about her that I can't explain and it draws me to her, but I admit, I love the way she makes me feel when those eyes smile at me."

"Oh girl, you've done gone and gotten smitten haven't you?" Kaitlin teased as she wrapped an arm around Tia's shoulder.

"I don't even know her, Kaitlin, or even if she's the slightest bit interested in me."

"I have no doubt. The air between you crackles with electricity when you two are close."

44

Tia looked at her friend in surprise, but remained quiet the rest of the walk home as she contemplated Kaitlin's observations.

"I'll see you at nine." Tia turned to her front stoop. She watched Kaitlin walk to the house next door and then sat down on the stoop to look up at the nearly full moon. She felt her blood begin to stir in her veins as she looked up at the bright orb. Thoughts of Devin rushed into her brain. She shook off the image of her golden eyes and unlocked the door to her home.

Chapter Five

Devin woke prior to her alarm sounding and showered before dressing in jeans and a navy blue tee. She quickly repacked her duffel and checked out of the hotel after loading her bike. It was still too early to arrive at Kaitlin's so she took another ride through the Garden District and then through the Quarter. She was amazed that some of the bars never closed and there were customers stumbling out at half past eight still shitfaced from the night before. She had to dodge more than one of them as she drove through the narrow streets searching for Kaitlin's address.

†

Kaitlin was enjoying one of the few cigarettes she allowed herself each day when she heard Devin's bike approaching. Sitting on her stoop, she looked down at her watch to see that Devin was early. She had not made it downtown to get the beignets yet, so when Devin pulled up to the curb and turned off the bike, she approached her.

"I haven't had a chance to get the beignets yet."

"Hop on then and I will give you a ride," Devin suggested.

Kaitlin looked down at her cut-off jeans and flip-flops and back up to Devin.

"You're fine, just mind you don't burn your leg on the exhaust." Devin dropped off her duffel and offered her hand to assist Kaitlin onto the back of her bike.

Kaitlin settled onto the bike, her hands encircling Devin's waist as the engine roared to life. "Hold on." Devin twisted the accelerator and the bike flew down the street.

Kaitlin let out a short squeal and scooted in closer to Devin as they rounded a corner and started for Jackson Square.

Devin smiled when she felt Kaitlin press against her back. She picked up a little speed and within minutes, they had arrived at Jackson Square. Their luck held out and Devin slipped into a small parking spot.

"Sit tight, these are on me." Devin stepped off the bike.

She skipped across the street between the slow-moving traffic and got in line at Café Du Monde for the sumptuous pastries that defined New Orleans. The aroma of rich coffee filled the air as wait staff hustled to serve hungry patrons. The lines of Café Du Monde moved quickly and within ten minutes, Devin emerged wearing a smile and carrying a bag full of the hot treats.

"Those smell sinful," Kaitlin said as Devin mounted the bike. Her stomach growled in anticipation and Devin grinned at her.

"No cheating until we get home," she teased.

"Not even a little taste?"

"Nope, hang on tight and I will get us home before they get cold."

"Turn left here, it's a shortcut," Kaitlin said.

When they returned, Kaitlin pointed to a small driveway. "Park there."

Devin killed the engine and dropped the kickstand before helping Kaitlin off the bike. "Wow, it's been a long time since I've been on a bike."

"You did well."

"It's still just as big a thrill as it was years ago."

"You can ride with me anytime."

Inside the small kitchen area of Kaitlin's home, they found Tia waiting for them. She had poured three cups of coffee and handed Kaitlin a cup. "How do you like yours?" she asked Devin.

"Sugar and cream please, ma'am."

Tia dropped two sugar cubes and two teaspoons of creamer into the mug and handed it to Devin.

"I didn't know they still made sugar cubes," she said.

"This is sugar city, honey, they make sugar every way possible here."

Devin hadn't thought of it before, but she did remember seeing a sugar manufacturing plant during her ride through the city.

"This is perfect, thank you." She gave Tia a sweet smile.

Tia returned her smile. "I smell beignets."

"Let me pull out some plates," Kaitlin said as Tia ripped open the bag.

"Heaven in a paper sack." Tia picked up a pastry and took a bite.

The three of them knocked out the beignets in record time. Carrying fresh cups of coffee and a bucket of cleaning supplies, they walked outside to climb the outside staircase to the small apartment.

Kaitlin turned to hand Devin a set of keys. "You might want to go ahead and bring your bags up. This is a pretty decent neighborhood, but it's still New Orleans," Kaitlin advised.

"I will be right up then." Devin retrieved her bags from the bike and on her way back to the stairs noticed a small garage. She hoped there would be room inside to park her bike. She made a mental note to ask Kaitlin about it as she climbed the stairs. Worst-case scenario was she would have to buy a good bike cover. She cherished her bike and the thought of leaving her out in the elements was not at all appealing.

She hiked the small duffel over her shoulder, stepped onto the small landing, and walked inside. The apartment was small but had plenty of windows that let in ample light. "This is great." She set the bags on the floor.

"Let me show you around," Kaitlin said.

The tour did not take long. A decent-sized bedroom with a queen bed and ample closet space for her meager belongings, a small bathroom, and a functional kitchenette was all she would need. They returned to the small breakfast area and den.

"This will be perfect for me." Devin grinned at Kaitlin.

"I bought some new blinds for the front windows, but never made time to hang them. Why don't you start on that while Tia and I start cleaning?"

"That sounds wonderful. Where can I find some tools?" Devin asked.

"In the garage downstairs, you can also park your bike there. I have no car so there should be plenty of space for your Harley."

"Thanks. I will be right back."

Devin descended the steps and walked to the outer door of the pull-up garage door. She pulled the cord and lifted the door. Inside she found a sexy, sleek black and red Ninja street bike. Surely, this couldn't be Kaitlin's. Was there a man or an ex in her life, she wondered? She walked over to the tool chest against the wall and opened drawers to find every tool she could possibly need. No ordinary woman created a tool chest like this she thought as she gently closed a heavy drawer.

She set the tools she'd selected on the ground and then rolled her bike in beside the Ninja and closed the door. After retrieving the tools, she returned to the upstairs apartment to find Tia and Kaitlin busy cleaning.

"I put the blinds on the kitchen table," Kaitlin hollered as she carried cleaning supplies to the bathroom. "I have some clean sheets downstairs in the dryer. I'll go get them when I finish here."

"Thanks." Devin carried the blinds into the den.

Tia was busy cleaning the kitchen. "I will give you the number to a small local grocery that still delivers, unless you want to make several trips on foot to get stocked up."

"Delivery sounds good. I can carry small stuff on my bike, but I need everything for starters."

"Yeah, I can't help you there. I can't get much on my bike either."

Devin realized then who owned the Ninja. "Is that sleek Ninja yours?"

"Yes, ma'am, bought and paid for," Tia answered with a smile. "That's my baby."

"I can relate." Devin took the first set of blinds from the package. "Maybe we can take a ride together sometime."

"I'd like that. So what brings you to town?"

Devin picked up one of the braces and began installing it as she contemplated her answer to Tia's question. She decided to go all in and answer her questions fully.

"I was born and raised just outside Baton Rouge, mostly by my older brother after our parents were murdered."

"Oh my God, I'm sorry, Devin."

"That's okay, you had no way of knowing."

"Did they catch the killer?"

"All of them but one. She escaped justice, but the others got death sentences," Devin said as her thoughts went back to the night of her parents' death. "What about you? Are you a native of N'awlins?"

"No, not me. I came here from Monroe two years ago to go to school."

Devin tensed up at the mention of Monroe, but relaxed when Tia continued.

"I'm slowly, very slowly, working my way through nursing school."

"That's a very noble career. Do you want to specialize?"

"I think I would like the emergency room, with all the wild and weird things that happen there. If not I could fall back onto pediatrics. I love kids."

"Do you plan on having a few yourself?"

Tia chuckled. "I said I loved kids, but I'm not sure I'm mother material."

"I think you may be selling yourself short." Devin lifted the first blind into place.

If she had been facing Tia she would have seen the blush rise to her face, but she finished hanging the blind and turned around to find Tia and Kaitlin watching her. "What? Did I hang them backward or something?"

"No, you did just fine. You work well with your hands don't you?"

"I never thought about it, but hanging blinds isn't that difficult."

"Would you consider helping us out with some repairs around our houses then?" Tia asked.

Devin smiled warmly at both women. "Is there food involved? I'm not the greatest of cooks."

"You keep our houses up and running and we will keep you well fed," Kaitlin promised.

"Start your honey-do lists and I will get some groceries."

"You have so got a deal. It's much easier to cook for two or three anyhow," Kaitlin said. "We may need to buy some additional tools and supplies."

"It looks like you have a great start on the tools."

Kaitlin chuckled. "They used to belong to my ex before I gave him the boot."

"So you kept the best of him?" Devin teased.

"Exactly." Kaitlin grinned. "I figured they were worth the thousand dollars he stole from the club."

"You came out good on that end, but it sucks that he ripped you off."

Kaitlin shrugged her shoulders. "You live and you learn, I guess."

Devin kept working as they chatted and had the other three sets of blinds installed in no time. "Is there anything else that needs repair in here?"

"The toilet needs to be tightened down."

Devin's stomach growled. "I will take care of that if someone orders some lunch. My treat for your help," she added. "Who delivers?"

"That depends on what you want," Tia said.

"I can eat almost anything, but I'm starving so lots of whatever you choose." Devin pulled forty dollars from her pocket. "Will that be enough?"

"I can feed you for days on that," Tia said.

"I am so going to love living here." Devin walked to the bathroom. The wax seal on the toilet was not broken, but the bolts needed tightening. She went through the kitchen to go downstairs for more tools and heard Tia placing an order for Chinese.

"Lunch will be here in thirty minutes. I hope you like Chinese."

"That will work just fine."

"I'm going downstairs to help Kaitlin with the linens and then we'll get your bed made." Tia started down the steps.

"Thanks for all your help."

"My pleasure." Tia entered Kaitlin's back door.

Devin went on to the garage and returned the tools she no longer needed and grabbed a socket set to take back to the bathroom. She followed the two women up the stairs and tightened the toilet as they made the bed and stocked towels and other linens in her linen closet.

"There. All set," Kaitlin said. "Welcome home."

"This looks fantastic, ladies."

"We will go back to my place and start on our lists and wait for lunch if you want to put your stuff away and then come on down."

Devin placed her duffel on the bed and opened it carefully, taking out the few personal items along with her clothing. She set photographs of her parents and Damien with his family atop the small dresser. As she hung her clothing in the closet, she realized she would need to do some shopping soon. *Maybe Tia could accompany her on a shopping trip tomorrow.* She closed the door and started for the stairs.

Devin made it to the bottom of the stairs just as a delivery driver exited Kaitlin's home.

"There you are. Now I don't have to climb those stairs again." Kaitlin handed Devin several full bags of food.

Devin followed her inside and placed the bags on the kitchen table.

"We have sweet tea or beer," Kaitlin said.

"I'll take tea," Tia said.

"Me too," Devin answered.

"Three teas coming up. Tia, you want to get some plates and utensils?"

They settled down to a feast and simple conversation. Tia agreed to take Devin on a shopping spree the next day to purchase the clothing items she needed. She suggested they do some grocery shopping after the meal.

"We just go in and select what we need and pay, then wait for it to be delivered," Tia said.

"Is there anything in particular you two enjoy cooking?"

Tia looked at Kaitlin. "Between us we can cook just about anything."

"I can grill up some fine meat and that's about it," Devin admitted.

"There is a relatively new charcoal grill in the garage," Kaitlin said.

"Another present from the ex?"

"You got it." Kaitlin grinned.

"Do you want me to come in at eight tonight?" Devin asked.

"Yes, that will be great. Maybe you and Tia can ride in together. We use the jukebox until she arrives."

Devin looked at Tia. "Does that sound okay to you?"

"Sure as long as we use your bike. Mine is not comfortable for two."

"Plenty of room for two on Devin's," Kaitlin said.

"Yeah, I saw you two pull up this morning."

Kaitlin brushed her hair back in dramatic fashion. "It was quite a ride too." All three of them broke up at her antics.

Devin finally pushed her plate away. "I better stop if I am going to be good for anything the rest of the day."

"I'll put the rest in my fridge in case either of you get hungry after your shopping trip."

"Kaitlin leaves a key under a planter on the back porch," Tia said.

Devin nodded. "Let me run back upstairs and I'll be ready to hit the grocery." She picked up the short list of things to repair in their homes. "Mind if I start on these tomorrow?"

"That will be fine. I suggest you both get a nap in later before work. It's almost the full moon so it will be a good crowd tonight."

"I'll help Kaitlin put away this food and meet you at the garage," Tia said.

✝

An hour and two hundred dollars later Devin had purchased everything she could possibly need to start her new apartment life. She and Tia sat around Kaitlin's kitchen table drinking tea while they awaited the grocery delivery.

When the young man pulled the grocery van into the driveway, Devin jumped to her feet and carried a large box upstairs. With everyone working together, it only took three trips up the stairs to deliver the groceries. Tia volunteered to help Devin put them away. Devin tipped the young man for the delivery and Kaitlin followed him downstairs.

Devin went to work unpacking and placing the items on the counter while Tia took control of putting items away. Their hands touched briefly as Tia transferred the box containing toiletries into Devin's arms. Devin's eyes locked on Tia and she smiled when she saw the blush rise to Tia's cheeks. Remaining silent, Devin took the box and disappeared to put the toiletries away.

"Thanks for the help," Devin said when she returned to the kitchen.

"You're very welcome."

"What time do you normally leave for work?"

"Seven thirty or so."

"I think I'm going to rinse off and get in that nap Kaitlin suggested."

"I'll see you downstairs at seven thirty then." Tia walked to the door.

"Sweet dreams," Devin said as Tia closed the door behind her.

†

Devin rarely remembered dreaming. Mostly her dreams just faded into darkness so black she could not make out any shapes or figures. Until today. Devin felt herself moving toward a light that grew brighter as she approached.

She sensed more than saw Were-folk lingering in the shadows as they appeared to watch her movements. She smelled Tia's scent, vivid and strong as it flooded her senses. Her dream world filled with a fog that made the light dance in front of her eyes as she searched for Tia to no avail. Devin was searching the fog frantically for Tia when the jangling of her alarm brought her back to reality.

Her eyes fell to the clock to find it was six o'clock. Devin climbed from the bed and pulled a loose-fitting robe around her shoulders before walking to the kitchen. Her stomach rumbled with hunger, so she pulled out lunchmeat and made a hearty sandwich. She wished she had taken a container of the Chinese leftovers, but a sandwich and chips would have to do. After downing the meal, Devin went to the bathroom to prepare for work. She showered more thoroughly this time, running some conditioner through her hair to give it a disheveled look that worked well with her strong jawline. The jeans she slipped over her slender hips fit snug in all the right places, and were only slightly worn in the knees. A quick spritz of her favorite cologne and slipping on her most comfortable boots and she was ready to roll. She caught a glimpse of herself in the full-length mirror and was pleased with her look. Tough but not decked out in leather. "It'll do." She grabbed her keys before jogging down the stairs.

✝

Tia was already waiting for her on the steps of Kaitlin's back stoop. She was wearing tight black jeans and a white tank top. Devin's heart raced when Tia stood and walked toward her, her hips gently swaying to an internal beat. The cinnamon and apple scent of her soul filled Devin's

57

nostrils as it teased her senses with a brutal assault. "You look fantastic." Devin felt a rush of warmth surging between her thighs. They turned toward the garage.

"You're looking pretty damned sexy yourself." Tia chuckled. "I bet you rake in the tips tonight."

"Why is that?"

"This is ladies' night," Tia said with a grin. "Some of the ladies you will serve tonight would pay big money to be with you."

It was Devin's turn to chuckle. "You have to be kidding."

"I'm deadly serious, but just you wait and see for yourself."

Devin shook her head, raised the garage door, and backed her bike out while Tia closed the door. She turned the key in the ignition to start the motor then twisted to offer Tia a hand. Tia easily slid onto the bike behind her and pressed herself into Devin's back as her arms encircled her waist. *Now this felt right.* Devin put the bike in gear and turned onto the street.

She regretted it was such a short drive to work. Devin found the closeness of Tia's body to be very pleasant and was disappointed when they arrived at the club and she pulled the bike into a small alleyway.

Music accosted them as the door flew open and two men came barreling out of the club, laughing as they held hands and walked past them.

"Sounds like quite a night already. Are you ready?" Tia asked.

"I was born ready." Devin pulled the door open.

George, sitting at his post near the door, greeted them with a smile. "Evening, ladies."

"Hey, George, how's the night going?" Tia asked.

"A thirsty crowd, but well behaved so far."

"Good, let's keep it that way." The door closed behind them.

"Amen to that." George watched them enter the club.

"See you at break time." Tia headed in the direction of the sound booth.

Devin watched her go for a few seconds and then turned to the bar. Kaitlin already had lines forming, so Devin moved quickly to join her and provide some relief. As she settled into the rhythm of the bar, Tia got her equipment set up and when she was finished took the microphone in hand.

"Are we ready to party?" she asked the crowd.

"Hell, yeah," they shouted in unison.

"I can't hear you," she teased. The crowd shouted even louder. "Now that's what I'm talking about." She cranked up the tempo of the music and the dance floor went wild.

"Evening, boss," Devin said as she rang up a sale and deposited the cash.

"I'm glad you're here, this crowd is like a sponge."

"That's great for business."

"Yes it is." Kaitlin grinned and filled another order.

✝

Tia watched as the tip jars filled quickly. She noticed several small scraps of paper mixed with the bills in Devin's jar. She was certain they contained scrawled names and phone numbers with pleas to give them a call and a small pang of jealousy coursed through her. There were some incredibly beautiful women in the club tonight, but Tia had no intention of anyone stealing Devin's attention from her. Tia shook her head even as the thought crossed her mind.

Devin was certainly a grown woman and if she wanted to date someone else she had every right to do so, but it didn't mean she had to like it.

†

In between song sets, Devin heard a table with two women getting extremely loud. It appeared they were in an intense argument. The flow at the bar had subsided for a few minutes and Devin looked over at Kaitlin. "I'll be right back."

She walked over to the table just as the music began and one of the women reared back to strike out at the other. Devin caught her wrist and the lovely blond-haired woman looked up at her in surprise. She smiled. "Well, hello handsome."

"Good evening. May I ask you to dance?"

"Oh please," the woman's partner sneered.

Devin took her by the hand and led her to the dance floor. The crowd parted to allow them a space to dance and more than one pair of eyes turned to watch Devin as she moved seductively to the music. The blond-haired woman couldn't take her eyes off her. Devin danced two songs with her to allow both women time to cool down. When the second song ended, she walked her back to the table and pulled the chair out for her dance partner.

"May I send you ladies something to drink?" She took note of what they were drinking.

"Yes please," her partner said. As Devin left the table, she heard them apologize to each other. When she turned to walk behind the bar, she caught a glimpse of the women embraced in a deep kiss. She pulled out two beers and sent them by the server to their table. Devin pulled bills from her tip jar and went to the cash register to ring up the drinks.

"There's no way you're paying for those beers," Kaitlin said. "That was a great job of defusing a situation that was sure to get hostile so the beers are on the house. Nice dance moves too," she added with a wink.

Women crowded the bar around Devin waiting patiently for drink orders while getting a good look at the hot new bartender in town.

†

The rest of the night progressed smoothly. Devin emptied her tip jar more than once, carefully folding the bills and notes together and slipping them into her pocket. Around one, the lovers that threatened to start world war three stopped by to say thanks on their way home.

"Have a great night, ladies, and come back soon." Devin watched as they made their way through the crowd.

"Count on it, handsome." The blond disappeared in the crowd.

When the crowd thinned out, Kaitlin began showing Devin what needed done to close down the club. She showed her the secured money drop, and reviewed the checklist of what needed restocking before they left for the night.

The last customers left and George locked the doors and they all went into action. Kaitlin dropped the remaining cash as George cleared the last few tables and Tia shut down her sound booth. Devin went to work emptying glasses, wiping down the bar, and carrying a bin full of glass bottles into the storeroom. She carried cases of beer to stock the cooler, and checked the liquor bottles for what needed

61

replenishing. She was just straightening the bottles when she turned and found the three of them watching her.

"That'll do just fine, Devin," Kaitlin said. "How about some breakfast? My treat."

"I can always eat."

The four of them walked to a diner only a block away and feasted on pork chops and eggs. After the meal, they walked back to the club.

"Care for a quick spin?" Devin asked Tia.

Tia looked at Kaitlin. "Go ahead, George will walk me home."

"That's right, I have to go right past there on my way home," he said.

"Let's ride then." Tia followed Devin to her bike.

✝

They left the city going south across the river, the wind whipping through their hair as Devin took each curve with expert precision. They rode until she smelled the approach of rain and turned back toward the city. They were less than a mile from home when the rain started and she had to slow the bike on the slippery cobblestone streets. They were both soaking wet when they arrived back at the house.

"Sorry about getting you soaked," she told Tia.

"I enjoyed every minute of the ride, " Tia answered, "even the rain."

Devin found her hand moving toward Tia, intent on brushing a strand of hair away from her face. Tia turned her face and nuzzled her cheek into Devin's hand. Tia's soft skin against her palm ignited a fire in her and Devin felt herself leaning into Tia until their lips brushed. A soft moan escaped Tia as Devin's hand slipped into her hair to pull her head forward for a tender kiss. Tia's heated tongue tasted Devin's lips that parted to invite Tia inside. Their tongues swirled together in a sensual exploration as the kiss deepened and Devin's hand slid down Tia's back to pull her close. She could feel the slight trembling of Tia's body as she held her against her chest. Her keen sense of hearing picked up the pounding of Tia's heart as their tongues struggled for domination.

When the kiss ended, Tia looked up at Devin breathless. "That was intense."

"Yes it was." Devin had a sheepish grin.

Silence fell between them, neither of them knew what to do next. Devin finally broke the silence asking the only rational thought that came to mind. "Are we still on for some shopping tomorrow?"

Tia was disappointed that the encounter was so brief, but she sensed Devin's hesitance to take their friendship to another level. The kiss did confirm for her that Devin was interested in more.

"Yes, see you about ten?"

"Ten will be great."

"Thanks again for the ride." Tia started out of the garage.

"Anytime." Devin watched Tia make a dash for her apartment.

"Damn." She watched the door close and Tia's outside light go off and then pulled the garage door down.

Devin climbed the stairs and opened the door to her new home. She shed her soaked clothing in the bathroom and toweled the rain from her skin. She collapsed naked onto the bed and pulled a pillow over her head to muffle the moan that ripped from her. Lust burned through her as she chastised herself for not inviting Tia up to her apartment.

Devin had never experienced a sexual encounter, but she knew her body would know how to respond even if her mind did not. She could feel the fever of the approaching full moon coursing through her veins until she finally exhausted herself tossing and turning and fell asleep.

†

Kaitlin had finished a cup of coffee in her kitchen when she heard the rumble of Devin's bike. Taking her cup to the sink she smiled when she saw Devin pull Tia close for a kiss. "That's it, girl," she spoke into the darkness of her kitchen. She too was disappointed when the two separated and went to their own apartments. "Well, it's a start." She set her empty cup in the kitchen sink and went in search of her own bed.

Chapter Six

Devin showered and dressed in holey jeans and a black tank top before she went bouncing down the stairs in hopes of getting a cup of coffee from Kaitlin. As she expected, Kaitlin was sitting on the back stoop, cup of coffee in one hand and a cigarette in the other.

"Any coffee left?"

"Still half a pot left, so grab a cup."

"You need a refill?"

"Thanks, but I'm good."

"I'll be right back then." Devin disappeared into the kitchen.

She quickly filled a mug, dropped in two sugar cubes, and added a dash of creamer. Devin took a sip and sighed before walking back out the door. She took a seat across from Kaitlin on the stoop. "Those things are bad for you, you know." She pointed at the cigarette.

"Yeah, I know, it's just hard to quit completely." Kaitlin blew smoke away from Devin. "Did you two enjoy your ride last night?"

Devin took a sip of the coffee. "Yes, it was great until we got caught in the rain."

"You can never predict the weather this time of year."

"I hear ya."

"The moon will be full tonight." Kaitlin stubbed out her cigarette.

Devin didn't need Kaitlin to tell her that. She could feel the pull of the moon in her blood and would need to find a place that would be safe for a run. That had never been an issue at the compound where the pack owned hundreds of acres covered with trails. Maybe tonight after work she would ride south again to find a spot.

"I bet the crowd will be wild tonight," she told Kaitlin.

"They usually are in a full moon."

Devin had sensed many otherworldly beings during her short time in New Orleans. She could most easily sense other were-folk, which reminded her she needed to call the local pack to let them know she was in the area. She had intended to call when she first arrived, but things began moving so quickly, the call had slipped her mind.

She sensed movement behind her and saw Kaitlin's eyes shift to an approaching Tia.

"Good morning, ladies."

"Morning, grab a cup of coffee and join us," Kaitlin said.

"Hi there, did you get some sleep?" Devin asked.

"I did, thanks, and you?"

"Once I settled down I slept like a rock."

"Anyone need a refill?"

"I could use one," Kaitlin said.

"You can top me off too. I need to make a quick call before I forget, so I will be right back." Devin started for the stairs.

†

Devin went to her bedroom to find the phone number and contact name Damien had given her and pulled out her cell. She also needed to call home to give them her address, but that could wait until later in the day. She dialed the number and waited for someone to answer.

"Hi, this is Devin Benoit. I'm calling for Simon," she said to a woman who answered the phone.

"Hang on for a minute and I will get him."

"Simon here," a deep voice said after a few seconds.

"This is Devin Benoit from Baton Rouge. My brother is Damien, the Alpha of our pack."

"I know Damien, how is he?"

"He is well, thank you."

"What can I do for you, Miss Benoit?"

"I have come to New Orleans to live for a while and I wanted to let you know that I arrived and mean no disrespect to your clan."

"I appreciate your respect and hope that you will visit while you are in our fair city. Did Damien give you our address?"

"Yes, he did and I would love to visit after I am settled in."

"We will look forward to your visit then and don't hesitate to call if you need anything."

"Thank you for your kindness." Devin ended the call. She slipped some cash in her pocket and picked up her bike keys before returning downstairs.

✝

"Welcome back." Tia offered Devin the cup of coffee.

"Thanks," she said and sat down next to Tia.

"So where are the two of you headed shopping this morning?" Kaitlin asked.

"I thought we would start at the mall and then hit a Harley shop, if that's all right with you, Tia."

"Sounds good to me," Tia said. "I think you will find some end-of-summer sales."

"That's always a good thing."

"Yes, ma'am, it is. Is there anything you need while we are out?"

Kaitlin pondered for a second. "Not that I can think of, but thanks for asking."

"You're welcome." Devin took a drink of the coffee. The three women were quiet as they drank their coffee and enjoyed the morning sunshine.

Minutes later Devin broke the silence. "How about if I pick up some steaks tomorrow morning and cook them before you go in to work?"

"Mmmm, that sounds good to me. I'll bake some potatoes if Tia will prepare a salad."

"You so have a deal," Tia said. "Does everybody like ranch and honey mustard dressing?"

"It's fine with me," Devin said as Kaitlin nodded. "I thought I would get to work on your honey-do lists tomorrow too until it's time to start the steaks."

"You know," Kaitlin started, "Mondays and Tuesdays are slow days for the club. Tia is off those days so would you like them off as well?"

"If that suits you." Devin was trying to hide her excitement.

"I'd rather have you both around on the busy nights."

Devin nodded her agreement and drained her cup. "Are you about ready?" she asked Tia.

"Yes, I am. Let me drop these cups in the sink while you get the bike."

†

Devin parked as close as she could to the mall entrance and walked in with Tia. She felt a familiar tingling sensation, which alerted her to the presence of other were-folk. She surveyed the parking lot to find a young couple also walking toward the entrance. She caught the eye of the male and nodded to acknowledge their presence.

Tia watched the exchange. "Anyone you know?"

"Nope, just being friendly," she answered.

Tia chuckled at her response.

"What's so funny?"

"You don't have any problem being friendly. I noticed how many phone numbers you collected last night during ladies' night."

Tia's comment surprised Devin. Was that a hint of jealousy she heard in her voice?

"It never hurts to be friendly, especially when you work in the service field."

"That's true." Tia walked through the door Devin held open for her.

Tia was correct. Many of the stores had great sales going on, and before long they had two bags filled with new jeans and shirts. They were close to the food court when Devin asked, "Are you hungry?"

69

"I could eat."

They surveyed the offerings and decided on pizza. Tia ordered a slice and Devin ordered two and drinks for them both.

"You have a healthy appetite."

"I am blessed with a good metabolism, but it seems like I am constantly hungry."

"That is a blessing," Tia said as they picked up their order and found a seat.

"So with your work schedule, when do you find time for classes?"

"I took the semester off for the summer, but normally I take a couple of daytime classes. Kaitlin is great about working around my schedule."

"She seems like a really good woman to work for."

Tia took a long drink. "She's been really good to me."

"How much longer do you have in school?"

"At this rate, probably another three years, but I have to work full-time to afford the tuition."

Devin had no idea what she would do in her future, but college didn't seem an option for her. She knew if she wanted to go Damien would pay for it, but she had no desire, at least not in this point in her life.

As if reading her thoughts, Tia asked, "What about you? What do you want for your future?"

"I have no clue," Devin answered. "I hoped some time away from home would give me some insight."

Tia nodded her head. "I can understand that. I always knew that I wanted to go into the medical field."

Devin finished her second slice before Tia finished her first. "Do you always wolf your food down?"

If only you knew, Devin thought. "Yeah, I'm a fast eater, always have been."

"I promise to not steal your food if you want to slow down and taste it," she teased.

Devin broke out in laughter, which brought a smile to Tia's face. "I could use another slice. Would you like one?"

"Oh my lord no, I couldn't hold another bite, but you go right ahead."

"I'll be right back then." Devin walked back to the counter.

Tia admired the way the jeans hugged Devin's hips as she walked back to the counter. The new jeans they had bought also fit her well, molding to her form in places like a glove. She was surprised by her thoughts as she watched Devin interact with the cashier who practically drooled over her. Devin really had no idea the affect she had on people of both sexes.

After leaving the mall, they dropped their bags off back at the apartment then stopped at one of the area's Harley Davidson stores where she purchased another pair of well-fitting jeans and a few tees. When they finally returned home, Tia helped Devin carry her purchases up the stairs.

"I have a washer and dryer you can use whenever you want," Tia told her.

"That would be great. I'd like to wash these new jeans before wearing them."

They removed the price tags and size markers and piled the jeans on the small kitchen table. "I'll make you a deal."

"What's that?"

"You start on Kaitlin's honey-do list and I will wash and dry these jeans for you."

Devin looked at Tia. "She will be leaving for work soon, correct?"

"Yeah, she goes in around two, so you wouldn't be interrupting her."

"Are you going to try for a nap later?" Devin asked.

"I may after I get your laundry done. What about you?"

"I wanted to take a ride. I got enough sleep last night so I will see you at seven thirty?"

Tia was disappointed that Devin didn't ask her to ride, but knew she would need a late afternoon nap to prepare for the long night ahead. "Sounds good, I will bring your jeans up with me then."

Devin helped her carry the new jeans downstairs and then took Kaitlin's list into the garage in search of tools. Many of the items on her list would be relatively easy to fix without causing too much noise. While she was in the garage, she checked on the condition of the grill. Tucked away in the back, sat an almost new grill and a full supply of charcoal and lighter fluid. Her muscles ached for some rare red meat and she looked forward to cooking for her new friends. She picked up the tools and supplies and walked to Kaitlin's house.

Devin stepped inside the back door and saw Kaitlin sitting in the kitchen writing out some bills. "Will I bother you too much if I start on your repairs?"

"No, not at all Devin, come on in. I have a bag of outlet covers and other pieces you will need for the list." She walked to a small closet.

"This shouldn't take too long, so I hope you are working on another list."

Kaitlin was surprised at her eagerness to complete tasks for her. "Do you like to paint?"

"As a matter of fact I do." Devin grinned.

"This old place could use a fresh coat and some patching of the drywall."

"If you pick out the colors, I'll give you a list of supplies I will need."

"Maybe you and Tia can help me with the colors."

"I think that could be arranged."

"Speaking of Tia, where is she?"

"She volunteered to wash my new jeans for me while I started on your list."

"That was very sweet of her."

"Yes it was." Devin started to take outlet covers from the bag. "You both have been very kind to me."

Kaitlin chuckled softly. "I think we make a good team. You do what neither of us want, or can't, do and we will do things for you."

Devin smiled warmly at her. "That is a pretty good arrangement, isn't it?"

"I'm certainly not complaining. You can have leftover Chinese or I can prepare something hot for you if you want."

"Chinese is always better the second day."

"I will call Tia and let her know to come over before she lays down then and maybe the two of you can finish off the leftovers then."

"Wonderful." Devin took a screwdriver and several outlet covers and left the small kitchen.

†

Kaitlin called Tia to make arrangements and then followed Devin throughout the house as she made the repairs, retrieving tools and supplies for Devin as she worked. They had just finished off the list when Kaitlin's back door opened and Tia stepped inside carrying a large stack of clean, folded jeans.

"Whoa, that was fast." Devin took the stack of jeans. "Thanks."

"You're welcome," Tia said. "How are the repairs coming?"

"All done with my list." Kaitlin began reheating the food. "I need your help with something."

Tia cocked her head at Kaitlin. "What?"

"I want Devin to paint my interior, but I don't know what colors I want to go with."

"Why don't you pick up some paint color strips and we can help you decide," Tia suggested.

"Good idea and pick up a small tub of drywall patch, a putty knife, and some fine grit sandpaper and I will go ahead with the repairs while you decide on colors. Pick up some bathtub caulk and I will reseal your bathtub too."

"Get a big tube. Mine needs it too," Tia said.

Kaitlin grinned. "It's nice to have such good help around."

Devin smiled. "It's nice to have someone to feed me."

They placed the food on the table as Kaitlin poured tea and got paper plates down for them. "You are getting the fine china today," she teased.

"Makes it easy to clean up," Tia said.

The leftovers were more than Devin remembered, but with her appetite, they disappeared in no time.

"I swear I don't know where you put all that food." Tia shook her head.

"It burns off quickly. I will probably have a sandwich before we leave for work," she replied.

"Oh, what I wouldn't do for a metabolism like that." Kaitlin started to clean up the kitchen.

"I'm going for a short ride this afternoon. Would you like a ride to the club, Kaitlin?"

"That would be great if you don't mind."

"Not at all, just give me a minute to put away these tools and get the bike," Devin said as she picked up the tools. "I'll see you later tonight, Tia."

"Be safe," she said as Devin went out the back door. Tia watched Devin depart then turned to find Kaitlin watching her. She smiled and turned away from her friend.

"She is very handsome isn't she?" Kaitlin asked.

"Yes she is, and she doesn't even realize how sexy she is."

"That's what makes her so special. She's humble and down to earth."

With a deep sigh she didn't realize she was holding back, Tia smiled once more at Kaitlin. "I'm off to nap, I'll see you later."

"Sweet dreams," Kaitlin said with a devilish grin, fully expecting Devin to fill her dreams.

Kaitlin locked the door behind her and walked out to meet Devin in the drive carrying the stack of jeans. "You forgot these." Kaitlin placed the jeans on top of the toolbox. She stepped forward, then took the hand Devin offered to assist her onto the bike.

"Here we go." Devin pulled out of the drive to ride the short distance to the club.

✝

After Devin dropped Kaitlin safely at the club she drove north until she reached a crossroads that took her near a levee. Thanks to Katrina, the Corps of Engineers had rebuilt a large portion of the levees that protected the city from the muddy waters of the Mississippi and Devin had decided this would be the perfect spot to run in the city. After work, she would drop Tia off at home and then drive out to the levee for a long run.

Devin returned to the garage and wiped the water spots from the bike's chrome. Picking up her stack of jeans she climbed the stairs to her apartment. Once she was ready for work, she settled down with a bottle of water and picked up her cell phone. It was early evening, but it should be past dinnertime at the compound. She clicked on Damien's name and waited for him to answer the phone.

"Hello," a young girl said.

"Hey, Lizard, how are you?"

"Devin," the girl screamed. "Are you coming home yet?"

Devin laughed heartily. "No, Lizard, not yet. Are you doing well?"

"Yes, ma'am. I can't wait to start back to school."

"Are you helping your mom with the other kids?"

"I am," Elizabeth answered. "Will you be coming home soon?"

"I will try to visit soon. May I talk with your dad now?"

"Yes, ma'am. I love you, Devin."

"I love you too, Lizard."

Devin could hear Elizabeth calling for her dad and soft footsteps coming toward the phone. "Thanks, Lizard. Hey, Devin," he said.

"Hey, Damien, how are you?"

"We're all great and you? Settled in yet?"

"I have an apartment and a job in New Orleans," she answered proudly.

"Fantastic, so you think you'll be staying there for a while?"

"I think so, at least for now," she answered. She gave Damien her address and a rundown of her job.

"It sounds like things are going very well for you. Will you come for a visit soon?"

"You sound like Lizard."

"Well, we all miss you."

"I miss you too. If things continue to go well, I may plan to drive up for a day or so."

"Anytime you could stay would be welcome."

Devin looked at her watch and saw that it was time to meet Tia. "I have to leave for work, but I'll call again soon. I love you, Damien."

"I love you too. Take care, baby sister."

"I will." Devin ended the call.

†

The night went well. The crowd was wild and the tips flowed as freely as the liquor. As the time wore on, she found herself growing increasingly restless as the pull of the full moon roared in her veins.

By the time the last customers left and they had the club ready to close, Devin felt like steam was rising off her skin. Tia climbed on the back of her bike and she drove them home quickly. When Tia stepped off to open the garage door, Devin stopped her.

"I have something to do. I'll be back later I'll see you in the morning."

Tia looked at her with a question burning on her tongue, but she kept it to herself. Devin backed the bike in the drive and drove away. Tia watched her go then walked across to her apartment.

†

Devin rode to a spot near the levee where she could safely leave her bike without fear of it disappearing. She stood near the small copse of trees, undressed, and willed herself to change. Devin felt the shifting of bones and the fur as it began to shift through her skin. She had transformed enough times in her life that she had adjusted to the pain that accompanied the shift, most of it anyhow. The shift brought her down on all four legs. She took a tentative first step, and then as the muscles relaxed, she broke into a trot, then a full run.

The moon provided enough light that she could safely traverse the top of the levee at full speed. The night air near the water was cool and the breeze ruffled her fur as she ran. Devin lifted her nose in the air and breathed in the smells of the night. It wasn't a run through her familiar bayou, but it was far enough from the city nights and sounds to bring peace to her inner wolf.

Devin spied the bright blinking lights of a southbound barge and slowed her pace. The fog off the water would partially hide her from view, but to be safe she dropped down the side of the levee to continue her run. Her sharp eyesight caught a glimpse of a fast-moving object just inside the tree line and she picked up an alluring scent. She slowed to a trot then stopped completely hoping to catch her stalker on the move, but it had also stopped. Devin sensed eyes on her as she moved closer to the tree line and smelled

78

the distinctive scent of female. She shifted back into human form so she could speak to the stranger. "I have your scent," she spoke calmly. "I know you are Were-folk, so if you come in peace, approach or else I will assume your behavior aggressive and a personal threat."

"No need to get your fur ruffled," a sexy voice spoke from the dark. "I come in peace, my sister."

Devin watched as a dark-haired woman in jeans and a form-fitting black sleeveless shirt emerged from the woods. Her green eyes carried a smile as she approached. Devin took in the well-built body of the young woman as she stalked closer.

"My name is Lucia, friend." She stepped into the moonlight.

"I'm Devin from Baton Rouge."

"Please to meet you, Devin from Baton Rouge."

"Likewise. I assume you are out on a run too since you've been following me for a few miles."

"Perceptive aren't you," the voice teased. "Imagine my surprise when I arrive for a nice run only to find a stranger running along my path."

"Such a nice path it is too," Devin said. "I apologize for intruding."

"No need, the path is plenty wide for both of us. I would welcome the company."

"Are you from New Orleans?"

"Not originally. I'm from down near Houma. I came here to attend the university to become a physician," she said. "Our pack is growing and our physician is ancient."

"How long have you been in school here?"

"I'm in my fifth year."

"Very impressive."

"What brings you to New Orleans?"

"Something is missing from my soul and I'm on a mission to find it."

"Do you know what that is?"

"Nope, but I'm hoping once I find it I'll know." Devin grinned.

Lucia chuckled at Devin's quick wit. "Your pack must be trusting to let such an attractive, young female go rogue."

"My brother is the Alpha, but it took some talking for him to allow me to leave the pack."

"He must really love you to allow you to find your way in this world."

Devin smiled at the mention of her brother. "Yes, he loves me and trusts that I'll know what is right for me."

"You sound close to each other."

"Damien raised me after our parents were murdered." Devin saw the narrowing of Lucia's green eyes. "That was the assassination coordinated by a witch?" she asked.

"Yes, it was. My parents stood little chance to survive the encounter."

"Has justice been served?"

"To all but the witch," Devin said, the bitterness obvious in her tone.

"Maybe one day then." Lucia left it at that. "So, what are you doing in New Orleans?"

"I just arrived a few days ago, but I am bartender/bouncer at a local club."

"That was quick. You must have done something impressive."

Devin grinned. "Just being my usual charming self." Devin told her about Kaitlin's club, how she got the job and apartment so quickly.

"I know that place," Lucia said. "They have a cute little DJ there who's a latent."

Lucia's revelation caught Devin completely by surprise. "What did you just say?"

"The DJ at the club, she's a latent, but I'm not sure she's Were. Her father or grandfather must have been Were-folk or some other magical being."

Devin had never considered the possibility of Tia being anything other than one hundred percent human. She should have known by her unusual scent that there was something more. She must have had a shocked expression on her face after the realization hit home.

"You really didn't know?"

"I knew her scent was something unusual, but no, I didn't make the connection."

"I only spoke with her briefly, but I don't think she knows either."

"What can you tell me about a latent?"

"Not a lot. There has to be some Were-folk genes mixed in there somewhere. If she were, she would have some heightened senses, but would not have the ability to shift. I don't know any of this as proof, but that's what the legends say."

"Very interesting," Devin said.

Lucia's laugh turned into a low rumbling growl. "You are attracted to her, yes?"

Devin could feel the heat rising to her cheeks. "Yes, I think so."

"You are an interesting one, my friend."

"There is never a dull moment around me." Devin smiled.

"Should we get furry and get out of here?" Lucia asked.

Devin grinned. "You afraid of getting caught naked in the moonlight?"

They transformed, and began the long run back to Devin's bike.

Nearing the end of the levee, they came to a halt to transform back to human form. They continued walking, and talked about life in New Orleans, the local pack and made plans to meet up for a run once a week. When they arrived back at the start of the levee where she had concealed her bike, Lucia let out a low whistle. "Is that your baby?"

"Yeah it is," she answered. "May I offer you a lift home?"

"Might as well since I'm no longer in the mood for a run," Lucia teased.

"How did you arrive here anyhow?"

"I have two good feet and I don't mind the walk, especially on such a beautiful night. One of the city buses runs about a mile from here."

"Come on then, I'll drop you anywhere you wish."

Lucia located her clothing not far from Devin's and they dressed before she climbed onto the bike behind Devin and gave her directions to her place. The night had grown deep when Devin pulled in front of an apartment not far from hers and parked at the curb.

"It was nice meeting you. I hope you will drop into the club sometime for a drink."

"You can count on that, my friend. I can see you're going to need someone watching over you to keep you out of all sorts of trouble here," she teased.

"And you are just the person for the job, right?"

"Yes, as a matter of fact I am. Thanks for the ride. I'll be seeing you soon." Lucia turned to walk inside her home.

Devin rode the remaining few blocks home and wearily climbed the steps to her apartment. Tired, she kicked off her boots and stretched out on the bed for some sleep.

Chapter Seven

Devin had planned to sleep for just a short time, but the sun peeking through her bedroom window woke her at nine. She rushed through a shower and rode down to the grocery store to buy the steaks for later in the day. When she returned she placed the steaks to soak in a marinade in the refrigerator and went down to Kaitlin's kitchen. She and Tia were sitting at the table drinking coffee when she knocked on the back door.

"Come on in and grab some coffee," Kaitlin said. "You are too late for pastries though, we just finished them off."

Devin walked in, poured a cup of coffee, and joined them at the table. "Good morning."

"You have already been out and about, I see," Kaitlin said.

"I went to the store for our steaks and I've got them soaking."

"I can hardly wait to taste your cooking," Tia said.

Devin looked over at her for the first time that morning. "I hope I won't disappoint you."

"I doubt you could. I got the spackling or whatever they call that stuff to patch the drywall," Kaitlin added.

"Good. I'll start on the patching and then caulk the bathroom while it dries, if that's all right with you two."

"Sounds fine to me," Tia said. "Kaitlin and I have been discussing paint schemes. Would you care to hear our ideas?"

"Lay it on me." Devin sipped her coffee.

Tia and Kaitlin shared their ideas with her as she finished off her coffee. "I really like your suggestions. I think a gallon for each room should be plenty, except for the master bedroom. You'll probably need two for that room," Devin said.

"What other supplies will you need?"

"Bring me your notepad and I will make a list and then get to work."

Kaitlin chuckled at Devin's eagerness. "There's no hurry so enjoy your coffee. I will head to the hardware store and order the supplies to be delivered and then bring some lunch back."

"Is there anything I can help you with?" Tia asked after Kaitlin left.

"Not really, but you can keep me company and be my gofer." Devin picked up her coffee and the bag of supplies to carry to the living room with Tia right behind her.

"I can be what?"

"My gofer, you can go for this and go for that. Speaking of which, I could go for some more coffee." She handed Tia her empty cup with a grin.

"I got it now." Tia walked into the kitchen.

Devin poured the bag of supplies out onto a small table and began opening the container of spackle. She picked up the putty knife, scooped out a portion, and started laughing as she spread the mixture over a cracked area of drywall.

"What's so funny?" Tia asked as she entered the room.

"Just like a female to pick out the kind that goes on pink and turns white as it dries." Devin chuckled as she demonstrated to Tia.

"You have an issue with pink?" Tia asked defensively.

"None at all," Devin smirked.

Tia watched as Devin moved around the room filling holes and cracks with the spackling. "That doesn't look too hard."

"It's not, come here and you can give it a try."

There was a good-sized dent in the wall from where the doorknob banged into the wall. Tia moved closer to the dent and Devin stood behind her to coach her through the patching. "Take some of the mixture on the putty knife and place it in the indentation and then use the knife to smooth the mixture even with the rest of the wall." Devin guided Tia's hand across the surface, smoothing the texture. "Yes, just like that," she said as she removed her hand from Tia's. "Good job. Remind me to pick up a door stopper for this door to keep it from banging up the walls."

"Why don't you give Kaitlin a call on her cell and ask her to pick one up while she's there," Tia suggested.

Devin grinned. "I have a gofer for that," she teased.

"All right, I'll call her. You just better hope I get the message to her right and she brings home the right thing," Tia teased back.

"Just tell her to ask the guy for a round thingy to keep the doorknob from putting holes in her wall," Devin yelled out to her as Tia walked to the kitchen to call Kaitlin.

"Right," she said sarcastically. Devin heard her relaying the message word for word.

When she returned to the living room Devin said, "I think we are done in here. Would you like to tackle the bathroom walls while I caulk the tub?"

"Sure, this seems pretty simple."

Tia followed her into the bathroom. "I need to use your putty knife for a few minutes to scrape out this old caulk and then you can have it back."

Tia nodded and watched Devin pry out the dried strip of caulk that was in dire need of replacement, tossing the old pieces in the trash. She handed Tia the putty knife, retrieved a pocketknife from her jeans, and sliced off an angled piece from the tip of the tube of caulking.

"Hey gofer," Devin called.

"Yes master?"

Devin shook her head and chuckled. "Will you go to the garage and bring me a nail with a head on it, please? You can probably find one in the toolbox on the wall."

"Sure thing. Any particular size?" Tia asked.

"It doesn't have to be long, but has to have a head on it. I will use it to close off the caulk when I'm done."

"Oh, okay. I'll be right back then."

Devin proceeded to begin replacing the caulk, filling in the gap between the tile and the top of the tub with the sticky caulk. Once she felt like she had a good bead formed, she wet her finger and used it to smooth the surface of the caulk even with the tile. She was concentrating on the task intently and had not heard Tia return.

"Wow, that looks good."

Startled, Devin turned so quickly at the sound of her voice she appeared to blur. "I'm sorry I didn't mean to scare you."

She was thankful Tia had missed the deep growl that escaped her throat as she turned toward the noise. "I just didn't hear you return," Devin said. She took the nail Tia offered and slipped it into the tube. She caught a glimpse of her eyes in the bathroom mirror and saw how brightly they were burning and hoped Tia didn't notice. "I'm going to check the bedroom while you patch those few spots." She hurriedly left the bathroom.

Devin tried to regain control over herself. Her heartbeat raced as she willed her body to fight the urge to shift and she doubled over in pain as her wolf fought against her. After several minutes, the nausea passed and she was able to sit down on the bed to catch her breath.

Tia walked in and found her sitting on the edge of the bed soaked in sweat and flushed from head to toe. "My God, Devin, you look horrible are you okay?" she cried as she rushed over to her.

"Yes, I'm all right, it must have been something I ate that didn't agree with me."

"Do you need to lie down or drink some water or something?"

"A glass of water would be nice." Devin was clenching her teeth to hide the pointed tips of her canines. She needed just a few more minutes to regain control.

"I'll be right back then." Tia left the bedroom.

Devin ran her fingers through her hair and felt the heat evaporating from her body. "Damn that was close," she told herself.

When Tia returned carrying a large glass of ice water, she handed it to Devin and sat on the bed beside her. "Take slow sips," Tia coached.

"Thanks." Devin took the glass and drank a few sips. "That is much better."

"I still think you should go home and lie down for a bit," Tia said.

Neither of them had heard Kaitlin return home. Kaitlin rushed in and saw them sitting on her bed. "What happened?"

"Something Devin ate isn't agreeing with her system," Tia explained.

"Enough work for today for you then, young lady." Kaitlin's mothering instinct bursting through her normally calm demeanor. "You will go home and lie down for a bit until you feel better. These projects can wait."

"But—" Devin tried to protest.

"No buts, except getting yours upstairs and into bed," Kaitlin said.

"Fine, but I'm still cooking us steaks later this afternoon."

"If you're feeling up to it, if not they will wait until tomorrow. Now off with you two."

Tia walked Devin to the stairs leading up to Devin's apartment. "I can make it from here," Devin said. "Have your salad ready by two, because we are eating steaks today."

"If you say so." Tia watched Devin climb the stairs.

Devin checked the time and realized she had plenty of time for a hot shower and a quick nap. As she stripped off her sweat-soaked clothes she realized she hadn't anticipated how strongly the full moon would affect her wolf while away from the compound. It was normal for her to experience the transformation, but she reckoned the proximity to others of her kind had dulled the full force of the moon. Now out on her own, she would have to be more careful around humans during the cycle of the full moon.

She finished her shower and then welcomed the soft comfort of her bed. She set her alarm for one hour and closed her eyes as she listened to the whirring of the ceiling fan above her.

Chapter Eight

Images of the Devil's Tree haunted her sleep. She remembered the night her parents were killed; how the bloody handprint had glowed against the dark bark of the ancient tree and the images she saw were just as they had been that night. She knew someone had made a pact with the devil and it would affect her life, otherwise there was no reason for her to have the images flashing in her subconscious.

She bolted upright in her bed after she saw a brief image of Damien in her dream. Soaked in sweat, her heart pounding, she ran for her phone. It rang five times before Damien answered.

"Hey, baby sister, what's up?" he asked, sounding calm and healthy.

Devin breathed a sigh of relief at the sound of her brother's voice. "I was just calling to check on you." Her voice was still quivering with emotion.

"What's wrong? I can hear the fear in your voice."

Devin knew she could not keep the truth away from her brother. Damien had always been able to tell when she was not telling the truth.

When she hesitated, Damien asked, "Are you okay?"

"I'm fine, Damien. I had a dream of the Devil's Tree, and a fresh handprint, then your image came up and it scared me."

"Well, let me assure you I am fine," he said. "I have been thinking a lot about you today so maybe my image just got confused with your dream."

Devin thought about that for a few seconds. "I guess you are right, it just gave me a fright."

"Other than that, are you all right?" he asked.

"Yeah, I'm doing good. I went for a run last night and met someone from the Houma pack."

Damien chuckled softly. "I'm glad to hear you are making some friends, especially those of our kind."

"Lucia, the young woman I met, is going to med school to replace the pack's doctor when he retires. She's really nice."

"That makes me feel even better knowing she has medical experience in case you become ill."

Devin thought of the experience she had earlier and debated telling Damien.

"I sense there is more going on," he said.

"I had no idea how difficult it would be on my own during the full moon. I was startled today and had to fight back the urge to shift."

"Hopefully that will become easier for you to control. I'm sure you will have to adjust many things being out on your own. You could always just come home," he teased.

"Thanks Damien. I'll keep that in mind. How are Tara and the kids?"

"Missing you as well, but everyone is doing well. I swear Lizard grows an inch every time I turn around."

Devin chuckled. "She's growing up way too fast."

"They all are."

"I better get a move on. I promised to cook steaks for some friends before work. I'll call again soon."

"I love you, Devin."

"I love you too. Hugs and kisses to the family." She ended the call.

She was relieved to find Damien and her family well, but the images from her dream still worried her. She walked to the bathroom and started another shower. The hot water did little to rinse the images from her mind, but it did relax her tense muscles. She dried off and slipped into a pair of her well-worn jeans and a T-shirt. Going to the kitchen she removed the steaks from the fridge. She would store them in Kaitlin's refrigerator until she was ready to put them on the grill. She was about to knock on Kaitlin's door, when she heard Tia's footsteps coming up behind her. She was carrying a large bowl of fresh salad. Devin knocked and then opened the door for Tia.

"Are you feeling better?" Kaitlin asked as they walked in.

"Yes, I am. I don't know what came over me, but I'm glad it has passed."

"Me too. I'm really looking forward to a steak," Tia teased.

"Let me stick these in the fridge and I'll go set up the grill."

"Is there anything we can help you with?" Kaitlin asked.

"Nope, I've got it from here. Are the potatoes ready?"

"In a half hour tops. I also have some corn I'm cooking."

"My mouth is already watering." Kaitlin was smiling as she left the kitchen.

†

Devin walked to the garage and pulled the door open. She wheeled the grill outside onto the drive and started the fire. She walked back into the garage, pulled out three collapsible lawn chairs, and set them up under the shade of a tree. She looked up to see Tia and Kaitlin approaching with a cooler filled with ice-cold Abitas.

"We thought you might want some company and a cold beer," Kaitlin said. "Phew, thanks for putting these chairs in the shade, this damned humidity is stifling."

"This is a bit unusual even for this time of year," Tia admitted.

Devin dropped into a chair beside them. "I thought it was always hot and humid here."

"Ha, we actually had snow flurries last year." Kaitlin chuckled. "But you're right, it's almost always damned hot."

They sipped the beer while the coals were burning down. When they looked just right, Devin said, "It's time to start the steaks. Is everything ready on the inside?"

Tia looked at Kaitlin with a grin and then to Devin. "Yep, we are way ahead of you. All we need is the meat."

Devin just shook her head. As she walked toward the house to retrieve the steaks she heard the rumble of bikes coming down the street. She slowed her pace and smelled the scent of Were and something else as a group of four bikes drove by. She couldn't be positive, but the flowing blond hair that fell behind the female on the lead bike made her think of Cedra, and she felt her hackles rise. A low growl rumbled from her chest and her bones ached to change. Her mood darkened as she climbed the steps into the house and rushed to the front window, but there was no sign of the passing bikes. Devin returned to the kitchen and jerked the refrigerator door open with more intensity than she had planned and heard the hinges creak under the strain. "Take it easy, girl," she told herself. She closed the door gently after pulling out the steaks.

Tia caught her eye as she walked to the grill and a slight gasp escaped her lips, too low for Kaitlin to hear but as loud as a shout to Devin. *She must see the glow of anger in my eyes.* Devin turned quickly toward the grill and dropped the steaks onto the rack. *Maybe there was more to my dream after all.* She turned back around for her beer. When Tia looked at her this time there was no look of surprise in her eyes, but there was a look of uncertainty in them.

Devin remembered what Lucia had said about Tia being a latent and possibly having heightened senses. *Could she possibly sense the anger flowing through my veins?*

"Are you okay?" Tia asked from beside her.

Devin was startled at the sound of Tia's voice so near. She had not heard Tia approach, and when she spoke, it had brought her back to reality with a low snarl.

"Yes, I'm fine, thanks, just hungry all of a sudden."

Tia looked at her with disbelief in her eyes and Devin knew she did not believe her answer for even a moment. For a moment Tia looked like she wanted to press Devin for answers but instead let out a low whistle as she looked at the grill. "I thought you said you were cooking steaks, but I swear those look more like roasts."

Her comment brought a smile to Devin's face. "I told you I was hungry."

95

"Kaitlin and I can eat on those for a couple of meals." Tia punched Devin in the shoulder and handed her a cold beer.

"Lightweights," Devin teased and took a long drink from the bottle.

Kaitlin returned from setting the table and joined them in the shade. "You sure do have it smelling good out here."

"How do you two like your steak?"

"Medium rare for me please," Tia said, bringing a smile to Devin's face.

"Done, well done for me. I don't want to even think of it mooing," Kaitlin answered.

"Got it, boss," she answered.

Kaitlin looked up at the sky and saw a growing mass of clouds. Devin saw concern cover her face and sat down beside her. "Is something wrong?"

"I think it is time to check the weather. Those aren't our usual storm clouds."

Tia perked up at the sound of worry in Kaitlin's voice. "Do you think there's a hurricane brewing?"

"I hope not, but it is prime time in the season."

"What happens if a storm heads this way?" Devin asked.

Kaitlin looked at her with a strained look on her face. "After Katrina's lessons, we board up and get the hell out of Dodge." She took a drink of beer and continued. "I will close up the club and head up to my sister's in Jackson until it blows over."

Devin looked at Tia. "I will go home to Monroe and ride it out with my family."

"Let's hope it won't come to that." Kaitlin took another worried look up to the sky.

96

Devin walked over to the grill and lifted the lid to check the steaks. The steam rose from inside and released a heavenly scent. She turned the meat and returned the lid. "Ours will be done in a few minutes, but it may take a day or so to cook Kaitlin's," she teased.

"I heard that." She grinned. "I'll go check everything inside and bring out a platter. You can take your steaks off and I'll cover them with foil to keep them warm until mine is ready."

"I think that's a great idea," Tia said. "Do you need any help?"

"No, but you can come inside and bring the platter back while I check on the weather."

Tia reached inside the small cooler and took out a fresh beer to hand to Devin. "I'll be right back."

"Thanks." Devin took the beer and sat back in her chair.

Devin's mind wandered back to the passing motorcycles and then to her dream. Could there really be something about to happen? she wondered. She took a long drink of the beer and raised her head to look at the rapidly moving clouds. There was certainly one storm brewing on her horizon.

✝

Kaitlin confirmed that there indeed was a tropical depression brewing in the Gulf, projected to turn into a tropical storm and then Hurricane Irene. Forecasters predicted landfall just east of New Orleans in the Mobile, Alabama area in three days, but the potential warning for New Orleans was evident in their reports.

Her concern for her home and business showed on Kaitlin's face as they shared their meal.

"What does this mean for us?" Devin asked.

Kaitlin shifted in her seat and pushed a bite of steak around her plate. "We will close down the club after tonight and spend the next two days getting the club and our homes as protected as possible. Then we get the heck out of town. Do you have someplace to go?"

"Yes, I'll go to Baton Rouge and hunker down with my brother and his family." She looked at Tia. "We can ride up together and you can meet my family," Devin suggested, much to Kaitlin's delight.

"That would be fun, thanks."

"So, do we need to purchase supplies like plywood, screws, and such?"

"No, thankfully I used some of the insurance money I received after Katrina to purchase heavy-duty hurricane shutters. They will take some time to install, but are much easier than plywood."

"That's good news."

"I figured the three of us can work on those and we'll send George with his truck to the Corps of Engineers to pick up as many sandbags as he can. I'm not too worried about flooding here, but the streets in the Quarter will flood in a hard thunderstorm." She looked hopeful when she said, "The sandbags really helped during Katrina, so I hope they'll do the trick again."

Devin looked at Tia and then Kaitlin. "I know we'd normally be off today, but I think it best if we work today to help with the preparations."

"I'll never pass on good help."

Tia jumped into the conversation. " I agree. Is there anything we can get started on today before we go into work?"

"Your place has the fewest windows. If you want to pull out some shutters from the garage, you could probably shutter her place up in a couple of hours."

"Just show us where the supplies are and we can get them hung."

Tia nodded in agreement. "The anchors are already sunk, correct?"

"Yes, you just have to place the shutters through the rails and onto the bolts and then tighten them down with wing nuts. You shouldn't need a ladder for your windows, but you certainly will for Devin's."

"That ladder you have in the garage should do the trick."

"Yes, I bought it just for that purpose."

Devin looked at her watch and saw that it was a little after two. "If you'll take care of the kitchen while Kaitlin gets ready for work, I'll start bringing out the supplies."

"There are nail aprons hanging up by the ladder. I've found that they are very handy to put the wing nuts in and it leaves your hands free."

"So noted, boss lady," Devin said with a wink and then left for the garage.

"She is really helpful to have around, don't you think Tia?"

"Yes she is," Tia said as a blush rose to her cheeks. Kaitlin had caught her staring after Devin again.

"Come on, I have time to help with the kitchen and then you can get outside to help quicker." Kaitlin gave her a wink. "You load the dishwasher and I will put the leftovers up."

"Deal." Tia started to clear the dishes from the table.

✝

Devin entered the garage and walked to the back where she had noted large boxes stored. Opening a lid, she found the metal shutters for the windows. The nail aprons were exactly where Kaitlin said they were and she emptied the contents of one box of wing nuts into the large pockets. She tied the apron around her waist and, as an afterthought, picked up a pair of pliers to tighten the wing nuts. Her Were strength would have been enough to secure the hardware, but she didn't want to draw attention to herself. In the storage bin with the hardware were several pairs of leather work gloves. She picked out the largest pair and slipped them onto her hands. She tested the weight of the shutters and figured she could safely carry two at a time. She picked up the first set and headed out the door just as Tia emerged from Kaitlin's house.

"Wow, you went right to work." Tia saw her carrying her load. "Let me grab another set and I'll be right there."

"Better put on a pair of the gloves. The edges of the shutters could be sharp," Devin warned.

"Yes, ma'am." Tia disappeared inside the garage.

Devin walked to the farthest window and leaned the shutters against the house. She figured each of the windows would need three shutters for protection. She was inspecting the rail system when Tia arrived with two more shutters. "It looks like we'll need three for each window."

Tia leaned her pair up against the house. "I'll go back for more while you are studying the installation."

Devin nodded her head as she picked up the first of the shutters and slid it across the rails. With a minor adjustment, the holes in the shutters matched up with the bolts and slid snuggly against the frame of the window. She reached into the pocket of the apron and took out a wing nut. The bulkiness of the gloves made it difficult for her to slip the nut onto the top of the bolt and then twist it down over the threads. She put the tip of the glove into her mouth and pulled it off, freeing her hand to tighten down the nut.

Tia watched her thread the nut and then suggested that Devin get the shutters in place and she would tighten them down with the nuts.

"Good idea." Devin removed the apron from her waist and shoved the pliers in her back pocket before tying the apron around Tia.

Tia slipped her gloves into the apron and pulled out a wing nut. Within minutes, they had the first window covered and Tia tightened all the nuts.

"There that should do it. One down and five more to go."

"Let's carry out all the shutters we'll need and then we can get back to hanging them," Tia suggested.

"Sounds like a good plan."

When they carried the last of the shutters out of the garage, Devin had begun to sweat and the back of her T-shirt was soaked with perspiration. Tia found herself intrigued by how the sheen of sweat on Devin's body seemed to make her skin glow and the aroma coming from her was tantalizing instead of offending. She was so mesmerized that when Devin stopped abruptly, Tia nearly ran into her.

"Did you hear me?" Devin asked as she turned toward Tia.

"No, I'm sorry. What did you say?"

"I asked if you would mind going back to the garage for the can of wasp spray. There is a nest we need to get rid of."

"Oh, okay, I'll be right back then." Tia spun away.

Devin propped the last of the shutters against the house and waited for Tia to return. She eyed the nest closely and saw that it was active and there were several wasps weaving in and out of the nest. She hated killing anything, even insects, but the nest was in her way and she had no other choice if she did not cherish the thought of being repeatedly stung.

Tia returned and handed her the can of spray. "You better back up now," she warned as she took off the glove on her right hand and shook the can. With a careful aim, Devin pointed the can at the nest from what she hoped was a safe distance. The wasps swarmed angrily from the nest and flew in Devin's direction. She dodged the first swarm as they flew past, but one straggler landed on her arm and stung her before dropping to the ground.

"Shit," Devin cursed and stomped the ground to be sure the wasp was dead and would not return for seconds.

Tia rushed over to her and looked into her eyes that were aglow with anger. The abrupt change made her take a step backward as a soft gasp escaped her.

Devin turned away from her quickly as her hand flew to her arm. She fought against her anger until she regained control of her emotions. "Damn," she said as she turned back to face a wide-eyed Tia.

"Are you okay?"

"Yes, I just need to get this stinger out and maybe put an ice cube on it for a few minutes."

Tia ran inside her home, returning moments later with a pair of tweezers and a bag of ice. She used the tweezers to gently remove the barbed stinger from Devin's arm and then placed the bag of ice against her skin. "Come sit down for a minute." She ushered Devin inside to a kitchen chair.

"I promise I'm fine." Devin felt the venom from the wasp sting racing through her system. Her increased metabolism would deal with the foreign invader much more quickly than a normal human, but she did feel the sudden nausea as her body fought it off.

"Would you like something to drink? You haven't stopped working since we got started. I have some tea."

"Tea would be very nice." Devin grinned.

She lifted the bag of ice and saw the swelling was already beginning to subside as the redness also started to dissipate. "I think I'll live," she said when Tia returned with a glass of tea.

"That's good news." Tia handed her the glass of tea.

They drank their tea, talking about the impending storm, when the rumble of motorcycles interrupted their break. Devin's keen sense of hearing had alerted her to their approach. Her eyes turned to the cobbled street and she was several strides ahead of Tia as she crossed the kitchen. She looked out the window to witness the same crew of bikers she had seen earlier drive by the house, following a blond female in the lead. There was no doubt in her mind the males were Weres and the female something more. Again, the Devil's Tree image flashed before her as the scent was one and the same. The blond-haired woman on the bike was Cedra of Monroe. Without a single look her way, the group roared toward Bourbon Street and disappeared.

A low growl rumbled through her throat.

"Someone you know?" Tia asked as she caught up with her.

"I don't know. Maybe." Devin pulled her gloves back on. "Let's finish up here."

They worked well together and within an hour, they had finished installing the shutters around Tia's home.

"Are you up for a few more shutters?"

Tia looked at her watch. "Sure, do you want to start on Kaitlin's next?"

"I think we have enough time for the two on the back."

"Come on then, let's get started."

When they finished, Tia looked at Devin with a grin. "We got a lot done today."

"Yeah, we did. Do you think Kaitlin will want to take care of the club tomorrow?"

"Probably. Then she can head out of town when we finish here."

"That makes sense." Devin hung the nail apron back on the garage wall. "Do you want to walk to work tonight?"

"Sure, it may be the last time we can walk the streets for a while."

Devin pulled the door to the garage down and turned back to Tia. "I'll meet you back here in an hour then."

"See you then." Tia walked across the yard.

Devin climbed the stairs to her apartment and stripped down for a shower. The warm water pelted her skin and relaxed her tense muscles. The thought that Cedra could be in New Orleans had her muscles wound tightly and she wondered what she was doing here. She could feel her body's urge to transform and track down Cedra. For the moment, at least, her primal instincts would have to wait. She finished showering and dressed; the hair on the back of her neck prickled as adrenaline raced through her veins.

She made herself a sandwich and walked out to meet Tia. A light breeze welcomed them as they stepped out to the cobbled street and the musky scent of the Weres assaulted Devin's nose.

"The breeze feels nice," Tia said. "Too bad it's bringing in a storm."

"Kaitlin is really worried, isn't she?"

"Yeah, the club and her home are all she has."

Devin ran her hand through her hair. "We'll do all we can to protect them and then fate will take it from there."

"That's the best anyone can do." The sound of hammering filled the night air.

Devin pulled open the front door to the club and the music blared from the jukebox. The crowd was surprisingly large considering the ominous days ahead. It was just natural for the carefree residents of New Orleans to party first and prepare later, she thought. She nodded to George and walked to the bar to find Kaitlin filling an order.

"Evening, boss," she said with a smile. "Looks like a decent crowd."

"Yes, the natives are still thirsty and ready for a party. I checked for news on the storm and it is now officially Hurricane Irene."

"So should we whip up some pitchers of Hurricanes and have a special?"

"You know, Devin, that's not a bad idea at all."

They went to work mixing New Orleans' signature drink and poured them into tall glasses. As quickly as they filled a pitcher, drinks were on order and gone. Tia whipped the crowd into a wild frenzy on the dance floor and decided to take an early break. She was seated at the end of the bar, sipping a Hurricane and chatting with George and Devin about the preparations for the storm.

The night was moving along nicely until the wind blew the door open. Devin felt a tingling sensation from the amulet around her neck and looked up at the bar to watch as the witch and the Weres entered the bar, their movement appearing as slow motion as Cedra's head turned to the bar and her eyes locked with Devin's. The pounding of the music masked the growl that ripped from deep inside her as her face turned into a sneer. The crowd turned to watch the entrance of three large handsome men and a beautiful woman and instantly the pheromone levels tripled inside the club.

Devin's grip on the handrail on the bar tightened, threatening to crush the polished brass as her canines began to sharpen. "I'll be right back." She walked quickly from behind the bar.

"That looks like trouble," George said to Tia as they watched Devin approach the group that had taken possession of a large booth.

A heavily muscled man wheeled on Devin as she came near, but a quick command from the woman brought him to his seat in the booth.

"That's right, down, Fido," Devin snarled as she stopped at the table. The male growled and exposed his fangs.

"My, haven't you grown up to be a fine young woman," Cedra said. "Damien must have forgotten to teach you manners." Her voice was sickly sweet.

"You have no business in here," Devin warned.

"Relax, little sister, we are just going to have a few beers and we'll be on our way," one of the other males responded.

"I am no sister of yours," Devin snarled, "or any Were that would take up with a murdering witch."

"I have murdered no one." Cedra glared at Devin.

106

"You can't deny you and a band of mutts from Monroe murdered my parents."

"I repeat I murdered no one."

"You bargained with the devil for extra strength and trapped them in a force field which drained their energy until your mutts could overpower them."

Cedra's smile was unnerving. "You ran from the clearing like a whipped puppy that night."

"I promise, the next time we meet I won't be going anywhere until you are dead."

"Such nastiness from such a gorgeous female," one of the males said, then left the booth.

"You have your beers and then head out and no trouble will occur. But trust me, we will have our day," Devin promised.

"Yes, we will, and maybe you can bring that tasty little treat with you for a snack." Cedra motioned toward Tia.

"She has nothing to do with you and me." Devin felt her body expanding, her inner wolf threatening to explode.

"Maybe, and then again maybe not, but she would make a nice prize, don't you think boys?"

"I bet she'd be a wild ride in the sack," the youngest of the three joked.

Devin's hand flew down to grasp him by his leather jacket, her movements a whir to the human eye. "You will eat those words one day. Two beers and take your flea-ridden curs elsewhere," she told Cedra.

"Don't worry, we won't cause a scene in this little dump of a club. We have much better company to keep tonight."

Devin took note of the beer they were drinking and stalked back to the bar to get refills. "Is everything okay?" Kaitlin asked.

107

"Yes, everything is under control," Devin said a little more harshly than Kaitlin deserved.

She walked back to the booth and placed the four beers on the table. One of the males moved to pull out some cash. "I'm buying this round. Drink them and get the fuck out of my sight." She whirled on her heel and stormed back to the bar.

Devin went back to work serving the customers but kept a sharp eye on the booth until they stood to leave. She watched as they approached the bar and Cedra stopped to speak to Tia. "We will see you again soon."

Tia was speechless as Cedra smiled, and followed the others out the door.

"What the fuck was that all about?" George asked, the smell of his fear filling the air.

"Some riffraff that needed to be politely asked to leave. Hopefully they will be gone for good." The adrenaline was still pumping overtime through Devin and she needed some physical activity to purge her system. "Will you dance with me?" she asked Tia.

"I'd love to." Tia slid off the barstool.

"Be right back, boss," she said to a smiling Kaitlin.

They reached the dance floor and fell into the thumping, gyrating beat of the crowd and Devin felt herself begin to calm to normal. Tia was breathless and sweating when they finally emerged from the dance floor ten minutes later.

"Phew, that was fun. Girl, you didn't tell me you had moves," she teased.

"I can't give up all my secrets," Devin answered.

"On that note, I better get back to work. This is the last song I set up before break. See you at closing." Tia made her way back to her booth.

"Feel better now?" Kaitlin asked with a nudge.

"Yeah I do, thanks for the break."

"You do have plenty of secrets left, don't you?" She had a knowing grin.

"Maybe one or two," Devin answered shyly.

✝

An hour later, the crowd began to thin out and Kaitlin made the call to close the bar early so they could get some rest and meet back early to begin preparing the club for the storm. After they cleaned and locked up, they planned to meet George at seven to start work. Kaitlin would send him off with his truck for sandbags while they began to shutter the club.

The three of them walked home. The breeze had picked up and Devin could smell the salt in the air. "What's the latest on the storm?" she asked.

"She's a category one so far, but expected to strengthen to a two, possibly a three, by tomorrow."

"You mean later today," she teased.

"Yeah, later today. Maybe she will blow herself out before she gets here."

"We can only hope, but we will be as ready as we can," Devin promised.

"Good, I want us to leave here before dark tomorrow."

"How are you getting to your sister's?" Tia asked.

"George is going to drop me off on his way to Memphis."

"That should be an interesting ride," Tia smirked.

"Will you lay over with me in Baton Rouge tomorrow night?"

"It depends on what time we get out of town. If it's not too late I'd like to make it to Monroe to help the family if needed," she said.

Devin was disappointed. "We'll get you out in plenty of time," Devin promised as they reached home. "I will see you two in the morning." She turned and climbed the stairs to her apartment.

She waited until Kaitlin and Tia were safely inside and then changed clothes. She was in no mood to sleep and still had adrenaline to burn off. Devin had planned to go for a run, but instead decided to go ahead and shutter her apartment while Tia and Kaitlin slept.

Devin quietly opened the garage door, took the ladder out, propped it against the apartment, and then went back to gear up. She tied the apron around her waist and began carrying out the shutter panels for each of the windows. Devin moved as quietly as she could and began shuttering the windows.

Kaitlin had brewed a cup of coffee and was staring out her kitchen window when she caught sight of Devin's movements. She watched her for several minutes until she realized what Devin was doing. She drained the cup of coffee and walked across the yard.

Devin heard her approach. "I'm sorry if I woke you. I was trying to be quiet."

"You didn't wake me, you are quiet as a church mouse, but if you are determined to do this I can at least help."

"All right, grab a pair of gloves and hand me that next panel."

Within an hour, the two of them had the apartment shuttered. Devin was more relaxed and she saw that Kaitlin looked weary. "Let me set out the panels for the rest of your house and we can crash for a few hours of sleep."

Twenty minutes later, they had the panels staged and the ladder and supplies stored in the garage. "See you at seven, and go to bed this time," Kaitlin said.

"I will." Devin climbed the stairs again. She stripped naked and collapsed across the bed.

Chapter Nine

Devin woke to the rising sun and found that the wind had gotten even stronger. After a quick shower, she dressed and bounced down the stairs to join Kaitlin for a cup of coffee. Tia came into the kitchen moments later. "Did the shutter fairies pay us a visit last night?"

"No, Devin couldn't sleep so she went ahead and shuttered her apartment. She made so much noise I just had to go help," Kaitlin teased.

"I was not noisy, but I did appreciate the help."

"I feel cheated," Tia said with a fake pout.

"No worries, you will get all the work you can handle today," Kaitlin chimed in.

Devin looked at her watch. "Do we have time to stop for some breakfast?"

"The diner may be open."

"We won't get anything done this morning if we eat that heavy," Devin said. "Will you take your bike and make a run to the café?"

"I do need to give it a run and get some gas, so yes, I'll bring breakfast."

"Awesome." Devin began to reach for the money in her pocket.

"I got these," Kaitlin said. "Better get extras."

Tia finished her coffee and walked out to the garage for her bike. Devin accompanied her and picked up the nail apron and several pairs of gloves. "Don't forget the pliers." Tia backed her bike out of the garage.

"Got 'em," Devin answered.

"I'll see you at the club." Tia started the motor and pulled away.

Kaitlin met Devin in the yard and they walked to the club. George was already waiting on them and, after getting some cash from Kaitlin, was soon on his way for sandbags. Kaitlin showed Devin where the ladder and panels were stored for the club.

Devin smiled at the toughness Kaitlin displayed as she took the panel and slid it onto the rail. "Let's slide all three on and then I can move the ladder to start locking them down."

"Sounds like a plan." Kaitlin went walked to the back of the club for the next panel. "Give me a holler if you need anything then."

Tia returned and after a quick break for breakfast, the three women went back to work getting the club battened down.

Devin and Tia worked together well and quickly had the last shutters installed and were working on the second door when George showed up with a load of sandbags. "The girls have already finished the back and side doors. If you want to pull your truck down the alley, we can start stacking them near the doors," Kaitlin said.

113

"Me and Devin can handle this if you ladies want to finish up inside," George suggested.

"Fine, I'd like a couple of layers in front of each door and if we have enough left over I would like to add a layer along the foundation on the front side," Kaitlin instructed.

"We should have enough." George climbed onto the bed of his truck. "I'll hand them down to you if you want to lay them, Devin."

"Bring them on." Devin took two bags as Kaitlin and Tia disappeared around the corner.

George and Devin entered the club just as Tia and Kaitlin were finishing up.

"All done in here," Kaitlin said. "We just need to install the storm door on the front entrance and drop the sandbags."

Devin positioned the door in place and worked quickly to install the door then they all finished laying the sandbags. Sweat was dripping off all of them by the time they finished despite the steady breeze.

"Now we can go to the diner," Kaitlin said.

"What about finishing your house?"

"That won't take long and I would feel better if we all left today with a good meal under our belts."

"You're the boss," George said. "Load up, ladies."

When they finished eating, George dropped Tia at the club for her bike and drove over to Kaitlin's home.

"Are you sure you don't need my help to finish up here?"

"Nope we can finish here. Go clean up and pack your bag. I should be ready in no more than two hours," Kaitlin said.

"See you soon then, boss." He pulled away.

Kaitlin reached into her pocket and pulled out a set of keys that she handed to Devin. "You have done so much, but could I ask another favor?"

Devin took the keys from her.

"Being in Baton Rouge, you'll be the closest. Once the storm has passed and it is safe, will you come back to check on everything and let me know how things fared?"

"I would love to do that for you." Devin heard Tia's bike approach.

"Thanks. You don't know how much I appreciate that."

"Have faith that everything will weather the storm just fine."

"I keep telling myself it will." Kaitlin knew her confidence wasn't strong.

Tia pulled up and parked outside the garage. "Let's do this people. I need a shower."

"Yes, you do," Devin said with a smirk.

"You don't exactly smell like a bed of roses either, smart-ass," Tia tossed back.

"You heard the lady, let's get to work." Kaitlin grinned.

The last set of the shutters were a pain in the ass, but they were able to finish in less than an hour. "All right, time to clean up and pack our bags. See you both before you go." Kaitlin watched as they split and went their separate ways.

†

Devin planned to travel light and packed another set of clothes before she stripped for a shower. A visit home would allow her to bring some other stuff back with her, she just wished it was on different terms and she wasn't running from a potentially devastating storm.

After dressing, she prepared her apartment for the storm and picked up her bag. With a final look at her apartment, she bounded down the stairs. There was a suitcase sitting on Kaitlin's porch as Devin went inside the garage and fastened her bag to the bike. She rolled it out and parked beside Tia.

"You have my phone numbers programmed into your phone, correct?" Kaitlin asked.

"Yes, and you, Tia, and George have my number, correct?"

Devin's sharp hearing picked up the rumbling of thunder miles away and she looked in the direction of the approaching weather. "Did you see any news on the storm?"

"She's losing strength, but will still be a very large tropical storm when she makes landfall."

"That's good, at least," Devin said, trying to comfort Kaitlin.

"Could be much worse." Kaitlin watched Tia approach across the yard.

"Ready to ride?" Tia asked Devin.

"Always." Devin looked over at Kaitlin who was smiling at them. Devin approached her and took her in her arms for a hug. "Everything will be fine."

"I hope so." She patted Devin's back. "If not, I've got a very handy woman who will fix it all up again."

"You got that right, boss." Devin landed a kiss on Kaitlin's forehead.

Tia approached next. "You two be very careful on those bikes."

"We will. Have fun with George," she teased.

"Call or text to let me know when you both are home safe and keep in touch," Kaitlin made them promise.

Devin heard another rumble of thunder in the distance. "We better get moving."

Tia and Devin mounted their bikes just as George pulled into the drive. The motors roared to life and Devin turned for one last look to Kaitlin, who was waving as she watched them start their journey. When they disappeared from view, Kaitlin grabbed her suitcase and after a final look at her home, she climbed into George's truck.

Devin and Tia rumbled through the Quarter for a last look on their way to the interstate. Several bars were still open with patrons stumbling in and out. Devin hoped they had plans to evacuate soon. She was relieved find the majority of businesses closed, and boarded or shuttered in preparation for the storm.

They turned north and began winding their way through the traffic that was already beginning to clog up the roads and highways.

Chapter Ten

Droplets of rain began to fall as they reached the turnoff that would take them to the compound. Devin pulled off the road and turned off her bike so she could hear Tia, "Do you have time to stop by and meet my family?"

Tia looked at the storm clouds that had chased them since leaving New Orleans. Devin saw that she struggling with her decision. "I'd love to, but I'm afraid that storm will catch me if I stop now."

Devin knew she was making the correct decision and she would never put Tia in danger, but she was still disappointed. "I understand." The disappointment written all over her face. "Will you call or text when you make it home?"

"You know I will," Tia said with a grin.

"Be safe then and hopefully I will see you soon."

"You too. Enjoy your visit with your family."

"I will." Devin started her motor.

Tia dropped the shield on her helmet and pulled back onto the road, several hours of hard riding still ahead of her.

Devin watched until she disappeared from view and turned onto the road that would take her to the compound. Ten minutes later, with the rain falling steady, Devin made the final turn onto the drive that would lead her home.

Fortunately, the door to the garage had been left open and she pulled the bike straight in. As she turned the motor off she heard Lizard squealing on the front porch. Devin grabbed her bag and made a dash across the yard for the front porch just as the heavens opened wide and the rain began to fall in sheets.

"Devin," screamed Elizabeth as she ran across the porch to hug her aunt. "I am so glad you're back."

Devin took the small girl in her arms and spun her around in a circle. "It's good to be home."

"Welcome home, baby sis," Damien said and took them both into his widespread arms. "Looks like you have just beaten the first feeder bands of the storm."

"What's the latest news?" she asked.

"Irene has lost strength and is a large tropical storm, but the bad news is she has also slowed down. We may have pounding rains for several days." He saw her look of concern. "Did your friends all make it out of New Orleans?"

"Yes. Tia is headed to Monroe, we rode together until just a little while ago, and Kaitlin and George are headed north as well."

"Good, then they shall be safe."

"Is there anything left to be done here?" she asked.

"Nope, we are just hunkering down to wait out the storm. Tara is preparing a nice meal for your return, so we shouldn't keep her waiting." He grinned as he opened the door.

Elizabeth nearly dragged her through the door and the other children flocked to her immediately, squirming for her attention. Immersed in children, Devin sprawled across the floor wrestling and tussling with them until Tara came in to announce dinner.

"Hello and welcome home, little sister." She hugged her.

Devin hugged her back. "I really was making my way to the kitchen to help."

"You helped more by keeping the little ones out from under my feet." Tara's arm remained around Devin's shoulder as they walked to the dining room.

"I can't believe how they seemed to have grown in such a short time."

"It's never a dull moment around here." Damien joined them.

A brisk wind caught the front door to the porch and blew it open. "I'll get it." Devin walked back onto the porch to latch the door. Movement across the yard caught her eye and she watched as two large wolves loped across the clearing and disappeared into the woods.

"Patrols," Damien said. "Just to keep an eye on the weather conditions and any potential damages."

"Can I help out?"

"Sure you can take a shift with me later tonight," Damien said, much to her relief.

"Thanks." Devin walked with him back to the dining room. "Something smells terrific."

Devin joined her family for a feast and when all were stuffed to the brink of explosion, she announced she would help Tara with the cleanup.

"I have a better suggestion." Tara grinned. "I know some little ones who are in need of a nap, and I bet they would love to have a story ready to them by their favorite aunt."

"Yes, yes, yes," squealed Elizabeth and her siblings. "Please tell us a story, Devin."

"Okay, your room, now," she said to Elizabeth. The children flew up to the room previously occupied by Devin and piled into the large bed.

Devin crawled into the middle of them, surrounded by the children who cuddled up next to her as she began to speak, retelling one of their favorite stories. One by one they drifted off to sleep, the warmth of their tiny bodies snuggled up next to her made her eyelids begin to droop.

An hour later, when Damien and Tara climbed the stairs to check on them, they stood in the doorway and looked at the pile of kids draped all over a sleeping Devin. "They look so very natural, don't they?" he asked his wife.

"Yes, she's a natural with the kids."

"Should we take advantage of the quiet to catch a nap of our own?" Damien asked with a mischievous grin.

"I'm right behind you, handsome." Tara playfully swatted Damien's jean-clad backside.

†

Tia was concentrating so closely on the road that she never noticed the dark van that had been following her for the last hour. She pulled into a nearly empty gas station and slid her credit card to fuel up. She looked at the road behind her at the storm she was trying to outrun. When done filling her tank, the van pulled into the station blocking the view to the pumps from inside the store. She saw a tall, muscular man step out of the van, but didn't pay attention to him until his large arm wrapped around her neck and a damp, sweet-smelling cloth covered her mouth. Darkness overtook her as the man dragged her into the back of the van. Another smaller man inside the van removed her helmet, then mounted her bike, and started down the road as a blond woman chatted up the young man operating the cash register. She paid for her drink, returned to the van, and climbed inside.

"Is she out?"

"Yeah, we have her bound and gagged, but she will be out at least a half hour," the man driving the van said.

"Excellent. We will be back in Monroe and have her safely stored before she wakes."

"It may be close, but there will be very little traffic out in this weather." He pulled back onto the highway.

"Let the fun begin." Cedra tossed her head back with a laugh.

†

Two hours later, Devin woke and carefully extricated herself from the pile of children surrounding her and silently crept down the stairs. The wind was howling as it circled the house, the sound drawing Devin onto the porch. Clouds passed quickly in front of the bright moon casting rapidly changing shadows on the front lawn. The Spanish moss, desperately trying to hang onto the cypress trees, blew furiously in the wind as fragments of limbs and unidentifiable items tumbled across the ground.

She heard soft footsteps approaching behind her and turned to see a shirtless Damien walking toward her.

"It's beautiful in a dangerous way, isn't it?" He stopped behind her and rested his arm along the doorframe.

"Yeah it is," she answered. "So mesmerizing and yet a moment of indecision could be fatal."

"Do you still want to join me on rounds tonight?"

Damien watched her carefully for an answer. "I would be disappointed if you left without me."

Damien chuckled. "I wouldn't think of it, baby sister. I've missed you terribly and want to cherish every minute I can with you."

"Will you two at least have a cup of coffee with me before you seek out the night?" Tara asked from behind them.

"That's a great idea," Devin followed Tara into the kitchen.

"It's getting pretty wild out there." Tara motioned toward the window. "I hope you will both be very careful."

"Of course we will," Damien said with a glimmer of mischief in his eyes.

Tara looked from her husband to his sister and saw the same glimmer of excitement shining in her eyes. "I swear you two should have been twins." She shook of her head. "On second thought, I couldn't handle two of you," she teased and punched Damien in the arm.

Damien shot a look at Devin. "Are you ready to run, city girl?"

"Do you think you can keep up with me?" she teased back.

"I think I can manage." He placed his mug on the counter. "We'll be home around midnight." He bent down and kissed his wife.

†

Damien and Devin walked out of the house and started across the yard. "Stop if you sense danger and we will shift back to explore," he instructed.

"Yes, my Alpha." Devin lowered her head.

With a blur, they transformed into their wolves and began to trot toward the edge of the compound. Lights shone through windows as they passed pack members' homes and several watchers lifted their hands in recognition of their leader. All was well within the compound as Devin and Damien started to patrol the boundaries.

The rain pelted down and slid freely from their thick coats as they loped around the perimeter of the pack's property. They cleared a downed tree in stride as lightning streaked across the sky, its bright fingers reaching from cloud to cloud. Another bright flash illuminated two wolves approaching them. She and Damien came to a halt and shifted back to human form as the wolves also transformed to human.

Devin recognized Thomas and his mate Sara as they approached.

"Greetings, my Alpha," Thomas spoke.

"Greetings, Thomas and Sara, I hope all is well."

"The grounds seem to be holding up just fine although the northeast quadrant is experiencing some flooding."

Damien nodded. "I wouldn't be surprised to see more of that soon. The weatherman says Irene has all but stopped movement and is going to soak us with heavy rains for a couple of days."

"Do you think we have any serious concerns to worry about?" Thomas asked.

"As long as it is just rain, we will fare just fine, but if the winds pick up we could have some minor damage."

Damien nodded toward Devin. "We will continue the patrols and I would appreciate it if you would check with the pack homes to make sure everyone is safe and well supplied for a couple of days."

"Consider it done, Alpha." Thomas turned to his mate and they shifted back into wolf form and loped away.

They watched them leave and Damien turned back to Devin. "Are you doing okay?"

"Yes, I'm fine."

"Let's move on then and check on the few families that live outside of the compound on pack property."

Devin followed him with her shift and fell in behind him as another wave of hard rain began to fall. They trotted along the trail easily until they reached an intersection and Devin skidded to a halt. The hackles on her neck rose to attention when she realized where their travels had brought them.

Damien sensed Devin's anxiety and turned to walk back to her. Devin was staring down the dark path that led to the Devil's Tree, the place where their parents were murdered. Damien sent her a communication to ask if she was all right and when she turned to look at him her eyes were aglow with anger.

"That place still makes me feel ill," Devin responded to him. "Can't we cut down or destroy that tree somehow?"

"Many have tried to no avail over the years. The tree is protected by a strange energy that prevents any harm to it." He turned his head to look down the trail. "After our parents were killed I tried taking an ax to it and even the sharpest blade could not penetrate the stone-like bark."

"What about fire, could we burn it down?"

"Nope, tried that too and the flames won't ignite within several feet of the trunk."

"Well damn." A low growl followed Devin's words.

"Relax, everything is fine," he answered. "Do you want to go see it for yourself?"

"No, that damn tree haunts me bad enough already."

"Let's continue on then." Damien turned away from her.

Devin stared down the path for several more seconds and then galloped away to catch up with Damien.

Together they checked on several families, who welcomed them inside for warm drinks and hot fires burning in the fireplaces to ward off the damp cold. All were pleased to see Devin and hoped she was home to stay, but she quickly informed them she was just seeking shelter from the storm and that she would be returning to New Orleans once the storm passed. When they left the last home, they proceeded into the section reported to have flooding, and it was evident that the waters continued to rise as the ground saturated with the rain that continued to fall in torrents.

Satisfied that no major damage would result from flooding in this sector, Damien led them back toward the compound. They were within a quarter mile when they saw the approach of the next pair of wolves to take over the patrol. Damien gave them quick instructions and they continued back to their home.

Tara had left out thick towels for them and a full pot of coffee. Damien finished drying first and asked, "Will you join me for a cup of coffee before we head off to bed?"

"I'd love to." She followed him into the kitchen.

Once they had filled their mugs with steaming coffee, Damien sat next to his sister at the table. "So tell me how things are going in New Orleans."

Devin told him about Kaitlin and the club. He was quick to notice a softening in her voice as she talked about Tia and he didn't twitch a muscle when Devin explained how attracted she had become to Tia.

"So when do we get to meet her?"

"I had hoped she would come with me tonight, but she wanted to get home to Monroe before the worst of the storm hit. Maybe once we return to New Orleans we will ride up for a day or two."

"You know you are always welcome."

"Thanks, Damien. I can't explain it all, but I feel very right when I'm with Tia."

"She must be very special then," he said with a genuine smile.

"Lucia, the med student from the Houma pack, thinks she has some sort of latent tendencies."

Damien leaned in closer. "That would be very interesting."

"Her soul has the most intriguing cinnamon and apple scent," Devin said with a soft sigh she did not realize she was holding back.

Damien chuckled at her obvious attraction to Tia. "An earth scent is a good sign."

He watched a dark shadow fall across Devin's face. "Is there something wrong?"

"I forgot to tell you that I ran into Cedra the witch and her mutts in New Orleans."

This time it was Damien's turn to have his hackles rise. "What happened?"

"I thought I saw them on bikes a few times and then they came into the club one night. We exchanged a few unpleasant words and I convinced them to leave the club."

"Is she living in New Orleans or just passing through?"

"I'm not sure, to be honest."

Damien leaned forward and traced the outline of Devin's neck until his fingers caught on the necklace and he lifted it with a sigh of relief. "I'm glad you are wearing this."

"I promised you I would and I never take it off."

"Good, somehow I think we have some unfinished business with the witch."

Devin nodded. "I do too. I just wish I knew what it is."

"When the time is right I guess we will know. Just be extra careful where she's concerned, Devin."

When they finished the coffee, Damien suggested they try to get some sleep. They climbed the steps together and found that Tara had carried the younger children to their room, but Elizabeth was soundly asleep in the bed.

"She really loves you, and so do I." He leaned down to kiss her forehead. "Get some rest, baby sister," he whispered and walked on to the master bedroom.

Devin stood in the doorway for several more minutes, watching the gentle rise and fall of Elizabeth's chest as she slept until she noticed a light flashing on her phone indicating a message had arrived. Picking up her phone from the table next to bed, she found a text from Kaitlin letting her know she had made it safely to Jackson. Devin answered the message quickly then searched for a message or call from Tia to no avail. She was disappointed, but figured Tia was catching up with her family and had forgotten to call. She promised herself she would call if Tia hadn't checked in by lunchtime. Satisfied with her plan, she changed into bed clothing and slipped in beside Elizabeth.

Chapter Eleven

Devin woke to the feeling of a warm body snuggling against her. Opening her eyes she found Elizabeth curled up next to her and reached down to stroke her soft hair. The sound of the rain pounding on the roof assured Devin that the weather had not eased up during her slumber. She closed her eyes and let the falling rain lull her back to sleep.

The next time she awoke, it was to the smell of frying bacon and fresh coffee. She could hear the smaller children playing quietly downstairs, but the slow beating of Elizabeth's heart let her know her bedmate was still sleeping soundly.

She placed a warm hand on the child's shoulder and gently shook her awake. "Hey, Lizard, it's time to wake up."

Elizabeth's eyes fluttered as she stretched and then looked up to find Devin looking down at her.

"Good morning, Lizard."

"Morning, Devin," she answered and stretched again. "You're so warm and snuggly."

Devin chuckled. "I don't have to ask if you slept well, but if we lay here much longer we may miss out on breakfast."

"Um, and I smell bacon," she answered.

"Your father did mention cooking pancakes this morning," Devin said.

Elizabeth shot up. "Let's go then." With great excitement she jumped from the bed.

"You go on down and I'll be there in a minute." Devin made her way to the bathroom while Elizabeth ran down the steps. She used the facilities and washed her face with warm water. As she passed back through the bedroom she glanced at her phone and was disappointed to see no new messages. She slipped her feet into bedroom shoes and went downstairs to find the rest of her family clustered around the kitchen table.

"Hey sleepyhead," Damien said as he flipped a pancake. "Grab some coffee and join us."

Devin gratefully walked to the coffeepot and poured a cup. "Is there anything I can do to help?"

"You can pull some plates down." Damien pointed to the shelf that held the plates, as if Devin didn't know where they were.

She smiled and walked to the shelf. "I haven't been gone that long," she teased.

Damien shrugged. "Habit."

"Don't let him fool you, Devin, he's just used to bossing people around." Tara snagged a slice of bacon from the large pile Damien had cooked.

"I resemble that remark." He playfully swatted at Tara's hand with the spatula.

"You look like you are cooking for an army. Do we have company coming?" Devin asked as she set the plates on the counter.

"You have been gone too long. These pups are nearly eating us out of house and home."

Devin smiled. She knew how much her brother loved his wife and children. "Would you have it any other way?" she asked as she reached for bacon.

"Absolutely not." He swatted her hand. "You have to wait."

"That is so unfair." She pouted and leaned against the counter.

He flipped another pancake on the griddle. He caught her staring out the window. "It's been pouring all night."

"Any damages?" she asked.

"Just the anticipated flooding, but nothing else so far. The weatherman said this may move through by tomorrow. I stress the may part of his report."

"We need the rain to help prevent a drought, but we don't need it all at once," Devin said as she turned toward him.

"True dat. Good for crops and gators, but I'm ready for some sun."

Devin jumped as Damien's cell phone rang. It was some of the pack calling to report in and he was pleased that everyone was safe and settled in for the day. When he ended the call, he looked back at her. "Is everything all right, Devin?"

"Yeah, I'm a little concerned that I haven't heard from Tia yet, but I reckon she's tied up with her family."

"So why don't you call her after we finish eating so you can have some peace of mind."

"I think I'll do just that," she answered as the herd of children rumbled into the kitchen.

After breakfast, Devin went upstairs to shower and tried to reach Tia but her phone went straight to voice mail. Devin sent a text and after waiting for several minutes decided to go ahead and shower with hopes Tia would read the text and try to contact her.

✝

Tia woke to find she was bound to a sturdy straight-backed chair in some sort of warehouse building, her head pounding from the drug they had used. Her eyesight was blurry, but she eventually recognized the bikers who had been in the club.

She heard her phone ring once in her saddlebag as it went to her voice mail and then the text alert tone sounded. She knew it was likely Devin or Kaitlin trying to check in since she had not alerted her family that she was coming home. Damn poor planning, she thought to herself as the blond woman walked over to her bike they had parked inside the building.

"It sounds like someone is trying to reach you." The blond fished through her bag until she found Tia's phone. She looked down to see that Devin had called and then sent a text. "Your big bad protector, who isn't doing a very good job, is probably wondering where you are." She spun around to glare at Tia. "Such a shame she can't track you in this weather." She broke out in laughter.

"Are you going to call the bitch or let her stew for a bit?"

"I'll give her a few more hours and then I'll send her a text. This is going to be so much fun."

132

A door flung open and one of the men came inside swearing at the weather. "That damn rain isn't about to let up anytime soon." He dropped several bags onto a table.

Tia could smell fried chicken and her mouth began to water. She had no idea how long she had been unconscious, but her stomach was letting her know it was time to eat.

"Would you bring our guest over to the table and loosen her right hand?" she asked one of the men.

Tia assumed he would untie her and lead her to the table so she was surprised when he picked up the chair with her tied in it and carried her across the room. He sat the chair down next to the table none too softly.

"Easy, jerk," Tia said.

Maybe it was a trick of her eyes, but Tia could have sworn his canines were sharp and pointed as he snarled back at her.

"Shut up if you want some food."

He shoved a plate in front of her and Tia dug in, eating heartily of the semi-warm food. "What do you want from me?" she asked with her mouth half-full of food.

"You, darling, are just the bait." The blond woman laughed.

"Bait?" Tia asked completely confused.

"Your girlfriend's brother killed my lover and I intend to get some payback."

"What girlfriend are you talking about?"

"That wolf-creature Devin and her brother Damien," she answered.

"Wolf-creature, what the hell are you talking about?"

The woman looked in disbelief at Tia and then at her male friends. "You seriously don't know, do you, that your girlfriend is a werewolf?"

"Yeah right, and I'm the fairy godmother," Tia spat back.

The woman broke out in laughter. "This is priceless."

The men joined her in laughter, which left Tia even more confused. "Should we give her a demonstration?"

"That's not a bad idea," the woman said. "Go ahead."

Tia watched in horror as the largest man stood up from the table. He seemed to blur as his form began to change. When she saw the grotesque creature the man was shifting into and the evil in his red, glowing eyes, she screamed and passed out.

†

Devin was dressing after her shower when she was overcome with a strong sense of distress. Feeling that Tia was in some sort of danger she picked up her phone to try to reach her again. She punched in Tia's number and waited for it to ring. "Come on, come on, Tia, pick up please."

†

Cedra heard the phone ring and reached for it. When she saw it was Devin calling, she could no longer resist answering the call. "Well hello again, lover-girl"

The blood drained from Devin's face when she heard the voice at the other end of the line. How could Cedra have Tia's phone, unless…? She let that thought lay unspoken.

"Are you not going to speak?"

Devin ground her teeth in anger. "What have you done with Tia?"

"Oh, she's just fine. A little tied up at the moment, but she's fine." She chuckled.

"What do you want, Cedra?"

Damien heard his sister speak the witch's name and rushed upstairs to find her on the phone.

"Oh, darling, I want you and that cur brother of yours. We have some unfinished business to take care of."

"Tia has no part of our business," Devin snarled.

"Oh, but she does. I know how much she means to you, but I feel I must warn you, she is terrified of werewolves," she said, barely containing her laughter.

"What have you done?" Devin demanded to know.

"Nothing yet, but I don't know how much longer I can hold off the boys," she warned.

"I promise you will die a slow painful death if you harm her."

"Well, my dear, that all depends on you and how long it takes you to get here. If you and Damien come alone, I promise I won't harm her."

"I can't speak for my brother, but I'll be there. Just tell me where."

"That's no good. I want you both to come. We will meet where this all started years ago at the Devil's Tree at sundown tonight Cedra ended the call.

Damien walked over and took the phone from Devin. She was holding it so tightly he could hear the plastic beginning to crack. "What's going on?"

"Cedra has Tia somewhere and is holding her captive to get you and me to meet her."

"Well, let's get going then," he answered. "Where are we supposed to meet?"

"At the Devil's Tree, where this all began, at sundown tonight." Devin looked at her brother with tears in her eyes. "I cannot ask you to leave your family to fight this battle," Devin said.

"You are my family or have you forgotten? I think it's time we are done with Cedra of Monroe for good."

"Just give me a moment to explain to Tara and then we will make our preparations. You have your pendant on, correct?"

"Yes, Damien, but I can't ask you to risk your life. The kids need you."

"If we don't deal with her now, next time it could be one of the kids she takes. Besides, I won't let you have all the pleasure of killing that witch and avenging our parents."

Devin's smile was grim. "Okay, thanks Damien."

"Go play with the kids and send Tara upstairs, if you would."

Devin nodded and left the room.

Tara passed her on the stairs as Devin went in search of the kids. She found them playing in the living room and Elizabeth sat with her on the sofa. "Lizard, your father and I need to go out for a while, so I need you to help your mom," she explained.

"No problem, Devin. Will you be gone long?"

"I hope not. We will be back as soon as possible, I promise."

A few minutes later Damien and Tara came downstairs and joined them. "Thomas and a few others will join us in the garage in just a few minutes."

Devin nodded and walked with him to the door. Tara hugged them both. "Hurry back soon." She turned away before her tears began to fall.

"Let's go." Damien ran across the soggy yard to the garage.

Devin could see headlights approaching as they went inside. "You know we have to do this on our own, right, or she will harm Tia."

"She is in our territory. We will have a few of the pack embedded in case she tries to ambush us. You said she travels with three Weres, correct?"

"Yes, all mature males."

"You and I should be able to handle three, don't you think?"

"As angry as she makes me, I think I could do all three by myself," Devin said.

"Don't allow your anger to cloud your senses. Battling a full-grown male is much different than sparring," he gently reminded her.

"Let the others in while I make a quick call." He walked to his truck. Damien found his phone, and punched in a number given to him years ago.

"Hello Damien," a husky voice said when the call was answered. "I hope you are well."

"Hello, Lucas. No time for a social chat. I'm calling to tell you Devin and I've been summoned to meet Cedra at the Devil's Tree at sundown. She has kidnapped a friend of Devin's for bait."

"You aren't going in alone are you?" Lucas asked.

"I will have six of my best embedded in case she tries to ambush us. She travels with three Weres, but if she has recruited more we may be in trouble."

"I would like to bring a few of my most trusted to come with me to see this witch destroyed once and for all, if I may."

"Come in from the west. She won't expect you to be present, and will not be looking for you. If things go bad, I hope you finish her off," Damien said around the large lump in his throat.

"Damien, if you and your sister go down I promise you I'll die trying to take her myself."

"Thank you, Lucas."

"Good fortune, my brother," Lucas said and the phone went silent.

Damien joined the group huddled around the workbench. There were only a few hours before sunset and they had planning to do.

"Thank you for coming so quickly. Has Devin filled you in on her phone call?"

"Yes, she has." Thomas and the other five men nodded.

"Good. We will have company coming in from the west to observe and assist as needed. I have contacted Lucas and he is on his way with a few of his best, in case things get messy."

"Lucas is a good man," Thomas said.

Damien saw Devin flinch at the mention of Lucas. "He has every right to be here and he has promised to take her down if we fail."

"You said she has three with her. Do you expect her to bring more?" Thomas asked.

"No, but I want to be prepared if she does. Hopefully the three rogues are all she has under her spell."

"Speaking of spells," Thomas said, "how will the two of you be protected from her magic?"

"Hopefully with these." Damien lifted the amulet from around his neck. "Lucas's pack nearly caught her years ago and managed to bleed her enough to make these as protection. I guess it's time to see if they really work."

"What do you need us to do?"

"I want you to be embedded in the swamp around the Devil's Tree clearing. Be on the lookout for any ambush or tricks she may have up her sleeve. I fully expect her to use her magic to seal us off in a dome of combat like she did our parents." He looked at Devin and then back to his men. "If so, it won't be broken until her wolves are dead, or we are. If we lose this battle, I want you to be ready to attack as soon as the dome disappears."

"When you kill the ones with her, what do you want us to do?" Thomas completely ignoring the mention of failure.

"Once the battle starts, come as close as the barrier will allow. When it ends, we will rip her to pieces and scatter her remains throughout the swamp."

"May the gators feast well tonight then," another man said.

The door opened and Tara entered carrying a large tray of sandwiches. "If you're going to battle you will need plenty of strength."

"Thank you." Damien took the food from his wife, kissing her softly before she turned away. He prayed it would not be the last time he kissed his beautiful mate as he turned to set the food on the table.

✝

"Are we all set?" Damien asked.

"Yes, we have our plans in place," Thomas said.

"We will follow your route in a half hour, so ours is the only scent the Weres may pick up," Damien instructed as he walked his men to the door.

"Battle well, my Alpha." Thomas hugged Damien before fleeing out the door. The five men, each of whom embraced Damien, disappeared into the storm following Thomas.

139

Proud of the strength of the pack, Damien turned away when the last man left and looked at Devin, who was pacing nervously.

She stopped when she saw he was watching her and asked, "Any last words of advice?"

"You take the smallest of the wolves and go for his throat every chance you can while protecting yours. If you can't get to his throat, go for a shoulder to see if you can make him feel the pain of every step he takes. Stay on your toes. We don't know who is with her, so we don't know how they will fight."

"And the witch?" she asked.

"Let's get through her protectors first. When the barrier goes down with the last wolf's death, I'm sure she will flee for her life. Thomas and the pack will be ready and if she dares flee west, Lucas and his pack will cut her off and herd her back toward us. You take Tia to safety and we will handle the witch."

"But, I want…" Devin started to say, but her brother interrupted her.

"I know you want to be there, but Tia does not need to see what we do to Cedra. Trust me, baby sister, Cedra will the feel pain of our parents' deaths before she dies," he promised.

Devin nodded her head with understanding, knowing he was right. Tia would probably be in shock with what she was about to witness, and she kicked herself for not sharing more of her life with Tia to lessen the horror she would probably be feeling.

Damien looked at the time. "Are you ready?"

"Yes, I am," she said, sounding much more confident than she felt.

"Let's cover the scent trail of the pack well, so they remain undetected." He opened the door for her.

Damien stepped out and looked up at his house to find Tara watching from the porch. "I love you," he projected to her.

"I love you too, my Alpha," she returned.

Devin's and Damien's forms blurred as they made the transformation into wolf and dashed out into the fading light of late afternoon. They easily picked up the scent of the pack as they followed the trails they made, leaving their scents behind.

When they had covered the members of their pack, Damien and Devin met at the Devil's Tree. In the fading daylight, the ever-present handprint glowed against the dark bark, making the hackles rise on her neck. She saw Damien's wolf begin to blur and she changed back into human form to stand beside him.

She quickly pulled her dark hair flat against her head and tied it behind, out of her face and eyes. Then they waited.

†

"Get her in the van," Cedra instructed. "We need to get a move on."

One of the men checked the bindings at her wrists and then lifted her none too gently to her feet. "Do you want her blindfolded?"

"There's no need for that," Cedra said with an evil grin.

Placed on a backseat and surrounded by two of the men, Tia watched as Cedra and another man occupied the front. "You know where to go, correct?"

"To the Devil's Tree, right?"

"Yes, that's the spot."

"No problem then." He pulled the van out of the warehouse.

The rain continued to fall, but Tia recognized that she had been held captive only a few miles from her family home.

As they drove ever closer to Baton Rouge the air in the van became heated with the excitement coming from the men. When they passed the small gas station where she and Devin had stopped, Tia knew they were getting close.

"We will be there soon and avenge the death of our brother, Laurent," Cedra said.

One of the men had placed a hand on her thigh and Tia kicked out at him. The man snarled, showing sharp fangs and slapped her face.

"Save your strength for the fight. You can have that wench afterward. You can all have her." Cedra chuckled. "I will have no further need of her."

"Go to hell," Tia spat at her.

"Been there, done that, got the T-shirt," Cedra said. "Not a bad place at all."

"I'm glad you like it so well. That way you'll feel at home when Devin sends you there permanently."

"There is no way that whelp is going to defeat us, as you will soon see for yourself. Stop here," she told the driver.

One of the men roughly pulled Tia out of the van to stand in the rain. "Go ahead and release her hands. She has nowhere to go now."

The man grunted his disapproval, but did as told. Tia rubbed her wrists and glared at him. "Good boy, now sit."

The man rushed to pounce on her. "Stop," Cedra commanded and his form froze in mid-step. "Don't press your luck too far," she warned Tia.

A man pushed her from behind and she fell into step following the others with no hope of escape. Her feet sloshed through the soaked ground. They walked for twenty minutes as daylight faded and darkness grew thick around them.

✝

"I can smell the witch," Devin said.

"I know, I can too. I love you, baby sister."

"I love you too. Are you ready to kick some ass?"

"We don't have much choice, but yes. Be safe and follow my lead."

Devin felt a trickle of sweat mix with the rain and run down her spine as she first sensed then saw movement across the clearing. Cedra led the way, followed by the three Weres with Tia in between them. She looked scared but unharmed, which was a great relief to Devin.

When Tia saw Devin in the clearing, she attempted to run to her but was caught by the arm and jerked backward by one of the men.

"Go ahead and let her go. There is nowhere else for her to go," Cedra said.

Devin stepped forward as Tia ran into her arms. "Are you all right?"

Tia shook uncontrollably in Devin's arms, but managed to whisper. "Yes, I'm fine."

"I wish I had told you more about my life before now, but it's too late. I promise I will tell you everything later tonight, but no matter what you see in the next few minutes, remember this: I love you, Tia."

Tia's response caught Devin off guard. "I love you too, Devin, no matter what happens."

"I do so hate to break up such a lovely reunion, but we have business to attend to." Cedra clapped her hands above her head.

There was no visible sign, but Devin could feel the invisible barrier that trapped them in the clearing. "Stay behind me," she told Tia and returned to Damien's side.

They watched the three men spread out in front of Cedra and begin to blur. "Remember, you take the one on the left," Damien's form began to shimmer and he turned into a large black wolf.

Devin chanced a last look at Tia, whose eyes were wide with disbelief, then she also transformed. She was the same dark color, but with some lighter streaks, and was smaller in form than Damien, but no less dangerous and somewhat quicker than her larger brother.

Tia backed away several steps as the wolves began slowly stalking each other. The wolf staring down Devin was huge, but nothing compared to the pair stalking Damien.

The pair rushed forward but Damien leapt to the side to avoid the first, who went tumbling past him. He crashed into the second wolf, who was caught by surprise at Damien's quickness, and sank his teeth into the wolf's throat. Damien let his momentum rip the tissue away from the owner's neck. The beast fell to his knees and tumbled over as Damien spit the muscle tissue and blood from his mouth and spun to look at the larger beast.

Devin and her attacker were a blur of teeth and claws, neither making contact as they crashed to the ground. Mud and torn earth flew everywhere as the two wolves struggled to get their footing. Devin was the first to stand and lunged at her enemy, making a drive for his throat. With a burst of energy he shifted and she went flying over his body. Devin skidded through the mud, maintaining her footing, and wheeled around to face him.

She rushed him again. As they clashed, her teeth found a hold in his throat and his teeth ground into her left shoulder. The pain was intense, but she fought the yelp of pain threatening to tear from her lungs, fearing Damien would lose his concentration to check on her. Instead, she limped backward, pulling most of her attacker's throat with her, clenched tightly between her jaws.

Time seemed to slow as Devin's attacker struggled to his feet, foam and blood running from his muzzle. He looked at Tia and then back to Devin. She was out of position to defend Tia and both she and her attacker knew it. Devin couldn't believe her eyes as he took one tentative step after another toward Tia.

Without thinking, Tia raised her hand, now glowing white-hot, and shouted "No!" at the top of her lungs. The wolf didn't stop and Tia hurled a ball of flame at her attacker. The ball struck the wolf and he burst into flame and fell to the ground. Her hand was aglow with another fireball as she turned to take aim on Damien's opponent. He stood frozen with fear and Damien lunged in for the kill.

Surprised and mystified by what had occurred, Tia turned to look at Devin, who saw the wildness of the fire still burning in her eyes. Her opponent dead, Devin shifted back to human form, the blood from her wound quickly soaking through her shirt as she walked toward Tia.

The energy in the clearing changed again, and as the wolf took his last breath, the barrier collapsed, leaving Cedra unprotected. Thinking quickly, her lips began to move as she worked feverishly to cast a spell toward Damien.

Damien prepared for a blow that never arrived as the power of the amulet released, blocking her spell. Cedra screamed when she realized she was powerless and defenseless against Damien and turned to flee the clearing. Thomas and the Baton Rouge pack members stepped from their posts. She skidded to a halt and spun around to change directions as Lucas and the Monroe pack stepped into the clearing.

"Take Tia home, Devin, and see after that shoulder," Damien shouted to her.

Shrieks of terror rang from the clearing as the wolves surrounded Cedra.

"Now, witch, you will feel my wrath for the death of my parents," Damien said.

"And for the death of my son," Lucas added.

In unison, the wolves closed in on Cedra, biting and tearing at her limbs as bones cracked and tissue shredded. Her death cries filled the air and then fell silent as the growls and snarls of the wolves grew louder.

An eerie howl filled the air, signaling the witch was dead.

Damien shifted back to human form. "Enough," he commanded and the wolves came to a stop. "We are done here."

The two packs shifted back into men as Damien reached down and picked up Cedra's head by her blood-filled blond hair. "Will you find a bog for this on your way home?" he asked as he offered the witch's head to the Alpha of the Monroe pack.

"Gladly, my brother." Lucas took his offering.

"We will scatter the rest of her across the bayou." Damien's pack went into action. "Thank you for your assistance."

"My thanks to you for allowing me to be a witness and participant to her demise." Lucas offered his hand to Damien. "Maybe now our packs can live in peace."

"I hope so as well. Good fortune to you, my brother," Damien said.

With a nod, Lucas and his pack turned and left the clearing.

☦

Devin had never walked back to the compound in human form before and the distance and blood loss began to take its toll on her body. She was leaning heavily on Tia for support and was beginning to worry if they would make it back to the compound when she heard paws splashing through the mud behind them. Moments later, Damien scooped her up in his arms and they moved quickly through the woods.

Damien projected to Tara to get the pack physician ready for the arrival of a patient and when they reached his front porch, the light was on and the elderly man waited for them in the doorway. "What do we have here?"

"Devin took a bad bite to her shoulder," he explained.

"You look like you could use a little attention too." The doctor motioned to Damien's side.

Damien hadn't realized that he had several long gashes along his left side. "Could probably use a few stitches, when I get done with your sister," Doc added.

The door burst open and Tara came rushing in. Damien saw the panicked look on her face. "We are going to be just fine. Who is with the kids?"

"Sara is watching them," she said. "She and Thomas will keep them tonight." Seeing him covered in blood she kissed his face. "God, you look awful."

"Most of it is hers." He motioned to Devin.

The doctor had already injected a potent pain shot and Devin looked at Tara with glassy eyes and waved.

"What am I going to do with the two of you?"

"Better make that three. Tia, this is my wife Tara. Tara, this is Devin's friend Tia."

"Dear God, you are covered in blood too," Tara exclaimed.

"It's all hers." Tia pointed to Devin.

"Do you have any blood left?" Tara asked Devin.

"She probably could use a pint or two," Doc said as he finished cleaning her wound. "It will have to wait until I get her sewed up, though, or she will just spit it back at me." He began to stitch.

Devin responded by passing out. Damien helped Doc get her on her side so he could stitch her up. "This is going to take a while, Tara, if you'd care to make a pot of coffee."

"I don't want any."

"That's fine, but I'm not as young as I used to be and I will need it," Doc said with a grin.

"Oh, I'm sorry." Tara went to the kitchen to brew a pot.

"Is there anything I can do?"

"I could use some extra light. If you would bring that surgical light over, I'd appreciate it."

Tia picked up the light and moved it to the location that would cast the best light on Devin's shoulder. "I'm studying to be a nurse, is there anything else I can help with?"

Doc pointed at Damien. "Clean that up for me and we will see if it needs stitching."

Damien gingerly lifted his arms to pull the T-shirt over his head. "I could have just cut it off," Tia told him.

"Not his favorite shirt." Tara walked back in carrying a mug of coffee for Doc. "I have thrown it out several times, but he keeps finding it and bringing it back."

"I can understand that, I have a few favorites too." Tia looked at the gashes on his flank. "I hope your stitching fingers aren't worn out, Doc. He's going to need a few."

"I'm going to be a while yet here. Are you up for it?" he asked.

"I've not graduated."

"No time like the present to get some hands-on training. Come watch me for a few."

Tia watched him for several minutes, taking in his technique. "Just like sewing an apron."

She couldn't resist as she turned to Damien and said, "I flunked out of home economics."

He broke out in laughter and immediately regretted his efforts as his side lit up with pain. "Give me some of what Doc gave Devin and you can have your way with me," he teased.

"Not while I'm in here, or she will be doing plenty more stitching." Tara winked at Tia.

"Sorry, Alpha, but you just need a local anesthetic." Doc gave him several injections around his wounds.

"Just like Devin to get the good stuff," he teased.

The door opened. Thomas and two of the pack that had been at the clearing stepped into Doc's house.

"This is not a party," Doc chastised the men.

"We had to check on the Alpha and his sister," Thomas said.

"They will live, so be gone for now so we can work here."

"Everything has been taken care of in the clearing."

"Thanks, Thomas, I will see you in the morning."

Thomas and the others left as Tia began stitching the wounds on Damien's side. Doc stepped over to take a break and looked over her shoulder as she added a stitch. "I couldn't do better myself. Keep going."

"Thanks," Tia said, quite pleased with his praise.

Devin moaned and Tia looked over to see her face grimacing with pain. Doc caught her expression of worry. "Our kind metabolize drugs and alcohol quickly, so I have to give her another dose." He gave her another injection and Devin's face relaxed.

"Our kind is Were-folk, in case you didn't notice earlier," Damien said. "We have a lot to talk about tomorrow, including what happened with you."

"I would appreciate that, since I have no clue what really happened."

"We can explain it, but I think we all need a night to heal."

"I can wait."

Tia finished a stitch and reached for the scissors to cut the thread." One down and one to go."

Damien looked down at his side. "Doc's correct, you do stitch nice."

"Thanks, it's a work in progress."

"I think she's a keeper," Devin slurred from across the room.

Tia looked across at her and smiled.

"You do have skills that could be very useful here," Damien said.

"Lord knows I could use the help around here," Doc chimed in.

"Why do I feel like I'm being ganged up on?" Tia asked.

"Probably because you are." Tara handed her a mug of hot coffee. "Take a break."

Tia took the mug and turned on the stool toward Devin who had faded back into unconsciousness. "How is she doing, Doc?"

"She's going to be just fine in a few days. I will be done here in a half hour or so."

"Will she heal fast?"

"With her metabolism, probably in a week's time," he answered. "We heal slower when the damage is from another Were."

"So, if I had hurt her she would heal faster?"

"From you, no, you are not totally human either," he said, surprising her. "I can smell you are…different."

"Different how?" she asked.

Devin groaned in her sleep and Tia forgot her question as she walked over to her and brushed a stray strand of hair behind her ear. Damien watched the interaction and the loving way Tia touched Devin and he knew then that his sister had found what her soul was missing.

Tara read her mate's thoughts. She was smiling when he turned back to her.

Tia sat back down on her stool to finish stitching Damien's side and gasped, nearly dropping her mug when she saw his side. The smaller wound had closed on its own and was already in the beginning stages of healing. She looked up at Damien, who was grinning at her.

"Great genes."

"There, that should do it." Doc rolled back away from Devin.

"Can we take her home?" Tara asked. "I brought the SUV, so we didn't have to walk in the rain."

"I think that would be fine, but let me get you some meds in case she wakes up in pain. I've cleaned her up as much as I could, but I would suggest getting her out of these clothes and into something clean and fresh."

Tara looked at Tia. "Will you help me?"

"Of course," she answered.

Damien slipped the bloodstained shirt over his head before Tara took the opportunity to trash it again. "I will carry her out if you get the doors." He walked over to lift Devin into his arms. "Thanks, Doc," he said as he entered the rainy night.

"You're welcome, my Alpha."

"Climb in and you can keep her upright for the ride," Damien said to Tia.

Damien gently placed Devin on the seat and slipped in beside Tara who drove them home. "Thomas took the kids over to his and Sara's place for the night, so it will be peaceful for a little while." Tara pulled up close to the front door of a large log home.

Damien got out and opened the back door to take Devin into his strong arms. "Welcome to our home." He moved past Tia and started up a flight of stairs. "Will you stay with her tonight?" he asked as he set Devin on the bed.

"Of course I will," she answered.

"I'll help you. We can clean her up a bit and get her into some fresh clothes." Tara shooed Damien from the room.

"Call out if you need anything tonight, Tia." He left the room.

"I'll get these clothes off her if you will go into the bathroom and soap up a warm washcloth. We can at least get this dried blood off her."

"I can help," Devin said with a drug-slurred voice.

"Okay, lift your right arm so I can get this shirt off of you," Tara said.

It took several prompts, but Devin finally lifted her arm and Tara worked quickly to pull the shirt off. Doc had cleaned the general area of the wound, but dried blood caked her skin across her chest and down her side. Tia returned to the bedroom carrying several washcloths and a clean towel.

"You start on her side and I will work on her chest."

Tia went to work, gently scrubbing the dried blood from Devin's skin and tried hard to concentrate on the task and keep her eyes off Devin's small firm breasts. She could feel the rush of blood rise to her cheeks and was glad Tara did not mention her obvious embarrassment.

When they had the blood taken care of Tara said, "Let's get these shoes and pants off her and get her in something comfortable. I will work on the jeans if you will get a T-shirt from the top drawer."

Tara slipped off Devin's boots, socks, and unfastened her jeans. "Devin, can you stand so I can get these jeans off?" she asked.

"Sure." Devin used Tara's shoulder for support as Tara pushed the jeans off her hips.

"Okay, you can sit back now," she instructed as Tia pulled the jeans off Devin's legs.

Tara gently slipped Devin's left arm into the sleeve of the oversized shirt and then pulled it over her head, slowly guiding her right arm into the sleeve. "That's it, there you go." Tara guided Devin back onto the bed and pulled the covers over her as Devin turned on her side.

"I will take care of her clothes and the linens. Is there anything you need other than something to sleep in?"

"No, I will use one of Devin's shirts if that's all right?"

"That would be fine. Just call out if you need anything." Tara closed the door behind her.

Tia slipped out of her still damp clothes and put on a soft T-shirt that nearly came to her knees. Leaving a light on in the bath and the door cracked she turned off the bedroom lights and slipped into bed beside Devin.

This was not what she imagined their first night together would be, but she did not hesitate to snuggle into Devin's back and fell asleep listening to the soft rise and fall of Devin breathing.

†

Tara joined Damien in the kitchen as he sipped coffee and looked out the window at the pouring rain. "How are you feeling?"

"I'll probably be sore for a day or two, but it's such a relief to know that Cedra will bother our family no more."

Tara wrapped her arms around his waist and hugged him close. "I'm glad you both survived the whole ordeal. Do you want to talk about it?"

"With a little help from Tia we were able to defeat the rogues with Cedra and then the combined packs took care of the witch."

Tara noticed a mischievous grin on her mate's face. "What is that smile for?"

"Tia is not only a nursing student, but she is also a latent witch."

"What? Are you joking?"

"Not at all, she took care of Devin's attacker when he turned on her, with a fireball she created in her palm. She surprised everyone with her action, including herself."

"She had no idea?"

"I don't think so, but the terror of seeing Devin's attacker attempting to get an upper hand was enough to trigger her latent ability."

"That's incredible." Tara rested her head against his chest.

"We will definitely have some interesting conversations tomorrow." Damien drained his mug. "Are you ready for bed?"

"I thought you'd never ask?" Tara said with a grin.

Damien took his mate by the hand and climbed the stairs. They stopped off to peek inside Devin's room to find both women resting peacefully and then continued on to their room.

Chapter Twelve

Devin woke the next morning, her nerves on fire with pain from her shoulder injury. The medicine Doc had given her had worn off long ago and she desperately wished she had another one of his injections. Her only comfort was the warm woman snuggled up to her back. She slowly and carefully rolled onto her back, her movements wracked by jolts of pain, but Devin was eager to see that Tia was safe. She had little memory of the events that had occurred the previous night and the fog of pain running through her brain made clear thinking very difficult for her.

Tia's scent filled her nostrils as she lifted her painfully swollen arm to reach down and stroke Tia's soft hair. A flash of lightning filled the room, causing Devin to flinch, and when the loud clash of thunder arrived seconds later, Tia jerked awake. Another wave of thunderstorms had arrived in full force as Devin and Tia came eye to eye on the bed.

"Hey," Devin said.

"How are you feeling?"

"I'm stiff and sore as hell, but I think I'll live," she answered.

"You seemed to rest pretty well last night."

"Good drugs." Devin grinned. "I wish I had another of Doc's shots right now," she added as she tried to sit up in the bed. Her painful grimace was obvious even though she tried to tough it out.

"Wait, let me help you." Tia offered a hand to Devin and helped her to a sitting position.

"Thanks." Devin gave herself time to adjust to the new position. "I don't know about you, but I'm starved."

"I could eat and then I want to take a long hot shower," Tia said. "If that's okay."

"Of course it is. If you open that drawer you can find us both a pair of sweats." Devin pointed to her dresser. "We can eat and you can get your shower."

When they opened the door to go downstairs Tara was standing outside the door, holding a pair of jeans and a shirt, about to knock. "I thought I heard you two. I brought Tia some of my clothes to wear." She handed Tia the clothes.

"Thanks, it will be nice to have something clean to put on after a shower."

"Come on down, your brother is making omelets today."

"That sounds wonderful," Devin said. "Are the kids here? I don't hear anyone."

"They spent the night with Thomas and his family. Damien will go get them later this afternoon."

Tia put the clean clothes on the bed and then followed Devin and Tara downstairs. Devin walked gingerly down the stairs, thankful Tara had a grip on her elbow. "Doc came by with some pain pills for you this morning, but he made us promise to get you something to eat first. He will be back around lunchtime to check your wounds."

"I could use one of those pills," she said as they entered the kitchen.

"Sit and eat this first." Damien slid a huge omelet onto a plate with toast on the side.

"Good morning, Tia. Have a seat and I will have one up for you in just a minute."

"Thanks, that looks great."

Tara walked to the counter. "Coffee and juice for both of you?"

"Yes, please," Tia answered.

"How do you feel this morning?" Damien asked Devin.

She swallowed a large bite of the omelet before answering. "My shoulder burns like hell, but I'll be fine."

"How about you, Tia?"

"I'm fine, thanks."

He plated an omelet and toast for Tia and joined the three women at the table. He took a sip of coffee and looked at Devin. "Is this a good time to talk about what happened last night?"

Devin looked at Tia who smiled at her and she nodded at Damien. "I reckon it's as good a time as any."

"You two eat and I will bring Tia up to speed." He began the story of their parents' murders and Cedra's involvement in the process. Tia seemed to take the news about their being werewolves in stride and he worried she was still in a bit of shock.

"So, the reason you were abducted was to get to us," he said. "For that I am truly sorry."

"Everything ended well, so no apology needed. Besides, you had no control over what she did."

"No, but if it weren't for our friendship, you wouldn't have been put in that position," Devin said.

Tia shrugged and took another bite of her breakfast.

"You could have very easily been killed last night."

"I knew you wouldn't let that happen," she said with a smile to Devin, causing her to blush.

"If it hadn't been for you, I might not be here this morning to have this conversation with you. Thank you for killing my attacker," Devin said.

"I knew you could take him, but my anger seemed to get the better of me," Tia confessed.

"Did you have any idea you had special powers?" Tara asked.

"Not a clue and I still don't understand what I did or how it happened," she admitted.

"There obviously was a family member in your past with some magical abilities, and the trauma of last night's events brought your powers to a head," Damien said. "Other than Cedra, we haven't seen a witch in these parts for many years, but we may have an elder who can teach you about your abilities."

"Miss Anna?" Devin asked.

"If anyone would know, she would," Tara agreed. "She is our eldest and probably our wisest pack member."

Tia looked at her hands in disbelief as they talked. She remembered hurling a ball of fire from the palm of her hand, but there were no blisters or any signs of her previous night's events. "Do you really think I could do it again?"

"Once your powers have emerged, I don't think there is much chance of them going away," Damien answered.

"You will have to be careful with your temper until you learn to control your power," Devin added. "I'd hate for you to burn something down by accident." She smirked.

"Hey, I'm trying to be serious here," Tia growled giving them a stern look. "You may be comfortable being a supernatural creature, but this is totally new to me."

"She is absolutely right," Tara agreed. "We grew up knowing about the abilities we would grow into, but hers have been sprung on her without warning."

"I'm sorry." Devin hung her head.

Damien smiled. "So what's the plan?"

Devin looked at Tia and back to Damien then shrugged. "I have no idea. What do you suggest?"

"When do you have to go back to New Orleans?"

"That depends on the weather."

"The Weather Channel says the rain should end by late tonight, but officials are asking residents of New Orleans to stay away another three to four days until the floodwaters can recede and they can check the safety systems," Tara reported.

"I need to go to Monroe to check on my family and get my bike."

"Can I borrow your truck?"

"Anytime, where are you headed?"

"I thought I could drive Tia to Monroe."

"We could stay over with my folks and then come back tomorrow when the weather clears," Tia suggested excitedly.

"I think it would be best if Tia drives for now."

"Even if I don't take this?" Devin rolled the pain pill between her fingers.

Tara raised an eyebrow. "Especially, if you don't take that. Down the hatch."

"I will load the ramps and a tie-down in the back of the truck and you can load Tia's bike and ride back together."

Tara noticed Tia lift her hands to rub her temples. "Are you okay? I've seen you rub your head a few times."

Tia dropped her hands immediately. "I have this strange buzzing in my head that doesn't seem to want to go away."

"That is some of your power coming alive. Whenever you are in the presence of someone else with supernatural powers you will get a tingling or buzzing sensation to let you know they are near," Tara explained.

Devin grinned. "We can smell others with power to alert us."

"Will it go away?"

"Not entirely as long as you are with one of us, but you will learn to ignore it when you are with friends. Just be aware, you will feel it when you cross others that have powers," Damien warned.

"You will sense a lot of others once we return to New Orleans," Devin said. "The place is filled with vamps and other Weres."

"Vampires are real?" Tia asked with wide eyes.

"Very much so and like Weres, not all can be trusted."

"You can count on becoming very popular once your scent and powers are noted. Most otherworldly folk want to have a witch as a friend," Damien told her. "That is why it is so important you spend some time here with Miss Anna learning how to control your powers."

Tia nodded her head. "I understand."

"I had hoped we could spend the night in Monroe with my family, but now I think it would be best to return here tonight, Devin."

"I think your training can wait another day," Devin responded.

"Enjoy the time with your family and then come back tomorrow," Tara encouraged.

Tia took in a big breath and pushed back from the table. "I'm going to go shower and get ready. When you come up, Devin, I will help you if you'd like."

"I'd appreciate that," Devin said with a sparkle in her eyes. "I will be up soon."

Tia left the three Weres sitting at the table and climbed the stairs to clean up.

"She took that pretty well, don't you think?"

"I just wonder how much has really sunk in. I can sense she has very strong powers," Tara said.

Devin looked at Damien and Tara, the sparkle still glowing in her eyes. "Could you handle having a witch in the family?"

"You should know she would not be exploited here like she might be out in the world. Do you think Tia is what your soul was searching for?" Damien asked.

"I do. She makes me feel so complete."

"We would welcome her into the family with open arms. Does that mean you will be coming home soon?"

"I have not discussed anything with Tia yet. I'm not certain she has the same feelings I do," she answered.

Tara chuckled. "You may not see it yet, but she is madly in love with you."

"What's not to love about my baby sister?" Damien joked.

161

Devin blushed. "If she does share my feelings, I would like to stay in New Orleans until she finishes school and then, if she's agreeable, return to the compound so she can assist Doc. But again we have not discussed anything."

"I would be very open to the idea of her joining the pack and I know Doc was very impressed with her abilities."

"I guess we have a lot of talking to do yet," Devin said.

"How much longer does she have in school?"

"She can only go part-time because of finances—that's why she works at the club—so maybe two to three years."

"If she went full time would it be quicker?" Tara asked, following her mate's line of thought.

"Yes, I'm sure it would."

"Do you think she would accept money from the pack for books and tuition?"

Devin looked up at her brother with tears in her eyes. "I don't know, but it wouldn't hurt if you asked."

"I will do just that, tomorrow when you return," he said. "Now if you'll excuse me, I'll go make sure the truck is ready for you." Damien left the table.

Tara stood also to clear the table and Devin picked up her plate. "Let me take that and you go upstairs to get ready for your trip."

Devin kissed her on the cheek. "Thanks for everything." She walked to the stairs.

When she entered the room, Tia was slipping the shirt that Tara had loaned her over her head. Devin felt a lump in her throat as Tia's smooth skin was covered. She felt her inner wolf release a soft growl of pleasure. "Feel better now?" she asked.

Tia tucked the shirttail into the jeans that fit her like a glove. "Yes, nice and clean again."

"You smell wonderful."

"What do I smell like?"

"Vanilla shampoo and soap," Devin answered with a grin.

"You know that's not what I mean. What does my scent smell like to you?"

162

"Warm cinnamon and apples, a very pleasant combination to me."

Tia approached her slowly with an almost seductive sway. "How near do I have to be for you to smell my scent?"

"About a hundred yards or so, but the closer you get the more enticing the scent becomes."

Tia slipped her arms around Devin's waist. "This close, what does it do?"

"It makes you completely irresistible," Devin teased. "You haven't put a spell on me have you?"

"Not yet, but I may be tempted."

Devin chuckled. "I have been under your spell since the night I first saw you," she admitted.

"So did you know about me then, my powers I mean?"

"I knew there was something different about you, but I had no idea what it was."

Tia looked up into Devin's eyes. "Do I look any different to you now?"

"There is a glow about you that makes you even more beautiful to me," Devin answered.

"I can see that around you too, the glow I mean, but not the others. What does that mean?"

Devin took a deep breath and looked into Tia's imploring eyes. "In our society, when two can see the auras it means they were destined to be mated," she explained.

"So we are destined to be mates?"

"Yes, it appears so. Do you think you can handle that?"

Tia paused and then stepped back from Devin and looked her up and down. "Do you think you can handle me?"

Devin chuckled. "Handle you? Probably not. But love you? Yes, most definitely."

"Good." Tia stepped back into Devin's arms and kissed her softly. When they broke the kiss, she looked into Devin's eyes. "We have a lot to learn about each other, don't we?"

"Yes, we do, but we have plenty of time and don't have to rush things."

"Let's get you cleaned up and dressed then, and we can be on our way. I am excited for you to meet my family."

She carefully removed Devin's shirt, gasping when she saw her wounds for the first time in daylight. The angry tears in her flesh were much larger and deeper than she had previously thought, but she was amazed at how quickly they appeared to be healing. "How long will it take for these to heal?" she asked as her fingertips lightly touched the wounds.

"Longer than if they were made by a human, but I would guess the stitches can come out in a few days and the scars will eventually fade to a very small white line."

Tia looked up at Devin with a serious look on her face. "I'm almost embarrassed to ask, but since there is canine blood involved is there any chance of rabies?"

Devin roared with laughter, which caught Tia by surprise. "I would already be foaming at the mouth if I was rabid," she said with a deadly serious face. "Weres typically do not get the usual canine diseases because our metabolisms are so strong."

"That's good to know. I'd hate to think I had to shoot you," she teased.

Devin shook her head and started toward the shower. "I will be right back."

"Do you need any help?"

"I think I can handle the shower, but could you lay out some jeans and a shirt for me? Preferably an oxford to make it easier to get into, and something for tomorrow since we are spending the night."

"You got it." Tia went to work searching for clothes.

"There's a small suitcase in the closet," Devin yelled from the bathroom.

"Found it," Tia answered when she stepped into the closet.

When she turned around to leave the closet, Tia jumped in fright. A small girl was sitting on the end of the bed.

"Well, hello there," she said when she got her wits about her. "I'm Tia."

"I'm Elizabeth, but Devin calls me Lizard," the bright-eyed girl said.

"Would you mind if I called you Lizard too, then?"

The girl cocked her head and seemed to inspect Tia closely. "No, I guess that would be all right," she answered after a moment. "What are you doing?"

"Getting some clothes ready for Devin to put on after she showers," Tia answered.

"With a suitcase?" the girl asked, perplexed by Tia's answer.

"Oh, this." Tia put the suitcase on the bed. "Devin is going to give me a ride up to Monroe to check on my family, so she needed an overnight bag packed."

"Devin is leaving again already?" She groaned.

"We will be back tomorrow, I promise."

"Who are you talking to?" Devin asked from the bathroom.

Tia walked over to the door. "There's a Lizard in your room." She winked at the girl, bringing forth a chuckle.

"Is it a big one?"

"The biggest Lizard I have ever seen in my life," Tia answered dramatically.

"Two legs or four?" Devin asked.

"Hmm, let me check. Looks like two," she answered.

Devin walked to the door wrapped in a towel and was drying her hair with another. "Hey Lizard," she said with a grin.

Elizabeth's face went ashen when she saw the wounds to Devin's shoulder. "What happened?"

"Had to take care of some business and had a little scuffle along the way," Devin said. "Doc fixed me up good though."

"Tia says you are leaving today." She had a long face.

"Yes, ma'am, but we will be back tomorrow."

"Would you like to ride up to Monroe with us?" Tia asked.

"Could I, Devin?"

"Fine with me, but you better go ask your parents."

165

The child flew off the end of the bed and out of the room. "Are you really okay with that?"

"She seemed devastated that you were leaving. I think she really misses you."

"I miss her too, but will your family be all right with us bringing her?"

Tia folded a shirt into the suitcase. "You obviously haven't met my mom. The more the merrier she always says, and she will adore Lizard."

"I'm not sure she has ever been away from the compound without her parents." Devin stepped into her jeans.

"Will Tara and Damien object to her going with us?"

"I doubt it, especially since she's already running back up the stairs." Devin chuckled.

Lizard charged back into the room. "Dad says if you don't mind a tagalong I can go," she said, nearly out of breath.

"I guess you better pack your suitcase then," Devin answered.

Tara had also come upstairs. "You sure you don't mind, Tia?"

"Not at all."

"Come on then, Lizard, I have a bag that's just your size you can use. Let's go get your clothes together."

After mother and daughter left the room, Tia turned back to assist Devin. She noticed the excited glow in Devin's eyes as she pulled the shirt gently onto her body. "Have a seat and I will help you with your socks and boots."

They had just finished getting Devin dressed and the suitcase packed when Lizard returned with a small gym bag and a pillow. "Are we all set?" Devin asked.

Lizard nodded, her eyes wide and bright with excitement.

"Toss these in your bag in case you need them." Tara handed Devin the bottle of pain pills.

Devin reached for the suitcase. "I've got this." Tia swung it out of Devin's reach.

"Well, I guess we are all set then."

The group walked down the stairs together. They introduced Tia to the other children then Damien walked them out to the truck. The rain had temporarily slacked off so they loaded up without getting soaked.

"You are all gassed up and ready to go." He handed Tia the keys. "I don't know how much longer this rain will hold off though and it looks like you will be driving into some heavy rains, so be careful."

"I will. I have very precious cargo to protect," she answered.

Damien smiled at her answer. "That you do, my friend. Be safe and we will see you all tomorrow. Buckle up, Lizard." He then closed the door behind her.

Tia got in behind the wheel and adjusted the seat and mirrors as Devin put on her seat belt. "All set?"

"Onward to Monroe,"

"Okay, but you will have to give me some directions back out to the highway," Tia said.

"I think I can handle that."

Tia put the truck in gear and pulled out of the driveway, taking a left as instructed by Devin and they were on their way to Monroe.

Chapter Thirteen

Thirty minutes after leaving the compound Devin turned around in her seat to find Lizard sound asleep in the backseat. "That didn't take long."

Tia looked in the rearview mirror to see the sleeping child. "Not much to see but rain and swamp right now anyway."

"Thank you for inviting her to join us."

"You're welcome. I could see how disappointed she was when I told her you were leaving. I just couldn't stand not asking."

"She is very special to me."

Tia drove on for a few more minutes before asking, "Does she know about her heritage and who she will become?"

"She understands that our way of life is very different from others, but she won't start her real training until she is about ten."

"When will she change for the first time?"

"It is different for everyone, but it usually occurs when puberty hits. All those raging hormones and such," Devin explained.

Tia kept a tight grip on the steering wheel as she drove through the pouring rain. "Is it as painful as it looks?"

"To transform, you mean?" Devin rubbed her sore shoulder as she collected her thoughts for a response. "When you are first learning to shift, it hurts like hell. Your bones and musculature are completely changed in structure, but the more you practice, the faster your body learns to accept the pain, even welcome it."

She looked over at Devin, who was still rubbing her shoulder. "Do you need another pain pill?"

"No, I'll be fine, just stiff and sore."

"Could you transform now with that injury?"

"I could if it was an absolute life-or-death emergency, but I would not be at full strength and would be vulnerable to an attacker." Devin watched for Tia's reaction and was very pleased with the ease she had in accepting her answers and her eagerness to learn about the pack. "May I ask you something?"

"Of course," Tia answered.

"Do you have an aunt or grandmother that you've always thought was a little different from the rest of the family?"

Tia chuckled. "My entire family is a little different. Why do you ask?"

"I am trying to figure out where your powers come from. If it is from a living relative, they would be the perfect teacher for you since they would already know what abilities you have."

Tia remained silent for a long while as she thought about Devin's question. Devin saw her eyes light up when a memory came to the forefront.

"My grandmother used to make all sorts of weird jewelry and had a small pantry in her home that stored some really bizarre stuff."

"Like what?" Devin asked.

"Feathers from many types of birds, small bones, powders and all sorts of liquids in colored bottles. She didn't have a cauldron or a flying broom that I ever saw," she said with a grin.

"Those are so stereotypical of the old wives' tales used to scare children and are not accurate accounts of witches today." Devin's voice was solemn. "Is your grandmother still alive?"

"Yes, but she is in a nursing home and does not see many people these days."

"Do you think we could see her before we leave?"

"If you think it is important, we can only try," she answered.

Devin nodded her head. "It may help answer some questions."

"What other kinds of Were-folk exist?"

"Wolves are the most predominate, but there are Were-cats and rarely a shifter that can take on bird form, usually a very large raptor," she explained.

"Are there really vampires in New Orleans?" she asked with amazement.

Devin chuckled softly. "You'll find that out for yourself, but yes, there are dozens if not more living in New Orleans."

"I'll get a tingle or a buzzing in my head?"

"Yes, if you come close enough, but most are harmless and no longer feast on human blood. However, like our species, some vamps do go rogue and can be very dangerous," she warned. "Once word gets around about your powers, expect to meet more than a few other supernatural creatures."

"Why is that?"

"If a pack or clan has a witch working for them they are much stronger and are seen as much more powerful."

"What skills could I bring to the pack?"

"You are one helluva bonfire starter," Devin teased.

"I'm serious," Tia said with a pout.

"I know, I'm sorry, I just couldn't resist. It all depends on what your gifts are." She reached over and covered Tia's hand with her own. "I honestly don't know a lot about witchcraft. Unfortunately Cedra is the only one I have ever had contact with and she wasn't the best of examples."

"What powers did she have?"

"She apparently had some mind control over the rogues that were with her and had the ability to create and imprison others inside a force field that drained energy from those she saw as enemies. That was how she was able to murder our parents."

"But why didn't it have the same effect on you and Damien?"

"Because we were wearing these." Devin pulled the amulet from under her shirt.

"I saw that when you were getting dressed." Tia blushed. "What is it?"

"Lucas, who you saw last night, is the pack leader from Monroe. Cedra was directly involved in the death of his son, and he and his pack have been tracking her for years.

171

Once they almost captured her and were able to bleed her enough to make these protection amulets." She tucked the amulet back underneath her shirt. "Lucas knew that Damien and I, and his family, would be possible targets of revenge for Cedra so he gave us each an amulet. The amulet was filled with the witch's blood and gave us protection from her powers."

"I don't want to be evil like she was," Tia said.

"I don't believe you will. You have a strong heart and won't be greedy for power like Cedra was."

Tia looked over at Devin. "That reminds me. I meant to ask you about that huge oak tree that had a red handprint on it. What is it?"

"It's called the Devil's Tree, and legend has it when someone makes a pact with the Devil, their handprint in blood is their signature on their contract. That's how Cedra was able to murder my parents and every time she is near the tree, her handprint glows red to give her extra power."

"That's spooky," Lizard said from the backseat.

Devin was not aware the child was awake and listening. She turned around and looked at her. "Yes, it is, Lizard, but hopefully we will never have to worry about being disturbed by it again."

"Can't we just cut it down?" she asked the obvious question.

"No, that tree is centuries old and cannot be destroyed. It's protected by dark forces and can't be harmed. If it could, we would have destroyed it long ago. That's why the pack frequently patrols the area. Even though it is on the pack's property, those that know about the legend of the tree occasionally still come to tempt their fate."

"I guess that's why I get the creeps when I see it," Lizard said.

"Me too, the hair on the back of my neck stands up," Devin told her.

"Is that where my grandparents died?" she asked, to Devin's surprise.

"Yes it is."

Devin saw the solemn look on Lizard's face. "Am I the only one getting hungry?"

"No, I'm hungry too," Tia answered. "We are almost to Monroe. Would you two like a burger and fries?"

"Oh yeah," Lizard said.

"Me too." Devin laughed.

Tia found a burger chain and pulled into the parking lot. They feasted on burgers and fries before returning to the truck to continue their journey.

"Would you look at that?" Devin looked out the window.

"What?" Lizard asked.

"The sun is peeking through the clouds."

"I'm glad, I'm tired of all this rain." Tia smiled.

"I am too," Lizard said from the backseat.

Tia pulled into the driveway of a small brick house and announced, "Here we are."

Devin and Lizard followed Tia up to the front door and waited for someone to answer their knock. An older woman, who looked like Tia, opened the door and gasped in shock when she saw her daughter standing there. "Tia," she cried. "I'm so glad you're home." The woman pulled her into her arms for a hug. "Please come inside out of this weather." She gestured them into the house.

"Mom, this is my friend, Devin, and her niece, Elizabeth. They have given me a ride from Baton Rouge to check on you and Dad. Ladies, this is my mom, Ann."

"It's a pleasure to meet you both," she said. "Your dad is at the store. He was driving me insane so I sent him out for groceries."

Tia laughed softly. "Cabin fever?"

"Big-time. Have you eaten, can I get you anything?"

"Thanks, but we stopped for lunch," Devin said.

"Well, come on in and let's sit by the fire in the den."

"How have you fared in this storm?" Tia asked.

"Other than cabin fever, we've been fine. The power has flickered a few times, but we never lost it. I hope this is the last of the rain for a while."

"I think we're done with the worst." Devin let Lizard crawl onto her lap.

"How long can you stay?"

"Just tonight, unfortunately. I wanted to come to check on you and I wanted to visit Grandma, if she will see me."

Ann's face turned into a frown. "Mom's not been doing well and may not agree to see you," she warned. "You know how she can get."

"I know, but I really need to try," Tia said.

"The earlier in the day the better then, nights are not good for her at all. Why don't you and Devin go to the nursing home and Elizabeth and I can make a cake for dessert tonight," she suggested. "That's not a place for children to be."

"Would you like to do that, Lizard?" Devin asked.

"Sure, Devin, I like to help out in the kitchen," she answered.

"Excellent, you can help me cook dinner too then," Ann said. "How about some fried chicken, rice, and biscuits with gravy?"

"My mouth is watering already," Devin's stomach growled in appreciation.

"Let's plan to eat at six." Ann smiled.

Devin looked down at Lizard. "You sure you're all right?"

"Yes, ma'am, we will be just fine." Lizard crawled out of her lap to stand beside Ann.

"Okay, we will be back soon." Devin gave Lizard a hug. "Love you."

"Love you more," Lizard said.

Tia and Devin left the house and were on their way to the nursing home when they passed a pickup truck. "There goes Dad. Boy, will he be surprised when he gets home."

"In a good way I hope."

"Does Lizard like playing checkers?"

"Yeah, she does."

"They will be just fine. Dad will have her playing for hours if she's not careful."

Devin chuckled and hoped he was ready for Lizard's energy. "That was sweet of your mom to keep Lizard while we visit."

"She's like that. Besides a nursing home really is no place for a child." She pulled the truck into a lot and found a spot next to a dismal-looking gray building. Tia caught the expression of concern on Devin's face. "It's a little better on the inside but not much."

They walked into the building and signed in at the nurse's station. A heavyset black nurse looked up at her and smiled. "She's in a rare good mood today. Did she know you were coming?"

"No, she didn't. This is a surprise visit," Tia said.

"Good luck then." The nurse went back to her charting.

"Thanks." Tia guided Devin through a wide hallway where many residents in various stages of slumber were slumped in wheelchairs or moaning softly from their beds.

Devin's heart ached as she saw the elders in the final stages of their lives, alone and separated from their families. She had never been inside a home as the members of the pack lived and died within their homes inside the compound, tended by their friends and family until their time came to cross over. She swallowed hard and fought off the depression that hung heavy in the building.

Tia finally reached a closed door and tapped on it.

"Go away," a frail voice yelled from inside.

Tia opened the door and stepped inside. "Grandma, it's me, Tia," she said.

Devin followed closely behind and saw a waif of a woman with sharp blue eyes lying on the bed. Her expression instantly turned from anger to excitement when she saw Tia. "Tia, my child, I knew you would be here soon." She reached out her hand.

Tia took it and kissed the age-spotted, wrinkled hand. "Hello Grandma."

Devin felt the tingling as soon as the door opened and when the old woman in the bed fixed her with her eyes, she knew where Tia had gotten her gift.

"Grandma Ella, this is Devin."

"My, you are a handsome young pup," she said. "Pleased to meet you, have a seat."

"The pleasure is mine, Grand One." Devin bowed at the waist and then took a seat next to Tia.

The old woman smiled, very pleased at Devin's manners. Tia watched the interaction between them.

"The time has finally come," she said. "You have found your strength, just as mine is waning."

"Yes, Grandma, although I have no idea who or what I am," she admitted.

"That will come with time. I can feel your power through your touch, you will be a strong one," she added.

"I need you to teach me, please Grandma," she implored.

"My child, I do not have the time left to teach you, but I have two gifts that I want to share with you. You have to promise me something, though."

"What, Grandma?"

"My time is short and my wish is to be cremated and have my ashes spread in Baton Rouge, my birthplace."

Tia looked at Devin, who was smiling.

"You are from the Baton Rogue pack, correct?" she asked Devin.

"Devin Benoit, sister to the pack Alpha, Damien, who followed our father Darwin."

"Yes, I know. I met your father once many years ago," she said.

Both young women looked at her with shocked expressions.

"It's on your pack's ground that I wish to be spread and I want the two of you to do this. I have been dreaming of it for so long."

"I would be honored to assist," Devin assured her.

"Is Anna Blackburn still alive?"

"Alive and doing well," Devin answered.

"Open that bottom drawer and bring me the box inside." Devin quickly crossed the room to open the drawer and pulled out the requested box. She carried it back to the bed and handed it to her. "Thank you."

Devin nodded acceptance of her thanks and returned to her seat beside Tia.

177

"I want you to take this. It is a journal of my life and the gifts I've learned across my years. Read it and take it to Anna. She will know how to teach you."

Tia opened the box to find a beautiful leather-bound journal wrapped in a soft cloth. "Thank you, Grandmother, I will cherish this forever."

"Ha, forever is a long time, girl. Just learn from it what you can and, if you have a chance, pass it down to a next generation before you pass into the next world."

"I will, I promise." Tia's voice was full of emotion.

"Your mother was not born with the gift and knows nothing other than how odd her mother acted at times, and she knows not of this journal. I prefer to keep it that way."

"Yes, Grandmother," Tia agreed.

"There is only one other thing I can give you."

"You don't have to give me anything else," Tia said. "This alone is a treasure."

"I have no more need of my powers, Tia, and I would like for you to have all that I can give you. That along with some memories may be of help to you in your greatest times of need," she added. "You have a very busy future ahead of you."

She took Tia's hand between the two of hers. The room grew warmer as their hands began to glow softly. Tia locked in on her grandmother's gaze as her powers transferred from old to young. Devin was sad to see the light go out of Ella's bright blue eyes. She knew her time was drawing ever nearer.

The connection between them seemed to snap. Tia looked at Devin with a new light in her eyes and Devin knew Tia had inherited a lifetime of knowledge and power from her grandmother, the strength of which Tia had no clue, but would learn to manage in the coming years.

The woman in the bed looked drained as she lowered herself back onto her pillows. "I am a tired old woman and need to rest now. Thank you for coming to see me, Tia." She turned her gaze to Devin and spoke. "You are the protector and I expect you to love and cherish every moment spent with Tia."

"I will, Grand One," Devin said. "For as long as she will have me."

She turned her gaze back to Tia. "You will not find a stronger love than the one she offers. Cherish that and live a long life together."

Tia nodded through her tears and kissed her grandmother's cheek for what she knew would be the last time.

"Do not mourn me as I will cross over into a place more beautiful than you can imagine and my soul will be at rest once my ashes are home."

"We will honor your life and death." Devin and Ella smiled a knowing smile.

"Thank you."

"Goodbye, Grandma." Tia walked from the room before her tears began to fall. Once she was outside the closed door Tia collapsed in tears to Devin's arms, her body wracked with sobs.

Devin held her for several minutes, smoothing her hair until her sobs began to subside. "Rest easy, my love, that she will pass a very happy woman."

Tia nodded and allowed Devin to walk her out of the nursing home. Tia climbed into the truck holding the box tightly in her arms. Devin bit back the pain of using her left arm to weave her fingers with Tia's on top of the box between them as she sent her all the love and support she could muster through her touch.

179

When they arrived back at her parents' home Tia had her emotions under control. They walked in to find Lizard and Ann icing a cake as her father was setting up the checkerboard in the den. "Hey, Dad." Tia gave him a hug. "This is my friend, Devin, and I'm sure you have already met Lizard."

"Call me Eric, and welcome to our home." He opened his arms for a hug.

Devin embraced him warmly and turned away when she heard Lizard running toward her.

"Devin, you have got to come see what we have made." Lizard took Devin's hand excitedly to lead her into the kitchen.

"Whatever it is smells good," Devin told her.

"We made a cake," she said proudly.

"You did most of the work," Ann told Elizabeth with a warm smile.

"That looks delicious. I can't wait to taste it."

"I will start dinner in a few minutes. How did your visit go?" she asked Tia.

"It was very nice, but she tired quickly, so we didn't stay for long."

"I'm sure she was glad to see you."

"She seemed to be," she answered with tears beginning to pool in her eyes. "Can I help you with dinner?"

"Yes, I'd like that. Devin, why don't you and Lizard see if you can beat my old man at checkers," she said.

"Lizard is the checker champion of the family, so I will supervise to make sure she doesn't beat him up too badly," she teased.

She found a comfortable chair close to the fireplace and watched several checkers games before her eyes were drawn to the fire. She watched the dancing of the flames until her eyes grew heavy and she nodded off to sleep.

Tia heard Lizard chuckling and walked in to see Devin asleep. She lifted her finger to her lips. "Shh, she needs to sleep."

"Yes, ma'am," Lizard whispered and turned back to her game.

"Everything all right in there?" her mom asked when she returned.

"Yes, Devin has crashed for a nap and the other two are embroiled in a checkers battle." She grinned.

"She is such a well-behaved child. How did you meet them?"

"Devin and I work together and are neighbors in New Orleans. I stayed over at her family home in Baton Rouge when the storm got so bad and then she offered to bring me up so I wouldn't have to ride in the rain." Tia hated to lie to her mom, but she wouldn't understand what had happened over the last two days. There were still moments where it seemed a bad nightmare and not reality to her.

"That was very sweet of her," Ann said. "How is school going?"

"Not bad. I took the summer semester off to work full-time, but my grades have been good."

"I wish we had the money to pay for it so you didn't have to work at all." Ann sighed.

Tia smiled at her mom. "I know, but it's fine. I think I appreciate my education more having to fund it myself."

"That's a good point, but still I feel bad."

"Please don't, Mom, I'm really doing well, so relax."

"I hope you girls are hungry. I laid out a lot of chicken."

"We all have healthy appetites and if there are any leftovers maybe we can talk you into packing them for lunch tomorrow."

"Do you really need to go so soon?"

"Yes, but I promise I will visit more often."

†

Devin jerked awake and sat up in the chair, startled that she had fallen asleep.

"Welcome back. Are you all right?" Eric asked.

"I am so sorry for drifting off," she apologized.

"No worries, that chair gets me several times a week too." Eric grinned.

"Boy, something smells great." Devin stood and stretched, immediately regretting her movements as a pain shot through her shoulder.

"Dinner," Eric said.

Devin walked into the kitchen in search of what was putting off such a delicious aroma and found Tia and her mom hard at work. "Is there anything I can help with?"

"You can go ahead and set the table. I think Tia and I have the meal under control." Ann pointed at a cupboard and drawer. "You will find plates and utensils in there."

"I'm on it." Devin quickly went to work.

When she had finished, she returned to the kitchen to peek over the cooks' shoulders. "Dinner sure smells mighty good."

"It will be ready in five minutes if you want to ask the others to get cleaned up."

"Yes, ma'am." She set off in search of Eric and Lizard.

"Crown me," Lizard cried out as she walked back into the den.

"Do you think we can call a truce long enough to eat dinner?"

"I think we can."

"Time to clean up for dinner then."

"Come with me, ladies, and I will show you where the guest bathroom is." They followed him down a hall.

"Here you go. Everything you need should be available. If not just call me."

"Thanks Eric." Devin ushered Lizard into the bathroom. "So how are the games going?"

"All tied up for now. I hope to beat him in the tiebreaker after dinner."

"That sounds promising." She lifted her to sit on her knee enabling her to reach the sink.

A knock on the door alerted them to Eric's return. "Here, this may help." He handed her a small stool.

"Thanks Eric, this is perfect." Devin placed the stool in front of the sink. It was just the right height for Lizard to wash her hands. When done, they joined the others in the dining room.

When seated, Eric gave thanks for the wonderful meal and then the feast began. Devin couldn't resist moaning when she tasted Ann's fried chicken, which brought a round of laughter from Ann and Tia. "Can you cook like this?" she asked Tia.

"Probably not as good, but she's the one who taught me."

"I think this is the best I have ever eaten."

"I cut out the biscuits while you were napping," Lizard looked at Devin proudly.

Devin took a bite from a biscuit with an exaggerated expression. "Wow, these are great too."

Lizard beamed with pride.

Devin had seconds and was reaching for another biscuit when Tia reminded her they had cake for dessert. "I almost forgot." She shot Lizard a wink.

"Would anyone like coffee?" Ann asked as she and Tia started to clear plates.

"I would, Mama," Eric said.

"Sounds good to me too, please," Devin answered.

"Milk for you, young lady." Tia teased Lizard.

A few minutes later, Tia returned with plates full of cake, followed by Ann who carried a tray with coffee and a glass of milk. Devin eyed the slices and was excited to see a large slice headed her way.

"This was one of the best meals of all times." Devin swallowed a bite of cake. "If I don't stop soon though I might explode," she warned.

"There is plenty more for later if you get hungry." Tia smiled.

"I feel like I shouldn't eat for a couple of days, but you know me, I'll be starving again by breakfast."

"It's good to see people with good appetites and who know how to appreciate good food," Eric said.

After everyone finished dessert, the plates were rinsed for the dishwasher and fresh cups of coffee were poured and carried to the den for the big checkers playoff. The fire had warmed the room and the closeness of Tia on the couch next to her made Devin feel relaxed and comfortable in her family home.

With a final exuberant move, Lizard raised her hands in victory. "Gotcha."

"Yes, you did indeed." Eric looked on in amazement. "Congratulations."

"Thank you for playing with me," Lizard told him.

"I haven't had this much fun in years."

Lizard climbed into Devin's lap and for a short time listened to the adult conversation, but soon began to yawn. "I think it is time we got you bathed and ready for bed," Devin said. "Hop down and I will go get our bags."

"Sit tight and I will go get them." Tia stood.

"Do you need help, honey?" Eric asked.

"No, Dad, I'm good, thanks."

"Again, I want to thank you for allowing us to stay with you tonight and for such a terrific meal." Devin laid a hand on her stomach.

"It was great having you both and I hope you will come back soon," Ann said.

"That's right. I need a second chance at beating Lizard in checkers."

"I'd like that too," she answered.

When Tia returned with the two small bags, Devin turned to Lizard. "Let's go get you bathed and dressed for bed."

"There should be plenty of supplies in the guest bath and maybe even some bubble bath under the sink." Ann gave her a wink.

"We shall return then." Devin walked with Tia and Lizard to the guest room.

"Do you need some help?"

"I think we can handle this. Go spend some time with your folks."

✝

"Would you care for bubbles, madam?" Devin asked in a horrible imitation of a French waiter.

"Yes please," Lizard answered with giggles soon to follow.

"I will draw a bath for you if you will undress and get your pajamas out."

"Thanks Devin." Lizard walked over to the bed.

Devin walked into the bathroom and placed the stopper in the tub and began to draw water for Lizard's bath and then went in search of bubbles.

When Lizard returned to the bathroom, Devin picked her up and placed her in the middle of the bubbles. She poured some rich-smelling shampoo onto Lizard's head and sat on the edge of the tub where she began to lather her hair.

"When did you get so grown up?" she asked.

"When you weren't looking," Lizard came back with a witty reply.

"I guess so." Devin continued washing her hair.

She rinsed Lizard's hair and then leaned back against the wall as her niece played in the bubbles.

"Is Tia okay?" she asked.

"Yes, she is. Why do you ask?"

"When you came back I could tell she had been crying," Lizard said.

Surprised by the empathy Lizard was displaying, Devin answered. "We went to see her grandmother who is elderly and not in good health."

"Is she soon to cross over?"

"Yes, it probably won't be long," she replied honestly.

"Do you think she will be with Grandma and Grandpa then?" she asked so innocently.

Devin remembered the conversation she had with Ella earlier and smiled at the thought. "I'm positive she will be and will tell them hello from all of us when she gets there."

Lizard seemed content with her answer and played in the bubbles until they started to disappear. "We better finish your bath before the water gets cold."

They had just about finished when Tia knocked on the doorframe. "Are you two doing okay in there?"

"Come on in. We are almost done," she answered.

"All clean." Lizard finished brushing her teeth as she hopped down from the stool Eric had brought in earlier.

"You know, Dad made that stool for me when I was about your age. I didn't even know it was still around."

"Why don't you go say goodnight to Tia's parent and thank them for their kindness and come back and I'll tuck you in," Devin suggested.

"Yes, ma'am, I'll be right back." Lizard left the room.

Tia stepped forward to embrace Devin and kissed her softly. "How are you feeling?"

"Not bad, thanks."

"Do you need a pain pill?"

"No, I think I'm good. If not, I promise to take one."

"Are you going to be comfortable with Lizard in here? I only have a twin bed in my room."

"We will be just fine, I promise."

"What if I get lonely?" Tia asked.

"We can make room for you so just climb on in with us."

Tia ran her fingertip down the bridge of Devin's nose. "I'm not sure my parents would understand that just yet."

"No problem," Devin answered. "Lizard will keep me warm."

"Like you need any help," Tia remarked.

Devin was about to make a smart comment when Lizard walked back through the door. "Okay, I'm ready," she said and climbed up onto the bed. "Will you be here soon, Devin?"

"Yes, I won't be too much longer, so don't go hogging the bed."

"I won't if you promise to not drool."

"I do not drool," Devin insisted.

"You did when you were napping," Lizard said.

"Did not," Devin exclaimed.

"Uh-huh you did too, but I won't tell Dad."

"Good, he would never let me live it down," she answered as she pulled the covers over Lizard's small form and kissed her forehead. "Goodnight."

"Goodnight Tia and Devin." Lizard closed her eyes.

"She is so precious." Tia walked back to the den with Devin.

"Would either of you like more coffee?"

"No thanks, I'm good."

"Me neither, Mom," Tia replied as they sat down on the couch.

"It sure is nice having you home, even if it is such a short visit." Eric shrugged.

"I have a feeling I will be back again soon."

"Why, what's up?"

"Gran told me she wants me to spread her ashes in Baton Rouge after she's gone and cremated, and I don't think she will be around much longer."

"I really wish she would change her mind about cremation," Ann said.

"She won't, and those are her last wishes, so we will stand by them," Eric said in support of her decision.

"I know, I know. She will be happy that way. I'm just being selfish to want a gravesite to visit."

"Gran wouldn't want that and you know it deep down, Mom."

"You're right I just have a hard time knowing I will have to deal with that soon."

"She's ready to cross over," Devin surprised them by saying. "I could tell she was in peace when we left."

"She's led a long, productive life," Eric said, trying to console his wife.

"She said she didn't want a funeral or any fancy send-off, or for us to mourn her. I promised her that whenever her ashes were ready I would take them and spread them as she requested."

"I hope that's not the only reason you plan on coming back home."

"No, Mom, I will try to do better. Life has been hectic lately. I promise I will try to take some time off before school starts and spend a few days here."

"I can live with that." Ann looked over and saw her husband nodding off in the same chair that Devin had dozed in earlier. "If you will excuse us, I think we will head off to bed. Please check that the fire is safe before you retire," she added.

"We won't be too far behind you," Tia stated.

"Goodnight then, ladies." Eric followed his wife.

When they were alone on the couch, Tia snuggled in beside Devin. "Your parents are really nice."

"Yeah, they are and they really seem to like you and Lizard too."

"What's not to like?" Devin teased.

"I haven't found anything I don't like so far."

"That is comforting."

They sat together on the couch watching the flames dance until Tia started to nod off. "I think it's time we head to bed."

"Yeah, you're right," Tia said, stifling a yawn. "Let me close the screen on the fireplace and we can go."

They stopped just outside the guest room door and Devin kissed her sweetly. "I will see you in the morning."

"Goodnight, Devin." Tia headed down the hall to her room.

Chapter Fourteen

Devin woke the next morning to the smell of bacon. She looked over at Lizard, who was still asleep and decided to let her sleep while she showered and dressed. When she stepped back into the room after brushing her teeth, the young girl was starting to stir. Devin sat on the bed beside her. "Bacon, bacon, bacon, I smell bacon."

Lizard's eyes popped open and she started laughing. "Devin, you sound like that dog on TV."

"I smell bacon," she repeated. "Go wash your face and get dressed and then come see what we are having for breakfast."

"We know bacon for sure." She jumped off the bed and walked toward the bathroom while Devin straightened the covers.

When Devin walked into the kitchen Tia and her mom were drinking coffee and talking while the bacon cooked. Eric was enjoying the morning paper with his coffee. Sunlight was streaming in through the kitchen windows.

191

"Good morning," she said. "That sunlight is a pleasure to see."

"It certainly is," Eric agreed.

Tia handed her a cup of coffee and was about to ask about Lizard when she came bouncing into the kitchen.

"Good morning, everyone." Lizard had a warm smile.

"Good morning," they all answered.

"Do you feel like being my assistant again this morning?"

"Yes, ma'am. What can I do?"

Ann looked at her with a smile. "The bacon is almost done. I'll make my special scrambled eggs if you will make the toast."

After breakfast, Tia, Devin, and Lizard packed their bags and prepared to head back to Baton Rouge.

"Please remind her to call home more often," Ann asked Devin. "I hope you and Lizard will come back with her to visit soon as well."

"Thanks, we'd like that," Devin answered. "Thank you both for your hospitality," she added as she hugged both of Tia's parents. "We will go load up, so take your time," she told Tia as she and Lizard left the house.

"The sun is finally out," Lizard said as they walked to the truck.

Devin opened the back door of the truck. "I know I was beginning to think we wouldn't see it again," she teased. She lifted her niece up onto the seat. "Can you get buckled in?"

"Yes, ma'am," she answered proudly.

Devin placed their bags and Lizard's pillow on the backseat then turned toward her niece. "You kick like a mule in your sleep." She reached in to tickle the young girl.

"And you snore," she said between giggles.

Tia walked up behind Devin. "Hey, what's the ruckus out here?"

"Payback for kicking like a mule last night."

"Well, Lizard is right, you do snore."

"What? Are you two ganging up on me?"

"Nope, we are just telling the truth as we heard it," Tia said with a grin.

"Whatever." She rolled her eyes dramatically, closed the back door, and turned to Tia. "I thought I would drive and let you do some reading."

"Do you really feel up to that?"

"Yes, I feel pretty good today. Do you have any idea where your bike is?"

"I'm pretty sure it's down in the industrial park. I will show you the way." She walked around to the passenger side.

Devin climbed in behind the wheel and began adjusting the seat and mirrors. "Dang, a munchkin must have driven this last." She moved the seat back to accommodate her long legs.

"I got you here, didn't I?"

"Yes, as a matter of fact you did."

"Enough said then." Tia winked at Lizard.

Devin cranked the truck and pulled slowly out of the driveway as Tia gave her directions. As they were leaving town, Tia instructed her to turn left and pointed out a particularly decrepit building. "There."

"What are we doing here?" Lizard asked.

"We are stopping to pick up Tia's motorcycle," Devin explained. "It shouldn't take long, but I want you to stay in the truck, all right?"

"Yes, ma'am."

Tia and Devin climbed out of the truck and Devin locked the doors as they walked toward a door hanging partially open.

"My bike better damned well be safe here." Tia's voice had a note of concern.

"It doesn't look like much has been happening around these parts lately." Devin pulled the door open and they walked inside. "This must be the place. I can still smell a faint scent of Were."

Tia's heart lifted when she saw her bike still parked in a back area, where she had last seen it. "Thank goodness," she said as she inspected it closely.

"Ride her out and I will get the ramps ready and the tailgate down."

Tia mounted her bike and her smile spread wide when the engine purred to life. Devin pulled the door wider and then dropped the tailgate of the truck and slid out a ramp. Tia carefully rode the bike up the ramp and into the bed of the truck and worked with Devin to secure it.

"All set." Tia jumped down from the tailgate.

"Let's go home then." Devin loaded the ramp and closed the tailgate.

"That is a pretty bike," Lizard said when they got back into the truck.

"Thanks, that's my baby."

"Will you and Devin let me ride with you sometime?"

Devin looked at her niece in the rearview mirror. "I think we can do that when you get a little older. If we can convince your mom, that is."

"I know you can do it, Devin."

"I'm glad you think so, but your mom can be tough."

"But you're tougher." Lizard giggled.

"Uh-hmm." Devin pulled the truck back onto the road.

In no time at all, Lizard was sound asleep once more in the backseat. Tia had pulled her grandmother's journal out of the box and was reading it page by page. Devin concentrated on the passing miles until they reached the turnoff for the compound.

"I can't believe she slept the whole way." Devin slowly made the turn. "Lizard," she called to wake her up.

There was no movement from the backseat, so Tia turned and gently shook the child awake. "Wake up, sleepyhead, we are almost home."

"Already? That was a fast trip."

"You slept the whole way. Are you feeling all right?"

"Yes, Devin, I just fall asleep so easy when we go anywhere."

"Okay, just checking. Here we are." She turned onto the drive that led to the compound.

Several children were playing outside, now that the rain had finally moved through. Lizard was quick to join them as soon as the truck parked. Devin grinned hearing her tell the others about her trip to Monroe and her cooking adventures as Tia and Devin unloaded the bike.

"Glad to see you made it back safely." Damien walked out of the house.

"Not a bad trip at all."

Tia parked the bike and walked over to them. "Could I meet Miss Anna today?"

"I don't see why not. I'll take you myself."

Devin wasn't sure if she should feel slighted for not being asked to go with Tia or the fact that Damien taking her himself, but watched them leave before going inside. The kids were sprawled about in the large den area engaged in various activities. Tara was on the couch watching the latest storm news. "How are things looking?" Devin asked as she sat next to her.

"Some flooding in New Orleans, but nothing as nearly catastrophic as Katrina, thank goodness," she said. "Several parishes to the south got hammered pretty badly though. The work on the levees around New Orleans helped to protect the city, but the strain on levees further south was too much with the continuous heavy rains."

"Major destruction?" Devin asked.

"A lot of flood damage, as you would expect, and homes lost, but it looks like most of the residents were evacuated safely. I haven't seen any reports of lost lives."

Devin watched the scene on the television of a coast guard helicopter airlifting a family from the rooftop of their home, which was probably a one hundred percent loss for them. "I bet many folks watching this don't understand why we stay, when the dangers are so great."

Tara turned and smiled to her. "I guess they just can't understand how the blood of the bayou runs through our veins. I honestly can't imagine living anywhere else."

Lizard came inside and climbed up into Devin's lap for a hug. Her aunt looked down at her and then turned back to Tara. "I can't either and I hope I am never forced to choose."

"You can always live with us, Devin," Lizard said.

"This will always be my home," Devin assured her. "Even if I'm away for a while, I'll always return here. That's a promise."

"Will Tia be coming to live with us?" she asked.

Devin sighed deeply. "I don't know yet, Lizard, but I hope so."

"That would be cool, I like her."

Devin chuckled. "I do too."

"I hear you did a lot of helping in the kitchen for Tia's mom," Tara said. "Are you going to be my new assistant?"

"Yes, Mommy, I really like helping in the kitchen."

"She is going to make one awesome cook one day." Devin kissed her on top of her head. "You know what?"

"What?" Lizard asked.

"It is way too pretty to be inside. Would you like to take a walk with me?"

"Oh yes, please, Devin," she answered.

"All righty then, we will be back later." Devin placed Lizard on the floor.

"Hey, why don't you stop by Doc's and get him to look at your shoulder?"

"We will." Devin and Lizard walked to the front door.

"It is nice to finally have the sun out." Lizard slipped her hand inside Devin's.

"Yes, it is." The comfort of the child's hand in hers made Devin smile.

They walked through the compound speaking to several pack members as they went about their daily chores until they reached Doc's home. "Would you knock, please?"

Lizard reached her small hand forward and made a fist to rap softly on Doc's front door. Devin heard footsteps inside the house and a moment later Doc answered the door.

"Well, hello there," he said when he saw Lizard. "Did you drag your aunt back to see me?" he joked.

"No, Doc, she came on her own. She's too big for me to drag," she answered innocently.

"There's no need for her to drag me, Doc. You know she has me wrapped around her little finger."

Doc laughed loudly. "Don't they have a way of doing that?"

"Especially this one." Devin reached down to ruffle her hair. "Tara suggested we stop by so you can check my wounds."

"Wise woman, that one," Doc said. "Come on in and we'll take a look."

Devin and Lizard followed him into a small exam room and he pointed to a chair. "How is that shoulder feeling?"

"Still a little stiff and sore, but not as painful as before," she replied.

"You were very lucky, another inch or two and you would have suffered some serious tendon damage. Take that shirt off and let's have a look."

Doc noticed the grimace as she lifted her left arm to remove it from the sleeve. "Have you been taking the pain pills I gave you?"

"No," Lizard said.

Devin looked at her. "Tattletale," she teased.

"I'm just telling the truth."

"Uh-huh," Doc said. "She's right, if you take them, you wouldn't still be having the soreness."

"Okay, I will start taking them."

"Just for another day or two, but it will help you heal quicker if you are not in pain," he continued. "Now let's see. These stiches look like they could come out if you're ready."

Doc used the scissors to cut the stitches one by one and Lizard, whom Doc had asked to assist, pulled them free without a flinch. She placed each piece in Devin's waiting hand.

"You're a natural," he told her as they removed the last of the stitches. "Thanks for your help."

198

"You're welcome, Doc."

"You have healed well from the outside." Doc took out the last stitch came out, "but it will be several more days before you are completely healed on the inside, so don't do any major physical activity just yet and keep some good ointment on the wound to minimize the scarring."

"Thanks, Doc." Devin slipped her arm back into the shirtsleeve.

"For goodness sake, take the medication," he added.

"I will remind her, Doc," Lizard said.

"Good girl, two times a day at least."

"You got it." Lizard slipped off the stool.

"Thanks again, Doc." Devin walked with him to the door.

"You are very welcome. Have a great day and let me know if you have any problems."

"I will." They stepped back into the sunshine. The glint of shining metal caught her eye as they turned away from Doc's house. The sun was shining on the nameplate on her parents' crypt and smiling, Devin started toward the cemetery. Lizard slipped her hand back into Devin's as they walked. "I haven't visited your grandparents since I have been home," she said.

"I pick some wildflowers when I can and bring them here." Lizard's words really surprised Devin.

"That is very sweet of you."

"Dad tells me often how much I remind him of my grandmother. I wish I could have known them," she said as they arrived at the family crypt.

"You do look a great deal like our mother. She was beautiful and would have loved to have been here to see you grow up." Devin's voice was full of emotion. She reached out and traced the nameplate on the front of the crypt as tears filled her eyes. Her parents were very dear memories for her and she wished they were here with them today.

"Where do you think they are?" Lizard asked.

Devin knelt down beside her niece. "You can't see them during the daylight, but at night, when the skies are clear and the stars are shining, they are running together through the heavens watching over us."

Lizard listened intently to every word and then looked up at the sky. "Do you think we might see them tonight?"

"That's a possibility," she answered.

Devin watched Lizard as she pondered her thoughts. "I know you say the Devil's Tree gives you the creeps, but I need to go there. I will be all right if you would rather stay here."

"You will protect me, Devin, so I have nothing to fear," Lizard said proudly.

"Let's go then." Devin grinned.

They left the cemetery and started down one of the many trails leading from the compound. Ever since their return from Monroe, Devin had felt a need to visit the clearing. Something was drawing her for some reason, and knew she'd not be content until she completed the visit.

"Tell me about growing up with my dad, please, Devin," Lizard asked.

As they walked, Devin told her stories of her father and her grandparents as she remembered them. Talking about her parents made Devin feel their presence around them as they walked through the dense woods and it warmed her heart.

When they reached the clearing, Devin stopped at the edge as her eyes drew to the tree. She was relieved to see the bloody handprint had almost completely faded from the bark.

"This is where they died, isn't it?" Lizard asked as she looked up at Devin.

"Yes, it is." Devin was fighting back tears and the memory of that night so long ago. She dropped to a knee beside her niece. "They fought a hard battle, but were tricked by the powers of an evil witch and were killed here." She stood and took Lizard's hand and walked into the clearing to a spot that in her memory would be forever stained with her parents' blood. "They died right here, together, lying side by side."

Lizard bent over and touched the ground. "It feels so warm." She looked up at Devin.

"A part of them will forever remain here," she explained. She hoped Lizard could comprehend how their spirits would roam freely over the compound and especially here.

Lizard stood and wiped away a tear that had slipped unnoticed down Devin's cheek. "Is this where you and Father were injured?" she asked.

"Yes, we battled the same witch that killed our parents, but luckily we were prepared for the battle and not ambushed as our parents were."

"I'm glad you killed the evil witch," she said.

"I hate to kill, but our family can live in peace now," Devin explained. "The witch had haunted many of our kind for years and needed to be punished for her behavior."

"I think I understand."

Lizard's words reminded Devin that she was still a very young child, even if she did act older than her age. She reached out to take Lizard in her arms. "Have I told you today how much I love you and how proud you make me?"

"I love you too, Devin." Lizard hugged her tightly.

"If I ever have a little girl, I hope she will be just like you," Devin told her.

She could tell by the puzzled look on the child's face that she didn't see Devin as a mother, but the confusion cleared and Lizard stepped back from Devin. "Part of me will always be your little girl, I promise," she said with such sweetness.

"I hope you will always speak with me so freely," Devin said, "even when you get older and think you know it all."

"Devin, you are so silly."

"Yeah, but you love me anyhow, you can't deny it," she teased. "Are you ready to start back to the compound?"

Lizard nodded and reached for Devin's hand. They had walked about halfway back when they stopped at the sound of movement in the woods. Devin could pick up the scent of a deer and crouched down beside Lizard. "I think we are about to have some company."

She looked at Devin with wide eyes filled with excitement. "What is it?" she whispered.

"Just watch." She pointed to the trail ahead of them as a doe and two spotted fawns stepped onto the trail. The doe froze when she caught the scent of humans and turned to look at Devin and Lizard. When she saw they meant them no harm, she and her babies took a giant leap, and cleared the remainder of the trail and disappeared into the woods.

"That was cool." Lizard started to walk again. "Hey Devin?"

"Yes, Lizard," she answered with a grin.

"Do you think we could take an airboat ride tomorrow?"

"I haven't done that in years," Devin said. "Yes, that would be fun. We can ask your father when we get home, but I don't see why not."

When they came within eyesight of the compound, Lizard saw her father talking to several men and raced forward to jump up in his arms. "Hey, my little Lizard, what have you two been up to?"

"We just went for a walk," she answered. "Can I ask him?" She looked down at Devin from her father's arms.

"Go ahead, it was your idea."

"Can Devin and I go for an airboat ride tomorrow, please Daddy?"

Devin smiled. She knew there was no way Damien could turn down such a sweetly presented request. "That depends," he said with a worried look.

"On what, Daddy?"

"Is this a girls-only affair, or can your father come along?" he asked.

Lizard looked at Devin who shrugged her shoulders. "Fine with me, but it's your decision."

"I would love it then, Daddy, if you would go too." She kissed his cheek.

"It's a done deal then. We can make a picnic lunch and spend the day out on the water. Maybe even bring some mudbugs home for dinner."

She climbed out of his arms to run toward the other children who were playing in the compound. "I would like to take a spin around the bayou to check for damages if you don't mind me tagging along."

"It will make my day perfect," Devin said as he slipped an arm around her shoulder and they started to walk. "Have you heard anything from Miss Anna or Tia?"

"When I left them earlier, they were deep in conversation. It may be late tonight before she comes home. I know how excited she is about learning who she is and what abilities she may possess."

"Thanks for being so accepting of Tia," she said. "I know Cedra left a bad taste in everyone's mouth, but I don't think there is an evil breath in Tia."

"I agree, and I think she is going to be a very special person, not to mention how cute and likeable she is," he teased.

They walked back to the house together and when they stepped inside, Damien took a deep breath. "Smells like taco night."

"They were Lizard's choice," Tara called from the kitchen.

"Do you need any help?" Devin asked.

"Sure, you can help me chop ingredients to go inside the tacos."

Devin went to the sink to wash her hands as Damien slipped his arms around his mate's waist and bent down to caress her neck with his lips. It was obvious how much in love they were, even after many years of marriage. A smile crossed her face when Devin heard Damien's inner wolf growl with pleasure. "You two need to get a room," she joked.

"Turning in early does sound good to me." Damien smirked.

"Go ahead and I will get the kids in bed." Devin grinned back at him.

"You take care of Lizard and I will handle the two little ones," Tara said.

Devin helped with the dinner prep and ate a hearty share of the tacos. "I need to make a phone call before it gets too late. Leave the kitchen and Lizard and I will clean it when I get done."

"You have a deal." Tara smiled as she picked up the baby.

"Hang tight, Lizard, and I will be right back." She climbed the stairs to her room and located her cell phone. She hit the button to call her boss and waited for an answer.

"Hey Devin, how are you?" Kaitlin asked when she answered the phone.

"I'm doing fine and you?"

"I'm glad this rain has finally let up. How is it down your way?"

"Still soggy but getting better, I thought I would ride down to New Orleans day after tomorrow when they open the city back up and check on things."

"I would really appreciate that. I'm having a blast shopping with my sister, but I'm anxious to get back home."

"I can understand that. The news reports aren't showing too much damage so be hopeful and try not to worry. I will call you as soon as I arrive and give you an update."

"Thank you, Devin. Have you heard from Tia?"

"She's doing fine. She came back from Monroe today and is staying with my family until we can get back home."

Kaitlin couldn't hold back a chuckle. "I'm glad to learn you both are doing fine. Call me when you can."

"I will, I promise." Devin hung up the phone.

She went back downstairs and found Lizard patiently waiting for her in the kitchen. Devin started carrying dishes to the sink to rinse and then opened the dishwasher. "Will you load while I rinse?"

When they finished the dishes, she and Lizard wiped off the table and counters. "You know what? I think we should pop some popcorn and see what is on television."

"I love popcorn," Lizard said.

"Grab a couple of bags from the pantry then." Devin pulled down a large bowl.

With the popcorn and two drinks, Devin and Lizard settled onto the couch to watch some TV. They found a good movie to watch, and were snuggled together on the couch sound asleep two hours later when Tia quietly entered the front door.

Hearing her arrive, Devin carefully separated herself from Lizard and walked over to her friend. "Welcome back. Are you hungry?" she whispered.

"No, Miss Anna fed me well."

She looked tired to Devin, and when she checked the clock and saw that it was nearly eleven, she understood why. Tia had spent a very long, intense day under instruction from Miss Anna and was probably exhausted. "Let me take these dishes to the kitchen and carry Lizard up to her bed."

"I'll get the dishes and the lights if you want to go ahead and take her upstairs."

Devin nodded and gently carried Lizard upstairs and placed her on the bed, carefully removing her slippers before covering her tiny body with the bed linens. She kissed her forehead and silently crept from the room.

She was changing clothes when Tia entered the room. "You got your stitches out today." Tia saw Devin's bare shoulder. She stepped in for a closer look. "That's amazing how quickly the wounds have healed."

"Doc was very pleased too, but he made me promise to take the pain pills two more days," she replied.

"It will help you heal faster."

"How was your day?"

Tia let out a deep breath. "Miss Anna and my grandma knew each other as children and even though Grandma never actively practiced her craft, Miss Anna knew all about her."

Devin slipped a T-shirt over her head. "Was she able to help you understand your gifts better?"

Tia bent down to remove her shoes and sat on the side of the bed. "She was very helpful and wants me to spend the next few days with her. Is that fine with you?"

Devin nodded her head. "Damien, Lizard, and I are going out on an airboat tomorrow and then I am planning to drive to New Orleans the following day to check on everything for Kaitlin, so that will work out great. I called Kaitlin tonight to give her an update and she sends her love."

"Is everything all right with her?"

"Yeah, she's having fun with her sister but is getting antsy to get back home." Devin stretched out on the bed while Tia changed clothes.

Tia turned off the light and climbed in next to her, snuggling in close as Devin's arm encircled her waist. "You are so nice and warm."

"You will never freeze to death with me around." Devin enjoyed the comfort of Tia so close to her. She was about to say something else when she realized Tia had slipped off to sleep. Devin smiled as she listened to the chirping of the crickets and Tia's soft breathing until sleep returned to capture her.

Chapter Fifteen

Devin woke and climbed quietly from the bed and took a shower before waking Tia. When she walked back into the bedroom, Tia was tangled up in the sheets and her soft hair had fallen to cover her dark eyes. She sat on the bed and gently called her name. "Tia, it's time to wake up."

"I know, but it's so warm here." She brushed the hair out of her face.

"You can sleep in a bit you know."

"I don't want to waste time when I can be learning from Miss Anna," she said with a sleepy voice.

"Okay, sleepyhead. I'm going down to help with breakfast. Come down when you're ready."

Tia mumbled an incoherent response and snuggled deeper into the covers.

"Good morning," Devin said entering the kitchen.

Damien and Tara both wore big smiles as they turned toward her. "Good morning. Did you sleep well?" Tara asked.

"Like a log." Devin stretched.

"Your brother is making pancakes this morning. He said the three of you are going on a picnic today. Do you still love egg salad?"

"Oh most definitely."

"I thought I would whip some up for your lunch while he makes breakfast," Tara said.

"That sounds wonderful. What can I help with?"

"Set the table and pour some juice for the kids. Pancakes will be up in a minute. Is Tia awake yet?"

"Just barely. She had a very late night with Miss Anna and found Lizard and I crashed out on the couch when she got home."

"Did she have a good time with Miss Anna?" Tara asked.

"Very much so, she plans to spend the next two days with her."

"Miss Anna was very eager to meet her. She knew Tia's grandmother when they were children."

"That's what I heard last night before Tia conked out," Devin added.

Damien laughed softly. "I bet she was exhausted. Miss Anna can be very intense for a woman of her age." Devin chuckled as she spread plates across the table.

Devin poured the juice into glasses. "I was planning to ride down to New Orleans tomorrow to check on our homes and the club."

"I hope you're not planning on taking your bike," Damien said.

"Of course not, I was hoping to borrow your truck." She grinned.

"Only under one condition."

"Which would be?"

209

"That you say yes to Lizard when she finds out you're going," he teased. "She will sulk around all day if you leave her behind, you know."

"Well that was going to be my next request. Has she ever been to New Orleans?"

"Probably not that she can remember. She was tiny when we went."

"It will be a treat for both of us then," Devin said.

Tara called the kids to the table as Damien put pancakes on each plate.

"Devin's got a question for you." Damien leaned against the kitchen counter to watch over his brood.

Chewing on a big bite of pancake, Lizard looked over at her. Devin had the forethought to wait until she swallowed to ask, "Do you want to ride to New Orleans with me tomorrow?"

The young girl responded with such enthusiasm that she would have coated everyone around the table with pancakes if Devin had not waited. "Good, that's settled then."

"Something smells good." Tia walked into the kitchen still wiping sleep from her eyes.

"Guess where I am going tomorrow?" Lizard said.

"Where?" Tia asked.

"To New Orleans with Devin," she shouted.

"Was that what all the whooping and hollering was about a few minutes ago?"

"She was a little excited," Tara said.

"Lizard's becoming our little world traveler," Damien added.

Lizard beamed up at Devin as she placed a cup of coffee in front of Tia. "She's very good company on an adventure too," Devin added.

Damien set a plate of pancakes in front of Tia and she dug in to them with a ravenous appetite.

"I thought you said Miss Anna fed you last night." Devin laughed.

"She did, but these pancakes are awesome." A drop of syrup was trailing down Tia's chin.

"My daddy makes the best pancakes ever."

"Hear, hear! I fully agree." Damien took a bow.

"What time are we heading out?" Devin asked.

"As soon as you gals are ready."

"I'm ready." Lizard jumped off her seat.

"Go brush your teeth and grab a jacket. It can get cool out on the water," he instructed and she flew out of the kitchen.

"I'll be right back too." Devin left the kitchen.

Tara poured a cup of coffee and sat at the table with Tia. "Devin says you have learned a lot from Miss Anna."

"Yes I have, she's a great woman," Tia said between bites. "It amazes me how much knowledge she has of so many things and so many people."

"Anna's like a sponge, she soaks up everything she sees or hears. She is probably one of the wisest elders this pack has ever had."

"I can believe that," Tia agreed as she wolfed down the last of the pancakes and reached for her coffee.

"Would you like that to go?" Tara asked with a smile.

"No, I'll finish it while I help you pick up the kitchen."

"There will be none of that. You are a guest in our home and you don't need to help."

"Need, maybe not, but I would like to help," Tia said when Devin walked back into the room.

"She's a stubborn woman, Tara, might as well get used to it," she warned.

"Very well, you can load the dishwasher while I clean the griddle."

Devin helped her carry the dishes to the sink. "Have a great day." She smiled and kissed Tia's forehead.

"I'll see you tonight." Tia started to rinse the dishes. Lizard ran back into the room, ready to go.

"If you will get the cooler, I'll handle the picnic basket," Damien told Devin.

"Got it." Devin followed her brother and niece out into the sunlit morning.

Tia was busy rinsing the dishes at the sink. "You have an amazing family," she told Tara. "Great kids and a good husband."

"The Benoit's make very good mates," she winked. "I could not ask for a more faithful husband and the kids are fantastic."

"Will there be more?"

"If Damien has his way we will have at least a dozen." Tara chuckled.

"Devin would really be in heaven then. She loves those kids."

"She will make a great mother one day."

"Yes, she will," she answered, as her thoughts became lost envisioning Devin pregnant. She shook her head in disbelief and finished rinsing the dishes. "Can I help you with anything else before I go?"

"No, but I really appreciate your help in the kitchen."

"My pleasure." Tia dried her hands. "I will see you later tonight then."

"Say hello to Miss Anna for me."

"I will." Tia stepped out into a beautiful morning. The humidity was still low and a cool breeze sighed through the cypress trees as she walked across the compound. She passed several of the pack as they moved about the compound and everyone was friendly, waving or speaking to her in passing. She was about to lift her hand to knock on Miss Anna's door when she heard the roar of an engine. She smiled at the thought of Devin, her midnight hair blowing through the wind as they rode through the bayou. *Be careful my love*, she thought.

"I will," came a silent response.

"Holy shit." Tia realized she had projected her thought to Devin.

When she turned back to the door, she found it open and Miss Anna was standing in front of her. "She does love you very much, you know," she surprised Tia by saying. "That woman would die to protect you."

"I hope it never gets to that," Tia said. "Hey, you read my mind."

"Yes I did, but it doesn't take a mind reader to see how much you two are meant to be together," the older woman answered with a smile. "Come in and let's get started. We have a lot to do today."

Tia followed her inside and closed the door.

†

Devin smiled too when she heard the thought Tia had projected to her, and before she could stop she answered the projection. *This was so weird, yet so natural.*

"Woohoo," Lizard hollered as her father gunned the airboat and they moved rapidly away from the dock. She sat on a small bench next to Devin as Damien guided the

213

powerful boat. Devin was glad Lizard had gotten a jacket as the wind had a chill to it and she did not have the full-blown Were metabolism yet. She snuggled in next to Devin and they watched the wildlife of the bayou come to life.

"Look, there's some nutria." Devin pointed to the large water rats as they swam along the bank.

"I see them." Lizard leaned forward.

Devin picked her up and put her in her lap for a better look.

"There's the gator that will have them for lunch." Damien indicated a large alligator sunning itself on the bank.

They toured the bayou for a couple of hours, checking for any storm damage and other than a few downed trees and a higher than normal water level, the bayou seemed pretty well intact. "These floodwaters will give those pesky beavers fits," Damien chuckled. "They have been blocking off several good ponds with their dams this summer."

"I suppose you have some mudbug traps out here."

Damien chuckled. "At least a couple dozen. I hope you don't mind but I asked Thomas, his wife, and Miss Anna to join us for dinner tonight."

It was Devin's turn to laugh. "That may be the only way I see Tia before midnight."

"We will have eaten well before then, I promise. You and Lizard have a big day tomorrow and you will need to be rested up."

Lizard squirmed in her lap at the mention of the trip to New Orleans, but was quickly sidetracked when a large blue heron took flight in front of the boat. "Wow, that's big." Her eyes grew wide.

"That is a big one," Damien said. "Look there," he pointed to a fallen log filled with a family of turtles out sunning themselves, "Looks like we are not the only ones enjoying this sunny day."

Damien turned the boat down a narrow canal and they saw a small boat with two men fishing. Devin recognized them as pack members, but could not remember their names as they pulled closer. "Hey, Leon and Leroy, having much luck?" he asked.

"Heck yeah, Damien, we got some nice catfish," Leroy lifted a string of large fish to show off their catch.

"Looks like the Dumont family will be eating well tonight," Damien said as they floated by. "Have a good one, boys." He started the engine. "All of this talk of food is making me hungry. Are you two about ready for some lunch?"

Devin grinned. "I thought you'd never ask."

"Let's check the beach and see if we can land there." He pointed to a spot and gunned the engine.

The beach was a hundred-yard strip of sugar-white sand along a small island where he and Devin used to play as kids. Devin had not been there in years and was anxious to see her old playground. When the boat turned a corner, they could see the white sand gleaming in the sun. The water here was higher than usual, but there was still plenty of solid ground for them to share a picnic. Damien aimed for the beach and landed the airboat on the soft sand. Devin stepped off the boat and reached back for Lizard.

"Let's head for that grassy spot." Damien handed her the cooler. "Watch for critters though, no telling what might have swam up here to higher ground."

Devin knew that he was referring to snakes, in particular water moccasins, which could be very aggressive creatures so she walked ahead of Lizard. "Looks like the coast is clear." Devin placed the cooler on the ground.

The trio ate their fill of sandwiches and chips while the sun shone down upon them. "Do you remember playing here when we were kids?" she asked her brother.

"We used to steal Father's pirogue and paddle out here and stay gone all day," Damien told his daughter. "One summer we even buried a pirates' chest of treasure and it took us weeks to remember where we had buried it after we got distracted for a few days."

"That's right. That was the summer grandfather took us gator hunting."

Damien smiled at the memory. "I still have the necklace you made from the gator claws."

"Do you really?"

"Yeah, it's hanging up in the garage above my tool chest."

Devin remembered spending several hours hand drilling small holes in the claws to be able to string them onto a length of leather as a present for her brother.

"That was one of the best birthday presents you ever gave me."

Devin smiled, pleased that even after all these years, Damien remembered her gift. "That was a great summer."

"Yes, it was. I hope Lizard and the other kids will have opportunities for days like the ones we shared."

"I don't see why not in a few more years. She's just as adventurous as we were at her age."

"Maybe even more so." He grinned at his daughter.

A blue heron gliding across the water caught her attention and she watched it gracefully land and wade through the water looking for a meal. "He's stalking something," she told Lizard. They watched the bird, his head disappeared beneath the water while he speared a large frog

216

in his beak. "Got him a frog," she said. He launched the frog in the air in front of him and swallowed it whole.

Lizard giggled, watching the bird. "That was funny."

He smiled at his daughter. "Maybe the next time you visit we can take Lizard frog gigging and cook us up some legs."

"That would be a lot of fun and good eating," Devin answered.

"Lizard and I will scout out some good sites and when you come back we'll get them good," he promised the smiling child.

They heard a rumbling in the distance. "We don't need any more rain, but it sure looks like we're going to get an afternoon storm. We better get some mud bugs and get on home before it arrives."

When they were loaded back on the airboat, Damien started the engine and they went skimming across the surface of the dark water, making sharp turns on a dime bringing screams of excitement from Devin and Lizard. When he reached the canal he was looking for he sought out the red markers that he used to signal his crawfish traps. He cut the engine at the first spot and let the boat glide up to a large cypress tree. "Let's see what we got here" He pulled up a trap, which was three-quarters full with crawfish. "Not a bad start." Devin held a five-gallon bucket while he poured the bounty inside. "On to the next." Damien started the engine.

After five more stops, they had all six of the buckets filled with crawfish and were ready to head for home. Lightning crackled through the bayou as they finally reached the dock and offloaded the cooler, picnic basket, and buckets of crawfish.

Thomas heard them approach and hurried to help them unload before the rains began pelting down.

217

"Would you and Lizard go inside and ask Tara if she has the potatoes and corn ready for the boil?" Damien asked her.

"Sure, no problem," she answered.

When they walked into the kitchen, they found Tara and Thomas's wife Sara working on the corn, breaking it in halves for the boil. "Is there anything we can do to help?"

"I think we have this under control. You can take the truck and go pick up Tia and Miss Anna," Tara said. "Oh, and tell Damien I will bring out the corn and potatoes in just a few minutes."

"Mama, can I ride with Devin?"

Tara looked at Devin and with a wink she answered her daughter. "I thought that was a given since you are Devin's shadow."

Lizard laughed, but followed Devin out the door close enough to be her shadow indeed.

"Lizard and I are going to Miss Anna's. Tara and Sara will bring out the veggies in just a few minutes," she said as they passed by on their way to the garage.

"Don't melt," Damien called out wearing a smirk.

"We won't, Daddy." Lizard reached the truck and Devin lifted her into the front seat.

Tara must have called ahead because Miss Anna and Tia were waiting for them on the front porch. Devin parked as close to the porch as possible and reached into the back to retrieve an umbrella. She opened her door and rushed to the porch as she opened the umbrella, dodging the quickly forming puddles in the yard. "Good evening, ladies." She stepped onto the porch. "Your carriage has arrived." Devin did a deep bow.

"You are ever so gracious." Miss Anna stepped underneath the cover of the umbrella.

Devin ushered her into the backseat of the truck and then returned for Tia. Her face lit up when she saw the smile Tia was wearing while she waited. "Hey there." She offered a hand to Tia for balance and then walked her around to the other side of the truck.

"I hope you have had as good a day as I did." Tia followed her around the truck.

"We had a blast," Devin answered. She opened the door for Tia before racing around to the driver's side.

She drove the short distance home while Lizard filled Tia in on the day's events with an excitement only a child could display.

Unable to get a word in edgewise, Tia and Miss Anna listened patiently and smiled at Lizard's exuberance.

When they reached the garage, Lizard bounded out of the truck and ran to the porch where her father was cooking. "Has she been like this all day?" Tia asked.

"I'm afraid so and she doesn't seem to be losing any steam. I hope she can get to sleep tonight and be ready for the big trip tomorrow."

"Yes, I hear you are going into New Orleans tomorrow," Miss Anna said.

"Yes, ma'am, Lizard and I are going to ride down to check on some property for my employer," Devin answered.

"Would you mind taking a side trip, if you have time, and pick up a package for me?"

"Of course not, Miss Anna, just give me the particulars."

"I will write the address down for you while we wait for dinner."

"That won't be too long," Damien said as he helped Miss Anna to a seat on the porch. "Lizard, will you go get a notepad and pen for Miss Anna?"

Lizard hopped off the stool she was perched on and ran inside to gather the requested material for Miss Anna.

"You sure have everything smelling good." Tia looked into the pot of boiling water.

"Thanks, I hope you like a good old crawfish boil," Damien said smiling.

"I do indeed." Tia returned his smile.

Tara and Sara were setting places at a long banquet table covered in plastic with paper plates and plastic utensils. "Y'all are getting the fine linens and china tonight," she teased.

"Makes for an easier cleanup," Miss Anna said. "I use the fine china often."

Damien lifted a heavy wire basket from the pot and rested it on the edge to allow the excess water to drain. "Okay everyone, stand back for a minute and let me get this first batch on the table."

Damien poured the contents of the basket onto the table and then placed the remaining vegetables and crawfish in the basket to prepare for the boil. "Be very careful, those are still extremely hot," he warned.

Tara went to work spreading butter over a cob of corn and some smashed up potatoes for Lizard while the piles of bright red crustaceans were allowed to cool. The rest of the adults followed suit and when Damien tested a mudbug, he pronounced them "fit for eating."

That was all it took for everyone else around the table to dig into the pile of bayou delicacies. Even Lizard, with her tender years, was proficient in peeling and eating the tasty treat. "You gonna suck the heads, Lizard?" Thomas asked.

"Eww, no Thomas, I can't do that."

"Dat's where the best juices are."

"No way, you can have them all," Lizard said, to a round of laughter.

"These are wonderful." Tia popped a mudbug into her mouth, "Sweet, with a nice kick to them."

"I am glad you like them and they aren't too spicy for your taste," Damien answered.

Devin chuckled and looked at her brother. "Are you kidding, she puts hot sauce on her eggs."

"That's my girl." Damien gave her a wink.

The small crowd ate for nearly an hour until every belly was full. Damien looked at the pile of crawfish remaining and looked at Tara. "Would you like me to peel these for some *etouffee* tomorrow?"

"That sounds like a splendid idea."

Devin looked at Lizard. "We will have to hurry back from New Orleans before your daddy can eat all the dinner tomorrow," she teased.

"I know, that's his favorite meal."

"Maybe, just maybe, I will save you some," Damien told his daughter.

"Don't worry, I will keep him busy frying some gator tail and hush puppies. He can munch on those while he cooks." Tara winked at her husband.

"You see how these women conspire against me, Thomas?"

"I see, my Alpha. You have your hands full with this bunch."

"Indeed." Damien let out an exaggerated huff.

Lizard climbed up in her father's lap finally beginning to wear down and looked up at him. "That really was a good meal, Daddy."

Devin could see her brother's heart melting as he held Lizard in his arms. "I am so happy you liked it, Lizard."

Thomas had been peeling crawfish the entire time the group was chatting and had finished off the pile and placed them in a bowl. He looked at Damien. "What you say we clean up this mess and have an adult beverage?"

"That sounds like a wonderful idea to me. Ladies, will you join us?"

Tara looked at Lizard who looked like she was ready to start dozing off. "Lizard, go get your bath and pajamas on and then you can come out to say good night to everyone."

"Yes, Mama." She slipped from Damien's lap after a kiss to her forehead.

Thomas and Damien cleaned off the table as Tia and Devin entered the kitchen for cold beers. "I could get used to this," Tia said.

"What's that?"

"Living here and having Damien cook for me all the time."

Devin failed to stifle the chuckle she was trying to hold back. "He is a good cook."

They returned to the porch and passed the beers around. "You know, Damien, Tia was just saying that she could get used to living here and having you cook for her all the time."

"Devin!"

Devin smiled as a furious blush came to Tia's face.

"Well, it just so happens I have an offer to make you." Damien followed Devin's lead.

Surprised at his comment Tia sat down beside Miss Anna without uttering a word.

"Well, aren't you going to at least ask?" Devin nudged her friend in the ribs with her elbow.

"Yes, I'm sorry, Damien, what were you saying?"

Damien looked at Tia. "I have consulted with the elders and we would like to offer to pay for your education as a nurse, if you will agree to return with Devin to the compound to assist Doc in caring for our pack."

"You could go to school full-time and be finished in two years tops," Devin said.

"Was this your idea?" she asked Devin, not showing any signs of emotion.

"Actually, it was mine," Damien told her. "I saw how well you worked with Doc and I know he would appreciate some assistance."

"He could also teach you a great deal about medicine," Miss Anna added.

Surprised by his offer, she stared at Damien for several seconds until Devin's impatience got the better of her. "Well?"

"That is a very generous offer," Tia answered, then paused.

"But what?" Devin asked.

"I almost feel guilty by wanting to say yes. Tuition and books are very expensive."

Damien smiled at her. "It will be a wise investment for the pack and it would be a time-limited agreement if that is what you are worried about."

"I am not worried about being able to leave if I needed to explore other avenues," she answered. "I feel very at home here and it would allow me to learn more of my gifts as well."

"In an environment that is safe to do that," Miss Anna chimed in.

"You have a deal then," Tia, still in shock answered. "I will register for full-time classes when we return to New Orleans."

"Fantastic." Damien had a wide grin.

Thomas lifted his bottle of beer. "To our future nurse."

"Cheers." Everyone tapped their bottles together in a toast.

They drank several rounds of beer while the rain tapped gently on the tin roof and the group mellowed out for the evening.

Thomas and Sara volunteered to take Miss Anna home. "I will see you tomorrow." Tia watched as the woman left the porch with her escort.

"I look forward to it." Miss Anna replied, her eyes bright with excitement.

They watched the group depart safely and then Damien turned back to Devin. "You have an eventful day tomorrow too, so I suggest you get some rest tonight."

"We will see you in the morning then." Devin led Tia inside.

When Devin turned off the lamp and crawled in bed beside Tia, she was welcomed into warm arms as Tia snuggled into her and placed her head on Devin's shoulder. "Pinch me."

Ever obedient, Devin pinched Tia's arm.

"Ouch, I didn't mean that hard." She reached up to rub her shoulder.

"I was just following your command," Devin said.

"At least now I know I'm not dreaming. Damn, that hurt," she growled.

"I'm sorry, I guess I don't know my own strength sometimes," Devin apologized.

"Did you know what Damien was going to ask me?"

"We had talked about it earlier, but I didn't know when he was planning to propose the idea to you."

Tia snuggled back into Devin. "I still can't believe all this is happening."

"It really is, my love," Devin stated. "By the way, thanks for warning me that you can get into my head," she teased. "You really surprised me this morning."

"I was surprised too. I had no idea and I was a bit freaked when you answered."

"You will get used to it in time and will learn to block me eventually."

"Why would I ever want to do that?"

"Trust me, you will sometime in the future." Devin chuckled.

"How close do we have to be to be able to communicate like that?"

"Distance wise?"

"Yes."

"Generally within a half-mile or so, though some couples can go further distances with practice."

"Couples hmm?"

"Yes, this means we have forged a very special bond to be able to communicate telepathically," Devin explained.

"I like the sound of that." Tia's body began to relax into Devin.

"I do too."

Tia had already drifted off to sleep.

Devin listened to the tapping of the rain against the window until the warmth of their bodies took its toll and she drifted into dream-filled sleep.

Chapter Sixteen

Devin had barely finished her coffee when Lizard announced she was ready to go to New Orleans. Tia had just walked into the kitchen in time to hear her announcement. "I guess I will see you two later tonight then. Did you pick up the address Miss Anna wrote down for you last night?"

"I have it right here." Devin patted her jeans pocket. "Is there anything you need while we are there?"

"Grab my backpack if you would. It should be on my kitchen table."

"I guess we will see you later. Have a great day with Miss Anna," Devin said.

"I will. You two be safe and have fun," she added.

"We will," Lizard answered.

"Time to rock and roll then," Devin said to Lizard.

They walked out into a beautiful late summer morning, the rain from the previous evening a distant memory. Lizard scrambled up into the passenger seat and fastened her seat belt while Devin climbed into the truck. It would take them a little over an hour to get to New Orleans and she hoped the roads and streets of New Orleans would be safely passable. She turned on the radio as she pulled out of the drive and she and Lizard sang along to songs as the miles disappeared behind them.

The Mississippi River had swelled from the torrential rains that had not only hit their area, but regions further north. Devin hoped the river would not exceed its banks to cause further flooding. She was relieved to see some river traffic, knowing that barges and other river crafts only traveled if conditions were no longer dangerous.

Devin was witness to the devastation to homes and property caused by the intense amount of rainfall the area received for several days from the tropical storm. Thankfully, Lizard was so content to be traveling with Devin she did not recognize the human trauma that had taken place in the remote parts of the state.

When they crested a bridge and the Superdome came into view she gasped. "Is that the Superdome?"

"Yes, it is. We will be driving right past there in just a few minutes."

"It is much bigger than I imagined."

"It is a big old place," Devin said as Lizard stared out the window. Once the storm damage was repaired and life returned to normal, Devin would plan to bring her back for a proper visit and show her the city as a child should see it.

The address in her pocket burned against her skin in her imagination, but Devin was anxious to see their homes and the club so she followed her heart until she reached the club. Besides a few trash piles and street gutters that needed to be cleaned, the outside of the building looked intact. "Let's go see what the inside looks like."

Lizard followed her from the truck and they worked together to move the sandbags away from the front door. Devin used the keys Kaitlin had given her to unlock the door. She was surprised when she hit the light switch to find the power was on. The club lit up and Devin was able to survey the area for damage. A small amount of water had seeped through the sandbags, but otherwise the club was intact. She went to the closet for the mop and cleaned up the water as Lizard walked around the club. Devin checked the coolers and everything was in good working condition. "We are in good shape here," she told Lizard. "Let's go check our homes."

There was very little traffic on the streets, which surprised her, and they made it home in record time. When she pulled the truck into the drive at Kaitlin's she saw a few branches down in the yard and some debris that had floated in from a neighboring area. The shutters were still intact and she decided to check Kaitlin's house first. She unlocked the door and Lizard followed her inside. The shutters on the windows prevented any sunlight from coming inside, so she reached for a light switch. She let out a deep sigh of relief when the lights revealed Kaitlin's home to be just how they had left it. "Everything looks good here." She decided they would go to Tia's apartment next.

"Don't forget her backpack," Lizard reminded her as they walked into the apartment.

"Thanks for reminding me." Devin picked up the bag from the table where Tia had left it. "Do you think you can handle this?" she asked as she held out the bag to Lizard.

"Sure I can." Lizard placed her arms through the straps and slung the backpack over her shoulders. It was nearly as big as she was, but she managed the size quite well.

Tia's apartment was secure and there was no evidence of damage. "Let's go check my place."

She locked the door behind them and they climbed the stairs to her apartment. They walked into the apartment and the first thing Lizard laid eyes on was a framed picture of her and Devin that had been taken a few months back. She smiled up at Devin. They continued to walk through the apartment. "Looks like everything is safe here too."

"You have a nice place here."

"Thanks, I'm getting used to it."

"Will you ever be coming back to the compound to live?"

"Yes, just as soon as Tia finishes nursing school in a year or two," Devin told her.

Lizard's face grew wide with a smile. "Tia is coming home with you?"

"Yes, she will be working with Doc to keep us all healthy."

"Awesome." Lizard followed Devin to the kitchen.

"You want a bottle of water?"

"Yes, please," she answered and Devin pulled out two bottles of cold water.

"Have a look around while I call Kaitlin," she told her niece.

Devin took out her cell phone and dialed Kaitlin's number. She was excited and relieved to hear that the club and their homes had survived with no damage.

"I will call George and we will head back that way tomorrow," Kaitlin said, eager to return to the city.

"Tia and I will plan on being back tomorrow as well. The traffic in town is still relatively light, so you should not have any trouble making it in."

"That's good news too."

"Tia and I will begin removing the shutters and storing them again. What do you want done with the sandbags?"

"I think we can line them up against the back of the building for now. Hopefully we won't need them again this year, but hurricane season isn't over yet."

"All right then, you two travel safe coming back tomorrow and we'll see you when you get here."

"Thanks for everything, Devin, and you and Tia need to be careful too."

"We will." Devin ended the call. "Decision time," she said to Lizard. "Let's go pick up Miss Anna's package and then we can decide what we want to do until it's time to head back home."

Devin placed Tia's backpack in the backseat and helped Lizard into the front seat. Taking the address from her pocket she smiled when she recognized the location as one in the French Quarter. She climbed into the truck and drove toward the Quarter. Many of the bars and shops were in the process of reopening and she was glad to see them stirring on the streets. She drove by a local voodoo shop and turned down a back alley to the address given by Miss Anna. She pulled the truck to a halt and turned to Lizard. "I will be right back."

Lizard nodded her head. Devin walked to the door of the shop and gave it a quick knock. She could hear and sense movement inside as she waited for the door to open. The sounds of a metal lock turning grated on her ears, but the door slowly swung open and a woman who appeared older than Miss Anna stood in the doorway. "You must be Devin," she said when she saw her.

"Yes, ma'am. Miss Anna asked if I would pick up a package for her."

"Come on in, I have it right here. How is Anna doing?"

"She is very well, thank you."

"My name is Marie and I have known Anna since we were very young." She had a knowing smile.

"It is a pleasure to meet you."

"Can you stay a while and chat?"

"Unfortunately no. I have my niece with me and we will be starting back to the compound soon."

The old woman seemed disappointed by Devin's answer. "Are you in good shape here from the storm?"

"Yes, I was fortunate to have no damage to my shop. Why?"

"We are headed back to the compound today, but I will be coming back tomorrow. Would you like to go back for the night and see Miss Anna?"

The woman chuckled. "These old bones don't let me travel that far, but do tell her I said 'hello'."

"I will, and maybe I can convince her to come down for a visit."

Marie's face lit up with a smile. "That would be wonderful. Feel free to stop in any time when you return too. I miss a good chat and these tourists just don't appreciate the art of a good conversation."

It was Devin's turn to chuckle. "I will stop in and see you then." For a moment saw the amber glitter in the old woman's eyes sparkle.

"I will look forward to your visit then." Marie walked Devin to the door. "Safe journeys."

Devin placed the package on the back floorboard and climbed in behind the wheel. "I don't know about you, but I'm hungry."

"I could eat." Lizard grinned.

"Let's go see what is open." Devin backed out of the alley.

They drove around for several minutes passing several places that had not opened back up yet until they arrived at Mama's, a local favorite for fried chicken. "Bingo. Are you hungry for some fried chicken?"

"Sounds good to me."

Devin located a parking spot, then they walked to the restaurant.

Inside the small, timeworn building a family of cooks from many generations served up fried chicken to die for, rice and gravy, biscuits, vegetables and some of the best sweet tea ever brewed. They consumed the hearty meal to the amazement of the server, who was further surprised to hear they still had room for some bread pudding. When they had finally eaten their fill, Devin paid the bill and they returned to the truck.

"How about a ride down by the river before we head home?"

"I'd like that."

They drove past the Brewery, Jackson Square, and the French Market where signs of life were becoming more evident. Devin was curious to see if the already devastated Ninth Ward had received further damage, but decided against taking Lizard to see such a depressing sight. Instead, she made a U-turn and headed back through the Garden District out to the zoo.

"Such pretty homes." She admired them as they passed by the antebellum mansions in the Garden District.

"Yes they are," Devin answered. "I still prefer the log homes in the compound over these any day though."

Lizard, surprising Devin, replied, "I agree. I'd be afraid to walk on the grass in one of these homes."

"Me too, Lizard. Are we ready to head back home?"

"Whenever you are," she answered sleepily.

Devin was quite certain her niece would be napping on the ride home as she turned north toward the interstate. They watched a cruise ship dock at the River Walk and then resumed the drive north.

Darkness had fallen when they turned into the drive of the compound. Devin reached across the seat and gently shook Lizard awake. "Wake up, sleepyhead, we're home."

"Already?" Lizard stretched.

"Yes already. You slept the whole trip home," she teased. She pulled into the garage and parked the truck. "Will you take Tia's bag up to our room while I take Miss Anna's package to her?"

"I will walk with you if you will wait a second."

"All right. Tell your father to save us some dinner on your way through," Devin teased.

"I will." Lizard giggled.

"I heard that." Damien stepped out of a shadow. "How was your trip?"

"It was great. Lizard and I are going to walk down to Miss Anna's to deliver her package," she explained.

"Please invite her to dinner, if you would. Tara assures me there is plenty."

"I will," she answered as the screen door to the porch opened.

"Hey, Daddy." Lizard came onto the porch.

"Welcome home."

"Devin says to save us some dinner," she told him.

"So I heard." He grinned. "Hurry back from Miss Anna's and dinner will be ready."

Lizard slipped her tiny hand into Devin's and they walked the short distance to Miss Anna's house together.

233

Welcome home, Devin," she heard Tia's voice say in her head. *I've missed you."*

I missed you too," she answered. *We are almost there. Would you ask Miss Anna to join us for dinner?*

She says she would be delighted, Tia answered with a giggle.

Tia opened the door before Lizard could knock. "Hey you two, did you have a good day?"

"We had a blast," Lizard answered as they walked inside.

Devin handed Miss Anna the package. "Marie said to come visit her soon. I told her I would try to convince you, and I hope you know you're welcome to stay with us."

"I might just do that," Miss Anna said. "I would have to get Damien to give me a ride. I don't think it would be proper for a woman of my years to be on the back of one of those motorbikes you ride." She grinned.

"You might just like it."

"I might at that." Miss Anna smiled. "Let's go eat. I'm starved."

"How is everything in New Orleans?" Tia asked as they walked.

"We are in good shape. I talked with Kaitlin. She said she will be returning tomorrow as well."

Devin thought Tia would be excited to return to New Orleans, but she sensed a hesitancy from her friend. "You do plan to go back with me tomorrow still?"

"Well, actually, I was hoping it would be all right if I spent a few more days with Miss Anna," Tia said.

Devin was disappointed, but understood Tia's excitement and eagerness to learn about her newfound gifts. "I'm sure it won't be a problem for you to stay, but I made a commitment to Kaitlin that I need to stand by."

"I promise it will only be a day or two."

Devin nodded. She was afraid if she verbally responded her disappointment would bleed through in her voice.

Miss Anna sensed the anxiety and broke the mood by stating, "I can smell supper from here."

"I do believe you are right." Devin grinned. "I'll race you," she said to Lizard.

Lizard took off at a dead run and Devin loped after the child. Tia looked at Miss Anna, who smiled to comfort her new friend. "She's disappointed, but she will be fine, so don't worry."

"I hate to think I have disappointed Devin."

"There will be plenty more disappointments in your lives, unfortunately. Devin knows you need to learn all you can right now, even if it means you will be separated for a short period of time."

Tia nodded her understanding, but she was still worried about hurting Devin's feelings. She tried to reach Devin through mental thought, but all she could feel was a closed door. Is this what Devin meant about blocking the other partner out, she wondered. She was not sure, but she knew she did not like it one damned bit.

Devin was pouring drinks for everyone when Tia and Miss Anna reached the dining room. Damien was carrying large platters of fried gator tail and hush puppies to the table as Tara dished up the *etouffee*. Lizard and the other children were already sitting at the table. Devin took a seat next to baby Edward, intent on feeding the young boy his meal instead of taking her seat next to Tia.

Damien noted his sister's behavior and raised an eyebrow at Tara when she caught his look of concern. He was not sure what had occurred, but would pull Devin aside for a talk after dinner. He could not let her leave in the morning if something had upset her that he could repair.

Dishes passed around the table and Devin filled her plate and took bites between spoonfuls for baby Edward. The conversation focused on Lizard's trip to New Orleans and she excitedly told her parents about her day.

When she was finished, Tia looked to Damien. "Would it be fine if I spend an extra day or two here before I go back to New Orleans?"

Damien instantly knew what was wrong with Devin. "You are welcome to stay as long as you need," he told Tia. He glanced down at Devin to find her tense with anxiety. *Calm down, baby sister,* he projected to her. *We will take a run together later tonight.*

Devin did not answer him, but he knew she had received his message. He picked up a hush puppy and looked at Tara as he took a bite. "You know, we make a pretty good pair of cooks."

"I will agree with that. This meal is splendid," Miss Anna said. "I haven't eaten this well in a long time."

"You are welcome to share our table anytime," Tara told her.

"Careful, I might show up every day," she teased.

"We always have room for one more," Damien assured her.

The rest of the meal passed with minimal conversation. Devin finished feeding Edward and took him to his room to clean him up and change his diaper. She placed him in his playpen and returned to help in the kitchen.

Damien met her just outside of the kitchen. "The ladies have the kitchen under control. You and I need to go for a walk." He ushered her out the front door. He slipped an arm around her shoulder as they walked. "I understand you are upset that Tia is staying behind a few extra days," he said to open the conversation.

Devin looked up to him. "I'm not really upset, I'm just disappointed. I'm really trying to understand things from her viewpoint, but I'm having a hard time."

"I can understand how you feel. You have someone you love very much and you don't want to spend time apart from her. But you need to give her the freedom to explore her gifts and right now Miss Anna is the one who can help her with that."

"I know I'm being selfish."

"Yes, you are, but I'm sure Tia will forgive you. Just remember, you have long lives ahead of you to establish your relationship. You don't have to rush into something neither of you are ready for."

Damien felt Devin's body tense and immediately regretted the words. "I'm not saying she doesn't love you, because anyone who sees you together can see how much you mean to each other, but you need to give her time to adjust to such a huge change in her life." He sensed his words were starting to sink in to his sister. "Do you remember when you first came into your powers to change and how new and unique they felt to you?"

"Yes. I was excited and terrified at the same time."

"Exactly, and you were prepared for the eventual change. Imagine how Tia felt when out of nowhere she realized she is a witch, can you imagine her surprise?"

"I see where you are coming from." Devin was becoming more relaxed.

"Do you think you are healed enough to shift?"

"Yes, I am, why?"

"Because I haven't run with my sister for a long time."

Devin looked at him and smiled. "Do you think you can keep up?"

He smiled, relieved that she was much more relaxed. "Try me." He shifted to wolf form.

Devin laughed and shifted before chasing her brother down a trail. Damien was right as usual, she needed a good long run to burn off the anxiety she was feeling over Tia and to defuse the hormones raging through her. Their run ended when they had made a full circuit of the compound under the shining moon.

Damien was the first to shift and he waited for Devin to change. "Feel better?"

"Much, thanks for the run. You're still pretty fast for an old married man."

"You're not bad for a young pup," he teased back. He took Devin in his arms for a hug. "Have faith in your love, baby sister."

"I will," she promised and wrapped an arm around his waist as they walked back to the house.

They walked inside to see Tara, Tia, and Miss Anna sitting on the couch watching TV. *I'm sorry,* she projected to Tia.

No need to apologize, I should have discussed it with you first, Tia answered.

"Would you mind walking an old woman home, Damien?" Miss Anna asked.

"I would be honored." He helped her up from the couch.

"I will see you tomorrow," she said to Tia and then turned to Devin. "I will send her back to you in two days."

"Thank you. Teach her well."

"I will do my best." Miss Anna bid them, "Goodnight, ladies."

They walked Miss Anna to the door and then Tara turned back to them.

"I'm going to wait for Damien if you two want to go on up. I told Lizard you would stop in before you retire," she added.

Devin nodded and followed Tia up the stairs. "I will be there in a minute." She stopped off to check on Lizard.

She stepped quietly in the room and found her niece sleeping soundly. She leaned down to kiss her on the forehead and the child stirred. "Do you really have to go tomorrow, Devin?"

"Yes, but I promise I will be back soon."

"Okay then, I will be waiting."

"I will see you in the morning, Lizard. I love you."

"I love you too, Devin," she whispered and went back to sleep.

Devin stood in the doorway and watched the child for several minutes until she was sure she had gone back to sleep, then she turned to walk to her room. Tia had already changed into her sleeping clothes and was sitting up in bed.

"I need a shower." Devin closed the door and walked into the bathroom.

Devin slowly peeled off her clothes. Shifting so soon after a major injury had left her feeling sore and aching and she prayed a hot shower would help loosen her muscles. She turned the water as hot as she could bear and stepped under the pulsing spray. She soaked until the water began to cool and then quickly washed her hair and body. When she finally emerged from the bathroom bathed and dressed in fresh clothes, Tia was sleeping deeply. Devin turned off the lamp and slipped in beside the woman she loved and watched the beauty of her sleeping form until the need for rest consumed her and she curled herself around Tia and succumbed to sleep.

Chapter Seventeen

The next morning Devin woke refreshed and eager to start on her journey even though she would be leaving Tia and the ones she loved. She wanted to have as much done as possible by the time Kaitlin and George returned.

She quietly slipped from the bed and packed her bag before dressing for the ride. Tia began to stir as Devin slipped on her boots.

"I know you weren't planning to sneak out without a goodbye."

"No, I wouldn't do that. I was just letting you get your rest while I packed."

Tia climbed out of the bed and began to dress. "I can smell bacon."

"Tara will have breakfast ready in a few minutes. Come down when you're ready."

Devin turned to leave the room, her bag in hand. "Devin," Tia called.

"Yes," she answered, turning back to Tia.

Tia rushed forward and wrapped her arms around Devin. "I'll miss you."

Devin lifted Tia's chin with her hand and looked into her tear-shined eyes. "I'll see you in two days." She leaned down to kiss her softly on the lips.

Tia closed her eyes as Devin's lips brushed hers ever so sweetly. "Be careful today, my love."

"I will." Devin left the room before she changed her mind.

✝

Tara was indeed cooking a huge breakfast with eggs, bacon, fried potatoes, and a mound of buttered toast. Lizard was sitting at the table waiting for her to arrive and her face lit up with a smile when Devin walked in.

"I was waiting for you. Would you like apple or orange juice?"

"What are you having?"

"Apple of course," she answered.

"Apple it is then." Devin sat next to her niece.

Tara served them a plate full of food. "Someone must think we are hungry." Devin chuckled.

"You are awake, aren't you?" Tara teased back.

"We're always hungry," Lizard said to Devin.

"I guess you are right, so we better dig in."

Damien walked in from outside and joined them at the table. "Your bike is gassed and ready to go," he told her as Tara placed a plate in front of him.

"Thanks." Devin took a bite of toast.

"When will you be coming back?" he asked.

"I would think within a month. Tia's Gran has asked that her ashes be scattered here and I don't think she will be alive much longer. When she passes, Tia and I will pick up her ashes and bring them here if that is okay with you."

"We would be honored to have her with us for eternity."

"Thank you."

"Will you call later so we know you made it back all right?" Tara asked.

"Of course I will."

Tia arrived and joined them at the table. Tara brought her a plate of food. "Good Lord, I can't eat all this."

"Here, let me help you then." Devin grinned and swiped a piece of bacon from her plate.

"I've been robbed," Tia cried.

"You two are worse than the kids." Tara chuckled as she placed two more pieces of bacon on Tia's plate.

"Thanks, Tara."

"You will need your strength to keep up with Miss Anna today."

"Tell me about it. That woman is amazing."

"Yes, she is," Damien agreed. When breakfast was finished, Devin pushed back from the table and hugged everyone goodbye. "Would you like a ride to Miss Anna's?"

"That would be lovely," she answered.

"I will see you all again soon."

Devin fastened her bag onto the bike and then mounted, holding her hand out for Tia to climb on. Tia wrapped her arms snugly around Devin's waist and rested her head on her shoulder. Devin enjoyed the comfort of Tia's body so near to hers and sighed when all too quickly they arrived at Miss Anna's house.

"I will see you day after tomorrow at the latest." Tia smiled as she stepped off the bike.

"I will be waiting." Devin turned the bike to head back down the drive. With a final nod and a wide smile, she started down the drive with Tia watching her departure. *Be safe*, Tia projected.

I will, Devin answered and sped toward the highway. When she turned south, she accelerated. The wind blowing through her hair felt wonderful and she met little traffic as she made her way to New Orleans. She stopped once to watch a barge float slowly down the river then she drove the rest of the way home.

†

When she arrived at the apartment, she pulled her bike into the garage and took her bag upstairs to her bedroom where she changed into work clothes. She was coming back down the stairs when she heard the approach of a deep-purring motorcycle. Lucia pulled into the drive and killed the engine.

"Hello, my friend. I was hoping you made it back safely." Lucia stepped off her bike.

"I've just now returned. I hope your family is well," Devin replied.

"All safe and sound, thank you. Are you alone here?"

"For now, yes. Kaitlin and George will arrive today and Tia will be back in a couple days. She stayed in Baton Rouge with my family. I'll take the shutters down while I am waiting for them."

Lucia cocked an eye at the news. "I hope all is well."

"So much has happened since we evacuated from the storm."

"Well, then, let me help you and you can tell me all about it."

"I'll never pass on help." Devin hugged her friend.

Devin told the story of Tia's kidnapping, her eventual rescue and the discovery of her gifts as they worked.

"So her latent ability turned out to be a witch?" Lucia asked.

"Incredibly so, if she hadn't come into her power I may not be here today." Devin, intensely proud of Tia, smiled.

"That's amazing. You do realize that you will have to be ever more vigilant, especially once the news of her abilities makes it through the city. Every clan and pack will want her allegiance and her strength."

"Yes, I know. That is why she has remained behind to be tutored on her abilities by one of our elders."

"That's a wise move. And what of your feelings for her?"

"They grow stronger every day," Devin grinned. "We are destined to be mates."

"That's excellent news, my friend."

Devin and Lucia worked well together, and had removed the shutters on all but Kaitlin's home, when George's truck pulled into the driveway.

"Welcome home, boss," Devin called out as Kaitlin stepped out of the truck.

"Thanks, it's great to be home. You've done a lot here already." She surveyed the property.

"I've had some help. This is my friend, Lucia and Lucia, this is Kaitlin and George."

"Pleased to meet you," Lucia said.

Kaitlin smiled warmly. "Thank you for all your help."

"No problem. It gave me time to catch up with Devin."

"Where is Tia?" she asked.

"She is still with my family in Baton Rouge finishing up something she started," Devin explained. "She'll be back in a day or so."

"All right then, let me get my bags inside and we will finish up here. Have you had any lunch yet?"

"Nope, we have been working straight through," Devin answered.

"Let me see if I can get something delivered then. The least I can do is feed you two for all your hard work."

George fell into stride and began carrying the shutter panels back into the garage for storage as Devin and Lucia removed them from the windows. When Kaitlin returned she helped Lucia and Devin remove the wing nuts from the panels.

"I'm glad we didn't suffer any damage from the storm," she said as they worked.

"It looks like most of the damage was further south, where the levees were breached," Lucia reported. "I plan to ride down there tomorrow to see if there is anything I can do to help."

"Would you mind some company?"

"Absolutely not. I don't know what we will find, but I feel like it would be worth a good day to at least try."

"Would you mind if I went?" she asked Kaitlin.

"Could I ride with you?" Kaitlin asked.

"Of course you can."

"I don't think we need to open the club until later in the week, so let's do it."

Just as they took down the last of the shutters, a car pulled into the drive and a deliveryman from a Chinese restaurant carried several large bags over to the porch. "I hope everyone is hungry."

"Constantly," Devin answered with a laugh.

Kaitlin paid the man and carried the food inside to her small kitchen table. "Let's clean up and get something to eat before we tackle the club."

"Sounds good to me." George stepped up on the porch.

Devin opened the refrigerator looking for drinks. "We have water, beer, or soda."

She took their drink orders and carried them to the table as Lucia and George washed their hands at the kitchen sink.

"I don't know what is in those bags, but it smells heavenly," he said.

"I got a little bit of everything," Kaitlin said.

"Man, you aren't kidding." Lucia began pulling containers from the bags. "Are you sure you weren't planning for more than the four of us?"

Kaitlin laughed. "You obviously have never seen this crowd eat. Besides it is always better as leftovers."

"You are assuming there will be something left uneaten."

"If you are still hungry I promise I will order more," Kaitlin assured them and took a seat between Lucia and Devin.

As they began to eat, a light cheerful conversation enveloped them. "George, is there anything we need to do at your place?" Devin asked.

"Nope, I paid my landlord's son twenty dollars to take my shutters down."

"Very good. And yours, Lucia?" Devin asked.

"All taken care of before I came over," she answered.

"So we can tackle the club and then come back for leftovers and some cold beer afterward then?" Kaitlin asked.

"Sounds like a good plan to me," George said.

Lucia noticed the cast on his arm and asked, "What happened to your hand?"

George looked at Devin with a sheepish grin. "A lady had to teach me some manners," he answered.

"Well, all right then." She shot a smile to Devin.

"He learned very well, the first time." Devin was teasing a very embarrassed George.

After they had eaten their fill Devin and Kaitlin placed the leftovers in the fridge, while Lucia and George loaded a ladder in the bed of his truck. "Hop in," he said. Devin and Lucia sat on the tailgate while Kaitlin joined George in the cab.

He drove slowly down the cobbled streets to the club and pulled into the parking lot. "If you and Lucia want to tackle the shutters, George and I will move the sandbags to the back wall."

Devin took the ladder from the truck to place it against the wall of the club and then pulled on her gloves. "You have nice friends," Lucia told her as she steadied the ladder for Devin.

"Yes, they have been like a family to me since I arrived. Even George after a less-than-perfect start."

"Remind me to never piss you off," Lucia teased.

"I have every confidence you could hold your own, but let's not give that theory a try."

†

Two hours later, the shutters were down and stored and the sandbags were stacked neatly against the back wall of the club. When the ladder was loaded onto the truck,

Kaitlin turned to George. "Will you grab us a cold case of Abitas from the walk-in?"

"Sure thing." George returned a moment later with the beer.

"George, if you'll take us back to my place we can all go home to get cleaned up and come back for leftovers."

They all nodded in agreement and when George dropped them, Devin carried the beer inside for Kaitlin. "See you in a bit."

She walked back outside to Lucia's bike. "Would you care for a run later tonight?"

"Yes, that would be nice. We might as well enjoy the peaceful night as long as we can."

"Hurry back then." Devin smiled as she watched her friend ride away. She pulled out her cell and dialed Tia as she climbed the stairs to her apartment.

"Hey," Tia answered. "How did everything go today?"

"Great. Lucia stopped by and helped me with the shutters until George and Kaitlin got back, then we all finished up."

"Lucia, hmm, I'm glad she stopped by to help out."

Was that a hint of jealousy she heard in Tia's voice or just her imagination, she wondered. "Yeah, she was a great help. We finished in record time."

"That's great. Miss Anna and I had a great day too. I swear that woman is amazing."

"Yes, she is. She is one of the wisest people I have ever met."

"What are you going to do tonight?"

"We are all getting cleaned up and will meet for some beers and leftover Chinese Kaitlin bought us for lunch. Later Lucia and I are going for a run."

This time there was no doubting the jealousy when Tia said, "The two of you are going for a run?"

"Yes, and tomorrow Kaitlin is going to join us for a ride down south to see if there are families we can help out from the storm."

"That is very sweet of you. Damien is going to build a bonfire and I promised Lizard we would roast marshmallows."

"Oh, she will love that. Please tell them I made it safely and I'll call soon."

"I will," she answered. "Have fun tonight."

"You too." Devin ended the call.

✝

Devin stripped out of her clothes and walked into the bathroom for a shower. Afterward, she put on the shirt she had worn earlier in the day and the smell of Tia's scent brought a smile to her face. She pulled on her boots and bounced down the stairs just as Kaitlin was pulling their lawn chairs out of the garage.

"Grab us a beer, will you?" Kaitlin asked.

"Sure." Devin went inside for three beers. She handed one to Kaitlin, who cocked her head at the third beer. Devin smiled at her. "Lucia will be here in about thirty seconds." Devin could hear the rumble of her bike as it approached. She sat down beside Kaitlin and opened her beer just as Lucia pulled her bike into the driveway.

Kaitlin looked at Devin with a grin. "You are just something else."

Devin's amber eyes glimmered with delight as she smiled back at Kaitlin. "Are you just now figuring that out?" she teased.

"No, smart-ass." Kaitlin smirked and tipped her bottle toward Devin. "I'm glad you're my friend."

"Ditto," Devin replied and took a long drink.

Lucia took a seat next to Kaitlin just as a soft breeze began to blow. Devin handed her a beer. "Thanks for bringing that breeze with you."

"It feels good doesn't it?"

"It's rare for a late summer evening to be so cool." Kaitlin grinned. "Better enjoy it while we can."

George arrived a few minutes later and Devin went inside for more beer. They sat together for an hour or more admiring the starlit sky without all the glaring lights from the New Orleans business district and finished off many more beers before Kaitlin suggested they have some dinner. "Will you help me heat the food?" she asked Devin.

"Sure," she answered and followed Kaitlin inside.

"It's so nice and peaceful outside. Why don't we make plates for everyone and eat outside."

"Fine with me." Devin started dishing up platters of food.

They sat together under the stars until about ten and Kaitlin stretched and tried to hide a yawn. "Long day, huh," Devin said.

"I forget how much the fresh air can take out of you."

"Let us help you pick up and you can get some rest for tomorrow."

"This will be easy, you go do what you need to do and I will see you both in the morning."

"Is seven too early?" Lucia asked.

"No, that will be fine."

"Goodnight then. Thanks for dinner."

"Thanks for all your help." Kaitlin walked inside to pick up and get ready for bed.

"Ready to run?" Lucia asked Devin.

"Yeah." Devin smiled as she walked to the garage for her bike.

When they reached the levee where they first met, she and Lucia parked their bikes and shifted into their wolf forms. They ran along the levee until midnight and when they parted, Devin went home to fall into a fully satisfied slumber.

Chapter Eighteen

Kaitlin was waiting on her with a cup of coffee when she went down to get her bike from the garage. "Good morning." She greeted her warmly as she handed her the drink.

"Yes, it looks like it will be a great day." Devin took the coffee. "Did you sleep well?"

"Like a rock. That fresh air really knocked me out. I didn't even hear you come back in last night."

"I tried to be quiet."

"I think I could have slept through anything last night."

Devin took a drink of her coffee and her eyes wandered over to Tia's apartment. Kaitlin caught her glance. "You miss her too, don't you?"

"Yeah, I've gotten used to her being around."

"Do you think she will be back tonight or tomorrow?"

"Probably tomorrow," Devin answered. "I know she had a lot planned."

Lucia drove up as they were finishing their coffee. "Good morning," she said cheerily. "Are you ready to ride?"

"We will be in just a minute." Devin handed Kaitlin the empty mug and walked to the garage for her bike.

Kaitlin took the mugs inside and then took Devin's hand to help her mount the bike. "All set." Devin watched as Lucia pulled out to lead the way.

†

Once they cleared the New Orleans traffic and drove south they passed very few vehicles. Kaitlin relaxed on the back of Devin's bike and pointed out the wildlife she saw along the banks of the bayou. The water was still high from the rains and runoff from the north, so many of the less commonly seen animals were on dry land and visible to those passing by, making it a special treat for them. It was nearly an hour's ride before they started seeing the devastation caused by the floodwaters. Several homes they passed were still under water and many of the vehicles they saw bore evidence of being abandoned in the floodwaters as their occupants attempted to flee the area.

Lucia slowed when she heard the sounds of a chainsaw as they approached a small home that had numerous fallen trees making the drive impassable by car. A young man was attempting to cut the trees into smaller sections so he could clear the drive. A young woman and small child were helping as much as they could, moving small branches away from the trunk of the tree he was cutting. Lucia stopped her bike in the middle of the road and motioned for Devin to pull up beside her.

"It looks like they could use some help."

Devin agreed and pulled her bike to the edge of the drive away from the road. The man stopped when he saw the bikes and turned off the saw. "May we offer some help?" Devin asked.

"I'd be mighty grateful if you did," he answered.

The women dismounted the bikes and Devin pulled three pairs of work gloves from her saddlebags. "I'm Devin, and this is Kaitlin and Lucia. We are from New Orleans and thought we might help."

"I'm Charlie and this is my wife Sue and our little girl Mandy. We don't have much to offer, but we'd be grateful for your help."

Devin looked at the small family and knew they were struggling to survive. "Just keep some cool water coming and we will help you get these trees cleared."

"Come with me, Mandy, and we will make a pitcher of ice water." Sue called to her daughter.

"You keep cutting and we will move and stack this wood," Lucia told Charlie.

Charlie nodded and cranked the saw and went back to cutting sections. Kaitlin took the branches and made a brush pile while Lucia and Kaitlin began stacking the logs away from the drive. When they had the first tree removed, Charlie killed the engine on the saw and turned to them, soaked in sweat.

"Let's take a break and get a drink. I can't thank y'all enough for your help," he said as Sue passed around glasses of ice water.

"No problem, we are just glad to help," Devin replied. "Did you have any damage to your home?"

"No, fortunately we were on high enough ground to keep it from flooding, but the ground was so wet from all the rain that the winds took these trees down like they were nothing," Sue answered.

"We were lucky they all fell away from the house," Charlie added. "It could have been much worse."

"Did you ride out the storm here?" Kaitlin asked.

"Yeah, we waited too long to try to evacuate to Houma."

"It was probably better that you stayed here then," Lucia told him. "I have family in Houma and they said it got pretty wicked down there."

"I'm just happy we are safe and alive."

"Amen to that," Kaitlin agreed.

They resumed their work and after another two hours, they had the driveway cleared enough where Charlie could get his old truck through. "We lost power two days ago, but we still have MREs if you would care to join us for a meal. I'm sorry we don't have anything better, but as you saw I couldn't get out of the drive to go anywhere."

"That's quite all right," Lucia answered. "We are planning to drive on to see if anyone else needs help. We will get some food along the way."

"Thank you all again for your help," Charlie said, truly grateful for their assistance.

"You're welcome and good luck." Lucia smiled to her friends as they turned to walk back to their bikes.

†

Another half hour's ride brought them to a small town that still had power and a small diner that was open for business. The place was full with customers as they walked inside and found a booth. Devin looked around at the tired faces that waited patiently for their orders. She had seen that look before on the faces of the survivors of Katrina as they desperately tried to piece their lives back together. Her heart went out to them as they were just beginning their struggles. When a harried server made it to the booth to take their orders, they ordered burgers and fries with a Coke. That seemed to be the special today with their limited menu.

"You ladies don't look to be from around here."

"We're not. We rode down from New Orleans to see if we could offer help to anyone who needs it," Kaitlin replied.

They were surprised when many heads of the patrons turned toward them. "I could use some help," an older man said. "I got an old oak tree I need to get off my roof."

"I could use some help too," another voice called out. "I have a foot of mud that I have to shovel out of my store."

"Where is your tree?" Devin asked the man.

"I'm about two miles down the road on the left." Her comment had him suddenly energized.

"And your store?" she asked the woman.

"Three doors down from here."

"Let us eat some lunch and we will help this lady with her mud and then we'll be out to help with the tree," Devin suggested.

"I should be done with my shift here about that time and I'll help with the tree, Mr. Herbert," the server volunteered.

"Thank you." The old man had tears in his bright blue eyes as he left the diner with his meal in a paper sack.

When their meals arrived, they ate hungrily, and even though they could all have eaten another burger, they decided the residents of this small town needed the food more. Devin walked to the register to pay their bill and the cook and owner of the diner looked out of the serving window. "This one is on the house, ladies. Thank you for your help and I hope you'll come back again."

Devin tried to insist on paying, but the man would have no part of her money. Defeated, she smiled at him. "Thank you."

"Let's go shovel some mud," Lucia grinned as every head in the small diner turned to watch them go.

They walked to a small hardware store and found the woman inside struggling against the heavy mud as she tried to move it out a back door. "Do you have some flat-head shovels?" Devin asked.

"Take anything you need." She pointed to a wall of shovels in varying sizes and shapes.

Lucia surveyed the back door and looked at the woman. "Do you have water?"

"Yes," she answered.

"Power nozzles?" Lucia asked.

"I have a store full of them," the woman said. "What's on your mind?"

"Let Devin and I move the mud out here and you and Kaitlin use the power nozzles to wash it off the back stoop. That will save us a few feet of shoveling."

"That's a brilliant idea." The woman smiled and went to retrieve two power nozzles and two lengths of hose.

"Open those doors wide and let's get busy." Devin picked up a shovel and handed it to Lucia.

"Wait a second," the woman called out. "We need to put these on to keep from getting covered in this stuff. Lord only knows what washed in with all this mud." She handed each of them a pair of knee-high rubber boots.

They slipped into the boots and went to work. She had not been joking when she told them there was a foot of mud in her store. They went to work clearing a path to the back door and then Devin and Lucia worked on both sides of the path slowly widening it and moving the mud more freely out the door. Kaitlin and the storeowner used the power nozzles to wash the heavy mud off the stoop and back into the bayou where it belonged.

The young man from the diner joined them after his shift and with a third shovel the work progressed even more quickly.

"A few good rounds of mopping should get the rest." The woman hefted the last shovelful of mud out the door. "Thank you all for your help."

As Devin, Lucia, and Kaitlin took off their boots, the woman walked to her cash register. "I don't have much, but will you at least take a little something for all you hard work?"

"No, ma'am, we did not come here for that," Lucia told her. "Good luck." They left the store to return to their bikes.

Tom, the young server from the diner, yelled out to them, "If you will wait, I will get my truck and you can follow me to Mr. Herbert's place."

"Wait!" They turned to see the hardware store owner rushing toward them. "You are going to need these once you get the tree off Mr. Herbert's roof." She handed Kaitlin a bag filled with blue tarps.

✝

When they reached Mr. Herbert's house he was sitting on the porch waiting for them with a cooler of cold drinks. "I have a chainsaw and a ladder over there, but my old bones won't let me up on the roof."

259

"No worries, Mr. Herbert. These ladies and I will have you fixed up in no time and Mrs. Benson sent some tarps to cover the damaged section once we clear the tree."

"Praise the Lord," Mr. Herbert said. "What can I do to help?"

"Show us where you want the wood stacked." Lucia smiled.

Tom picked up the chainsaw and followed Devin up the ladder. "You want to cut or carry?" he asked.

"I'll carry if you don't mind, those things scare the hell out of me."

Tom began trimming the branches away from the trunk and Devin carefully tossed them off the roof for Lucia and Kaitlin to drag to a burn pile. When all the branches were trimmed, Tom began working on cutting the trunk sections. When they reached the section that was close to the eave, he cut the engine on the saw. "I have an idea. Wait here." He returned carrying a long length of rope. "We cannot cut any more on the trunk while it is on the roof without causing more damage. Let's tie it off and pull it back with my truck."

"Not a bad idea," Devin agreed.

She helped him tie the rope to the top of the trunk and then explained what they were doing to Lucia and Kaitlin. "Move back under the porch in case this goes bad," she warned.

Tom tied the rope to the front of his truck and climbed inside the cab. When Devin gave him a thumbs-up, he put the truck in reverse and began to back slowly. Devin guided the top of the trunk as it lifted off the roof and made sure it cleared the eaves. Once clear, Tom gunned the truck and laid the tree on the ground in front of the house.

"That worked out beautifully," Lucia remarked as she looked up at Devin.

"Yeah it did," she answered with a smile. "Ask Mr. Herbert if he has a hammer and some roofing tacks we can use to secure the tarps."

A few minutes later Kaitlin came up the ladder with a rusty coffee can and a hammer with the bag of tarps looped over her elbow. "Lucia sent me up to help you as she and Tom finish off the tree," she said as the saw engine roared to life.

Fortunately, there was only one damaged area in the roof. Devin used one tarp to cover it, tacking it down tightly to prevent leaks. She and Kaitlin climbed down the ladder to join the others who were just finishing up as well.

"You are as good as we can get you, Mr. Herbert," Devin reported.

"Thank you all so much. Can I at least offer you something cold to drink?"

"Yes, you can." Lucia took a drink from him.

They sat on the porch with Mr. Herbert for a short while and then decided they would ride for home before it got too late.

Mr. Herbert hugged each of them and thanked them again. Tom walked them out to their bikes.

"What you did today was very special and I know the town really appreciates your help and kind thoughts."

"It was the least we could do to help," Lucia replied.

"It may not seem like much to you, but for this weary little town it was monumental. I hope you will all come back on a better day."

"We will," Lucia assured him as he hugged her.

"Next time it will be the best steak dinner money can buy on me," he promised.

"You have so got a deal." Devin smiled to him.

"Be safe, ladies. He turned to walk back to his truck.

"Let's go home," Lucia said.

Devin looked at Kaitlin who was completely exhausted. "Do I need to tie you on so you won't fall off?"

"No, but I promise I won't have a bit of trouble sleeping tonight."

Chapter Nineteen

"Come on in, breakfast is almost ready," Kaitlin hollered when Devin knocked on her door the next morning.

Devin walked inside to find Kaitlin toiling away as she fried potatoes, eggs, and bacon. "Something smells great." She walked to the coffeepot to pour a cup. "Is there anything I can help with?"

"You can set the table."

Devin grinned as she walked to the cupboard for dishes. It seemed like setting the table was her only way of contributing to meals here as well as at the compound. It was no wonder she could barely cook. No one ever gave her the chance, leaving Devin to wonder if they all knew something she did not about her domestic abilities. She shrugged off the thought and busied herself setting the table.

"What do you want to do today?"

Kaitlin slid two fried eggs onto her plate and turned back to the stove. "I thought we might take advantage of the club being closed today to give it a good deep cleaning and make any repairs we find."

"I have noticed that some of the electrical outlets are pretty loose," Devin said. "Can we afford to upgrade the lights in the ladies' room? I noticed it is pretty dim in there."

"I think I can afford a few light fixtures," Kaitlin said. "I will give you my credit card and you and George can go get what you need."

"I promise to go easy." Devin spooned out potatoes and picked up a piece of toast.

Kaitlin cooked her eggs and joined her at the table. "If the delivery trucks are running today, we should be well stocked for beer and liquor when we reopen tomorrow night."

"I bet they will be. You know those corporate types won't miss an opportunity to make money," Devin said.

"You are so right," she agreed.

"So cleaning and making some repairs. Is there anything else you would like to have done?"

"Do we have time for a fresh coat of paint?"

"With George and Lucia's help, I bet we could get it done."

"Do you think Lucia will be by today?"

"I'm almost certain she will be. With summer school not resuming until Monday, she is bored to death," Devin answered. "What color do you want to go with?"

"I thought we would stick with the sand color. What do you think?"

"That's fine with me, boss. Do I need to pick up the paint and supplies while I'm out?"

"Yes, the last time it was painted, I had it contracted out and boy was that a nightmare, so we need all of the supplies to paint."

Devin chuckled. "I will make a list after breakfast."

"George will meet us at eight," Kaitlin said.

"That will give us plenty of time to look around the club to see if we need any other items for repairs."

"I really do appreciate having you around, Devin. There doesn't seem to be anything you can't do."

"Except cook," Devin said, which caused Kaitlin to laugh.

✝

Breakfast done, kitchen cleaned and list made, Kaitlin and Devin were about to pull out onto the street when Lucia pulled into the drive. "Morning. Are you up for some painting today?" Devin asked.

"Sure, at the club?"

"Yeah, we want to give her a fresh coat."

"I'm right behind you then," Lucia said.

They rode the short distance to the club, completed a walk-through and added to their lists while they waited for George. They decided to upgrade the lighting in both bathrooms and give them a fresh coat of paint too if they had enough time.

"I will get started on the electrical outlets and help Kaitlin with the cleaning while you and George get the supplies," Lucia offered.

"I think I hear him pulling up now." Seconds later, George came through the front door. "Let's go shopping, my man." Devin spun him around on his heels as they walked back through the front door.

"How about a pot of coffee?" Kaitlin asked after they left.

265

"Sounds great to me." Lucia took a pair of screwdrivers out of the toolbox and began making a circuit around the club.

"Coffee's ready," Kaitlin said from the bar. "Come fix a cup."

"When I finish the outlets, what do you need me to do?" Lucia asked as she sipped her coffee.

"I would like for you to pull the beer out of the coolers for me so I can give the shelves a good scrubbing."

"That sounds painless enough." Lucia grinned.

✝

George and Devin made it back and carried in a few loads of supplies. "If you can handle installing the new light fixtures, I will start trimming the walls," Devin told George who was carrying in the ladder. "Then you and Lucia can start rolling."

"Okay, but if you hear a crash come running, I may have fried myself," George said with a laugh.

"I think you would look great with curly hair," Devin teased.

"Very funny." He grinned.

"Would you rather trim?"

"Heck no, I'd have paint all over the place and I don't do ladders well."

"I don't mind electricity," Lucia said, "if you want to pull the beer out of the coolers for Kaitlin."

A look of relief passed over the big man's face. "You have a deal."

"Should I paint the bathrooms first?" she asked.

"That might be a good idea. Do you want me to trim them out for you?"

"No, I think I can handle it." Lucia picked up a trim brush and a can of paint.

"I know it's still early, but do y'all have any special requests for lunch?" Kaitlin asked.

"I do so love you," Devin said. "Pizza is fine with me unless someone else has another idea."

"Nope, that's good for me," Lucia said and George agreed.

"Okay, I'll call in an order later."

Lucia disappeared into the women's restroom while George assisted Kaitlin. Devin opened a can of paint and climbed the ladder to begin trimming. She had made it halfway around the large club when the door opened and Kaitlin spread several pizzas across a large table in one of the booths.

"Let's eat."

Devin climbed down the ladder and smirked when she saw the paint frosting Lucia's hair. She caught her smiling. "Don't laugh at mine, friend, until you see yours in the mirror."

"She's right, you have a bit on your head too," Kaitlin said. "I'm sure before the night is through, we will all be wearing our share of paint."

"You are probably right."

†

The traffic outside had picked up from earlier in the day and on several occasions Devin had heard the purr of a motorcycle as it passed by and she caught herself looking toward the door. The familiar sound once more caught her attention and her heart raced briefly, but the sound moved on, so she was surprised when five minutes later Tia came striding through the door.

"I thought I smelled fresh paint." They all turned toward her voice.

"Welcome home. We thought we would give the club some attention while we were closed," Kaitlin explained.

"Only one thing is missing."

"Besides you?" George chuckled.

"Music," Tia shouted. "This work will pass more quickly if we have some tunes to work to."

"Get on it then, Miss DJ," Kaitlin chided.

Missed you, Devin projected.

You too, and my attention was not in the bayou, so Miss Anna sent me back.

I am glad she did, Devin answered.

"Have you eaten? We have pizza left over," Kaitlin told her.

"Let me get some tunes going and I will grab a slice. What else do you want me to do?"

"Grab a roller," Devin instructed. "I'll be done trimming in a few minutes."

"I don't think we are going to have enough paint," Lucia remarked as she emptied a can into a rolling pan.

"George, can you take Kaitlin to get three more gallons?"

"Sure, Devin, do we need anything else?"

Tia grinned. "Can I get my door repainted too?"

"What color?"

"How about a deep green?" she answered. "I can trim the window frame of the DJ booth to match."

"I think we can handle that," Kaitlin replied. "Ready George?"

"I'm right behind you, boss," he answered.

George and Kaitlin left the club and Tia walked over to Devin for a hug and kiss. "I missed you."

"I missed you too."

"No kidding, she's been moaning and groaning since she got back," Lucia teased.

"I have not," Devin insisted.

"Lizard begged to come, but Damien said she had to wait for an invitation."

"Lizard?" Lucia asked with a grin.

"My eight-year-old niece."

"She is Devin's shadow. She adores her aunt."

"Well, what's not to love?" Devin teased.

"You got that right." Lucia resumed rolling paint onto the wall.

Devin watched Tia who was looking at Lucia funny. "What's wrong?" she asked.

"I just realized I can smell Lucia's scent even through all the paint fumes."

"Well, I promise I showered this morning," Lucia said.

Tia punched her in the shoulder. "You know what I mean, silly."

"Did you feel the tingle when you pulled up?" Devin asked.

"I have been tingling ever since I rode back into New Orleans, but it was stronger when I pulled up here."

"I told you there were many vamps and Were-folk in the city." Devin grinned.

"Yeah you did, I just didn't know how many."

"Way too numerous to count," Lucia chimed in. "I imagine you will be meeting quite a few of them in the near future."

"Miss Anna warned me they would be drawn to me like a magnet."

"I hope she also taught you ways to deal with them," Devin said. "I really don't cherish the thought of fighting vamps."

"She said Were-folk don't think too highly of vamps."

"That's a kind way of saying we despise each other," Lucia said. "We have battled for centuries and maintain only the slimmest of a truce."

"The older vamps are genuinely brilliant and wealthy from their business arrangements, but the younger ones tend to be impatient and greedy. Quite a pain in the ass at times," Lucia explained.

"How so?" she asked.

"When a vamp goes rogue and starts feeding on humans, the existence of the entire population of supernatural beings in the city is threatened until it can be located and destroyed. Hunters are employed and the nights can be very dangerous."

"Who are these hunters?"

"Mostly Were-folk, but on occasion a human with knowledge of the vamps. Apparently it is a highly unpopular and unwise for a vamp to kill one of their own."

"What about the police, do they know about them and us?"

"There are several Were-folk on the police force who tend to govern the activities of supernatural beings in the city, latents mostly, who have the enhanced senses and strength, but not the power to shift."

"I see." Tia picked up a roller. "So much to learn." She lowered the roller into the paint.

"One day at a time, Tia," Devin promised.

"Does she know about the bonding?" Lucia asked truly concerned.

"Not yet, but we will have to wait to talk about it. We are about to have company."

She could sense Tia's burning curiosity and wished Lucia had not brought the subject up at this inopportune time. She looked at her friend. *We will discuss it later,* she projected to Tia.

Devin would have to come up with a gentle way of explaining bonding to Tia. Until Tia chose a mate and bonded with the One, she would be aggressively courted by vamps and other Were-folk alike who sought to have her as a mate to gain power for their clan or pack. Devin was certain of her feelings for Tia, but would need to be vigilant over her until Tia made up her own mind.

†

George and Kaitlin returned with more paint and supplies. "You know, Devin, I had an idea riding back here," Kaitlin said.

"That could be dangerous," Tia smirked.

"What's up?"

"If you aren't too tired, I thought one of your steaks would be great for dinner," Kaitlin replied.

"That does sound good. Let me finish trimming and, if George will loan me his truck, I'll go to the store and get what we need."

"Fine by me," George answered and tossed her a set of keys.

Devin finished off the trim work and climbed down the ladder. "Baked potatoes and salad?" she asked Kaitlin.

"Yes, and some corn to boil," she added and handed Devin a credit card.

"I'll get the steaks soaking and the potatoes in the oven and be back here as quick as I can."

"Take your time, I think we have things under control here," Kaitlin said.

"All right, I will see you soon then." She left the club.

†

Devin picked up the supplies they needed for dinner and drove back to Kaitlin's home. She placed the steaks in to soak and got the potatoes baking in the oven. The rest of the items she stored in the refrigerator before going to the garage to get the grill ready. Her mouth was watering as she climbed back into the truck. There was nothing like a rare piece of meat she thought with a smile. Well, there were things that were better, but she would not dwell on those right now.

When she walked back into the club, Kaitlin, George, and Lucia were painting the final wall and Tia was finishing the trim on her sound booth. "Wow, this place is looking great," she remarked as she entered.

Kaitlin smiled. "I am very pleased with it too. It's amazing what fresh paint and some elbow grease can accomplish. Go look at the restrooms to see how they are looking."

Kaitlin was right. The fresh paint and new lighting did wonders for the restrooms. She could not suppress a smile when she saw the stall doors painted green to match Tia's door.

"I like the green in there, it ready adds some contrast." She returned to the main room.

"That was Tia's idea since we had leftover green paint."

"Great choice," Devin answered. "What would you have me do?"

"We are almost done here if you want to start picking up. Those empty paint containers can go out to the Dumpster."

Devin picked up the empty cans to carry out back. The evening was arriving and bringing with it a soft breeze, which would make for a beautiful night for a cookout, she thought as she closed the lid and walked inside for another load.

"We can toss these rollers in the Dumpsters and put the rest of the equipment in my truck. I will clean it at home," George replied. "I assume we can clean up before dinner." He waved paint-covered hands in the air.

Kaitlin looked at her watch. "Everyone please meet at my place at eight for dinner. That should be plenty time to clean up and rest a bit."

Chapter Twenty

As she showered, Devin contemplated the best way to approach the subject of bonding with Tia. The impact it would have on both of their lives was tremendous, but in very different ways. For Tia, it would mean protection from others that coveted her powers, but for Devin it would mean a lifelong commitment to Tia once they were bonded. However, if Tia decided she no longer wished to be with her, Devin could not bond with another.

Devin was positive Tia was the one her soul was searching for, but she did not want Tia to feel pressured into making a decision. It was imperative however, that they have this conversation soon, so Tia could be aware of the consequences when she made her decisions.

We need to talk tonight after everyone has left, she projected into Tia's mind.

Yes, I agree, Tia responded back.

Devin finished showering and after dressing walked down to Kaitlin's house to check on dinner. Kaitlin was busy making salads for everyone. "The potatoes are nearly done."

"Let me go start the fire and I will be back to help."

"No rush," Kaitlin answered as Devin walked out the door.

Devin was lighting the fire when she looked up to see Tia approach. She looked beautiful under the moonlight and she felt her heart beating wildly in her chest. Tia could feel the change in Devin. "I take it you approve."

"Oh most definitely. You are beautiful," Devin said, causing Tia to blush.

"I have missed you." Tia slipped an arm around Devin's waist. "I could hardly sleep last night for thinking about you."

"I am so glad you are back here with me," Devin replied. "I did not want to leave, but I knew Kaitlin was counting on me."

"I understand, besides I needed that extra time with Miss Anna."

"I know you did and I was being selfish when you wanted to stay."

"That just told me how much you cared."

"I do love you," Devin admitted.

"Yes, I know, and I love you too."

The door to Kaitlin's house swung open and spoiled the moment for them as their friend walked over carrying three beers. "Don't you look nice," she remarked as she handed Tia a beer.

"I guess that makes me chopped meat," Devin teased.

Tia and Kaitlin laughed. "I don't know anyone that can make a pair of jeans look any better than you," Kaitlin said.

"I'll second that," Tia answered with a purr.

"Okay, enough." Devin's face went scarlet.

George and Lucia pulled up at the same time and parked in the drive. "I will get more beer if you two will set up our chairs," Kaitlin said.

Devin and Tia placed the chairs out on the lawn away from the smoke and welcomed George and Lucia.

"You're not the only one that cleans up nicely, Tia, take a look at George," Devin teased.

"I don't ever think I have seen you without a beard, George. But the goatee looks very nice on you."

"I thought it was time for a change." He took a cold beer from Kaitlin. "I guess it is back to business as usual tomorrow."

"Yes, we will open back up tomorrow night," she answered.

"I need to talk to you about that," Tia said to Kaitlin.

"Go ahead."

"Devin's brother, Damien, has loaned me money to go to school full time when the semester starts next month, so I won't be able to DJ except on weekends. I do have a plan though."

"That is wonderful about going to school! Don't worry, we can manage without live music."

"Well, I can set up tracks for the nights that I am not working and Devin can make sure they are playing once the crowd arrives and you switch off the jukebox."

Kaitlin looked at Devin. "I should be able to handle that."

"If the rent needs to go up, I should have money to pay a little extra."

"Nonsense, I will get my money's worth out of you, don't you worry. Your main concentration needs to be on school." Kaitlin was as proud of Tia as her own parents would be.

"Thanks," Tia answered.

"I want to thank you all for helping at the club today. I still can't get over how fresh and new everything looks," she said.

"We need to plan on doing a facelift every year then," Devin replied.

"That's not a bad idea. I'm sure we could come up with plenty of changes to make."

The conversation turned to different ideas for the bar and Devin got lost in the glow of the coals. She snapped back to attention when she realized Kaitlin had asked if she was ready for another beer. "Yes, I'm sorry I was a little out there for a minute. Is everyone starting to get hungry?" she asked.

"Starving as usual?" Lucia asked. "Do you want me to carry the steaks out?"

"Yeah, that would be great."

"Hang on and I'll help you." George followed her inside.

"Turn the corn up to high if you would please, Lucia," Kaitlin called.

"Got it," Lucia walked inside.

When they returned with steaks and fresh beers, Devin went to work cooking and paid little attention to the conversation. Something on the nighttime breeze was niggling at her nerves and she could not quite determine what it was. Devin felt like they were being watched but she could not pinpoint where the feeling was coming from.

Lucia noticed the distraction and tension in Devin's stance and walked over to the grill. "Is everything all right over here?"

"Maybe it is my imagination, but I feel we are being watched," Devin answered.

"I thought so too earlier, but I cannot pinpoint anything. It may be the first of the watchers attracted to Tia's power."

"I'd hoped for at least a few days before all of that started."

"She needs to be bonded soon. Are you going to talk with her tonight?"

"Yes, I plan to after dinner, but I will not pressure her into an answer."

"I never dreamed you would, Devin, but would you mind if I lurked around for a night or two, just as a precaution?" Lucia asked.

"I would appreciate it if you would, my friend."

"Consider it done then."

"What are you two plotting up over here?" Tia asked as she joined them at the grill.

"Not plotting, just arguing over who gets the biggest steak." Lucia grinned.

"I'm sure there will be plenty for all before the night is through. Don't forget we have other things to eat besides meat."

Lucia looked at her with a smirk.

"Yeah, yeah, I know, meat first for you carnivores."

"See, I told you she was trainable." Lucia winked, which earned her an elbow to her ribs from Tia.

"Careful Lucia, she throws a mean fireball," Devin warned.

"Ah yes, don't let my pretties get singed." She cowered away from Tia, who giggled at her antics.

"Tia, would you go inside for a large cookie sheet so I can put these steaks on it?" Devin asked.

"Sure," she replied and disappeared into the house.

Devin turned the steaks on the grill as she waited for Tia to return. When several minutes had passed and Tia had not returned, she gave Lucia a worried look. "I'm going to go check on her."

Devin walked into Kaitlin's kitchen to find Tia holding the cookie sheet under one arm as she held a note out in front of her. She nearly jumped out of her skin when Devin asked, "Is everything okay in here?"

Tia turned toward her with eyes wide with fright. "I found this on the counter with my name on it." She handed the note to Devin. "It appears to be an invitation or a summons."

Devin read the note and quickly stuffed it into her pocket. "We will discuss this later," she said. When she read the signature at the bottom of the note, Devin knew her senses were correct earlier. One of Lord Jordan's henchmen must have been the presence both she and Lucia felt while they were outside.

Lucia noticed the startled look on Tia's face when they returned and moved over to the grill.

"Kaitlin, if you and George will get the rest of the food on the table, we will bring the steaks inside," Devin said.

Kaitlin nodded and she and George went inside. Devin waited until they were in the house before she turned to Lucia. "It has begun. Lord Jordan is the first to send his invitation to Tia," she told her.

Lucia let out a low whistle. "Lord Jordan is ancient. Rumors have it he is nearly a thousand years old and very powerful. I am not surprised he is the first to sense Tia. He has the largest clan I have ever heard of and must have spies throughout town."

"Would someone please tell me what is going on?" Tia asked rather impatiently.

Devin pulled the steaks off the fire as she spoke to Tia. "Your new powers have already been detected and word of your arrival is spreading throughout the city. The invitation you received tonight was from one of the oldest vampires known to our kind. He wishes to speak to you tomorrow night."

"Lord Jordan. That sounds like some form of royalty."

"In the vampire world that is the title bestowed only on the most powerful. Dare not underestimate him, Tia," Lucia warned.

"Do I have to go?" she asked Devin.

"Unfortunately, unless you want him to come here and that would jeopardize Kaitlin," she answered.

"I would never want that to happen," Tia said. "What do I do?"

"You calm down, eat a good supper and we will make some calls after dinner. We need to speak to Damien for his advice and also Simon, the Alpha of the New Orleans pack," Devin answered. "And you, you need to remember what Miss Anna has taught you about vamps."

Devin carried the steaks inside and placed them on the stove. "Eat up everyone." She started dishing out steaks.

While they sat around the table enjoying the meal, Devin felt her wolf's low growl of approval for the delicious steak.

Did I just hear you purr? Tia projected.

Wolves do not purr. Devin was quick to correct her. *My inner wolf was growling to let me know she was enjoying the steak.*

"This steak is even better than the last," Kaitlin said.

280

"It is fantastic," Lucia agreed.

"I am glad you are all enjoying it."

When the meal was finished and the kitchen cleaned, Devin and Tia told Kaitlin goodnight and, trailed by Lucia, went up to Devin's apartment.

Devin took out the note and handed it to Lucia. "I think we need to call Damien first for advice and then we can plan what else needs to be done."

"Agreed."

Devin pulled out her cell and called Damien, placing him on speaker so the others could hear as she described the situation to him and request his advice.

"Lord Jordan is not only powerful, but he is wealthy and a scrupulous businessman," Damien reported. "He will want Tia in league with his clan and will pay whatever it takes to buy her loyalty."

"I don't wish to be in anyone's clan or pack other than yours," Tia told him, which made Devin smile with pride.

"Then that needs to be your message to Lord Jordan, but done in a diplomatic fashion," he warned.

"Do we need to let Simon know what is happening?" Devin asked.

"I'll contact him and bring him up to speed. Would you like me to come down as your future Alpha to meet with Lord Jordan?"

"I, for one, certainly would not turn down your assistance."

"What time do you plan to meet with him?"

"Just after sundown was his request, at his mansion in the Garden District," Devin answered.

"I'll drive down in the afternoon then and we can ride together. Devin, you and Tia need to discuss a bonding tonight or else this will go on for quite some time."

"Yes, my Alpha."

"And your brother who loves you both dearly," he reminded her. "I will see you tomorrow."

"Goodnight, Damien, and thanks."

"What is all this business with a bonding?" Tia asked when the call ended.

"That is my cue to exit," Lucia smirked. "I will see you both tomorrow."

"Thanks for your help tonight." Devin walked Lucia to the door.

"You're welcome and good luck with your chat with Tia." She walked out the door.

"I need something to drink. Would you like something?"

"Do I need a drink?"

"Possibly." Devin got two glasses and a bottle of Single Barrel from the kitchen and took them to the couch. She poured them a drink of the strong whiskey.

"So, tell me about this bonding stuff."

"In the ways of the Were-folk when two souls find their mates, they undergo what is known as bonding."

"Which is exactly what?" Tia asked.

"Well, for two wolves it would be the sharing of blood while making love, but since you are not Were, you cannot share my blood."

"How would you take my blood?" she asked.

"By a small bite to your neck," Devin explained. "The wound would heal quickly, but you will forever carry my mark, which lets others know you are bonded and protected by me."

"That doesn't sound too awful."

"It is different for you than it is for me." Devin took a long drink.

"Different how?"

"Once wolves are bonded they are mated for life to their one and only. You are not wolf-bound and can walk away at any time, but you would be my one and only mate."

"So if I left you, you would be alone forever?"

"Yes, that is how it is told," Devin said. "There is more."

"What else?"

"I have never heard of two females bonding before, so I cannot be one hundred percent sure the bonding would be forged."

"That would be horrible."

Devin took another drink and this time Tia joined her.

"So why does everyone imply that bonding is so urgent for me?" she asked.

"If you are bonded, you are marked and cannot be taken by any other creature without huge repercussions. So until you are bonded, Lord Jordan and others will try to seduce you."

"Oh, so what you are saying is that I'm free game until I am bonded to someone?" She shivered. "That makes me feel like fresh meat to a starving animal."

"You are the only one to decide what your future is. As long as we can, Damien, the pack and I will protect you."

"Is that the reason Damien is giving me money for school?"

"No. Damien is first and foremost looking out for the benefit of the pack, by having you educated to assist Doc with the medical care of the pack."

They sat in silence for a few minutes as Devin's words sank in.

Tia finally set her glass down and turned toward Devin. "Are you positive I am the one you want to spend your life with?"

Devin smiled the most beautiful smile Tia had ever seen, then spoke. "I have never been more certain of anything in my life. My soul brought me here to search for what was missing from my life. From the moment I laid eyes on you, I knew you were the one." She reached out to touch Tia's face. "I would love and protect you with my life to eternity if you will allow me."

"Oh, Devin, I love you too, but what if something happens between us? I can't stand the thought of you being alone forever."

"If you have doubts then I would not make a decision yet, but being alone is a risk I am willing to take."

"I don't and never have doubted you, not even for a second, Devin."

Devin leaned down to kiss Tia and felt her shiver as their tongues met and swirled together. She pulled Tia into her arms for a heated kiss, which left them both breathless and wanting.

"I want to be bonded with you, Devin. Please make love with me."

Devin stood and took Tia's hand to lead her to the bedroom. She lit a candle beside the bed and began to remove Tia's clothing, kissing each inch of skin as it became bare, making her tremble for more. When Tia was undressed, Devin quickly removed her clothes and pressed her lover onto the bed with hungry kisses.

Tia's hands explored Devin, stroking up and down her back as Devin's mouth and tongue ignited trails of passion as she moved down Tia's body. Her lust turned her breathing into rapid pants as Devin's tongue sought out the center of her soul, her hips gyrating against Devin's face, pressing her deeper as wave after wave of passion crashed down upon her. "Oh God yes, Devin," Tia cried out as she erupted into uncontrollable spasms. Never had a lover made her feel anything as intense or pleasurable as Devin. Tears of absolute bliss ran down her cheeks.

Tia's tears alarmed Devin. Fearing she had hurt her lover, she quickly moved up to lie beside her. "Tia, I am sorry if I hurt you," she whispered.

"Devin Benoit, if that is how making love with you feels every time then you can hurt me all you want," Tia said. "That was the most incredible experience I have ever had."

A smile of relief crossed Devin's face at her words. "I've been told it gets even better." She grinned.

Tia smiled and rolled Devin onto her back. Her fingers lovingly stroked down her skin, making her inner wolf growl with excitement. "Show her to me, please," Tia said.

"What?" Devin asked startled by her request.

"Show me the other half of my mate," she repeated.

Devin climbed from the bed as Tia sat up in the bed. The air in the room appeared to shiver and in a moment, the candlelight fell upon the most beautiful gray wolf Tia had ever imagined. She reached out with fingers trembling with excitement to stroke the soft muzzle and then buried her face in the wolf's furry neck. She breathed in the familiar scent she associated with Devin and pulled her face back to stare into amber eyes. "You are my wolf and my mate."

With those words spoken, Devin shifted back into human form and joined Tia on the bed. Their bodies entwined in a lovers embrace, kissing deeply.

Tia broke the kiss. "I'm ready," she whispered.

"Are you positive?" Devin asked.

"Absolutely." Tia's voice was full of emotion. "I have never wanted you more."

Devin nuzzled Tia's neck, slowly licking her skin as her passion rose to the surface. Their bodies moved fluidly together as Devin's teeth became sharpened canines and she bit Tia's neck, drawing blood and a small cry from her lover as they climaxed together. That was the first and only time Devin would harm her love. Devin's soft tongue lapped up the blood. When she tasted Tia's blood, mental flashes of Tia's life played through her mind as she truly witnessed her love and her life.

Tia's life as a child and a young woman played through Devin's mind like a movie reel as she witnessed the life of the woman she loved. Her only regret was that Tia could not benefit from the same information about her. There would be plenty of time in their future for Devin to share those precious memories with Tia.

When Devin's hunger was satisfied, she rolled onto her back and Tia snuggled into her. This was how her life was destined, Devin thought as her eyes grew heavy and she dreamed.

Chapter Twenty-one

Her ringing cell phone woke them the next morning and Devin picked it up to see Damien calling. "Good morning, big brother," she said with a relaxed and sultry voice.

Damien hesitated for a moment at the drastic change in his sister's voice from the previous evening and then he chuckled when he realized the reason for the change. "You did it, didn't you?"

"Yes, we did, and may I say it was the most wonderful experience." Devin was propped up on an elbow as her fingers caressed the skin of Tia's shoulder.

"Congratulations to you both. How is Tia?"

"Smiling like a Cheshire cat," Devin answered.

"Is she feeling okay?"

"Damien wants to know if you are feeling okay?" she whispered.

"Let me have the phone," Tia said.

Devin handed Tia the phone and waited for her to speak.

"Your baby sister is an absolute devil in bed." Tia could feel his blush coming through the phone.

"Well, I am glad to hear that and I take it you are feeling well," Damien managed to stammer.

"I feel terrific."

"Good enough to meet with a thousand-year-old vampire today?"

"I don't think anything could stand in my way."

"All right, well, let the devil know I will be leaving around lunch. Hopefully, the two of you will be out of bed and dressed by then."

"I think we can handle that. Is Miss Anna coming with you?"

"I don't know, but I will ask if she wants a quick visit with Marie," he said. "I love you both and will see you soon."

"We love you too. Goodbye for now." Tia ended the call.

She handed the phone back to Devin. "He says he will be leaving around lunch."

"Excellent. Would you care to take a shower with your mate?"

"I'd love to."

†

They walked into the tiny bathroom and Devin started the water as Tia looked at her image in the mirror. Behind her ear and at the base of her neck appeared to be a small bruise about the size of a quarter. She looked closer at the faint image. "This looks like a paw print," she said as she pulled her hair back for a closer look.

"It is mine," Devin said. "It will grow darker until it looks like a tattoo. The placement can be concealed easily enough by your hair, but for those who are bound by it, they will know it is there and you are off-limits to them."

"You mentioned last night that serious repercussions would take place if someone violated the bond. What did you mean by that?"

"It would basically turn into a race war between our pack and whoever violated the bond," she explained.

"We can never let that happen."

"No, for everyone's sake, we can't. That is why it was so important that it was done quickly once you left the compound."

"Thank you for loving me." Tia pulled Devin into the shower with her.

They made love in the shower, eager to explore the other's body in full light, until the water started to run cool.

"Do you think Lucia would like your apartment?" Tia asked.

"I don't see why she wouldn't. Why? What are you thinking?"

"My place is bigger, big enough for two, and I have more hot water," she said with a seductive grin.

"Ah, I see. I will ask her if she is interested when she comes by today."

"I think we should run it by Kaitlin first, but I don't think she will have any problem with it."

As they dressed, Devin turned to Tia and asked, "Would you like some beignets this morning?"

"I could eat a whole bag myself," Tia said.

"Let's ride down and get some and then we can share them with Kaitlin over coffee."

Tia followed Devin down the stairs. "How long do you think the meeting will take tonight?"

"I don't know for certain, but I hope it won't take long so we can get back to help Kaitlin at the club," Devin answered.

†

Tia knocked on Kaitlin's door and entered carrying a bag of beignets. She found Kaitlin preparing a pot of coffee.

"I was hoping I would have company this morning and here you are carrying beignets to boot." She turned to pull three mugs from the cabinet.

"We have a proposition for you and we thought these might sweeten the offer," Tia said.

"Oh this I must hear." Kaitlin took a seat at the table.

"Devin and I have decided to move in together, at my place since it is bigger. We were wondering if you would rent Devin's place to Lucia, if she's interested."

"Oh honey, you didn't have to buy beignets for that. Yes, I would welcome Lucia into our little pack."

Interesting choice of words, Devin projected to Tia.

Yeah, I thought so too. Maybe she knows more than we think.

"But, since you bought them, let's not let them go to waste." Kaitlin pulled a pastry from the bag.

Devin took a seat at the table while Tia waited on the coffee. "We have some business to take care of later with my brother Damien, but we will be into work as quickly as we can."

"That's no problem. I don't expect tonight to be a heavy night, at least not early. I imagine there are still a lot of folks moving back home today." She took a bite and continued. "Will I get to meet Damien?"

"I would think so. He'll be here after lunch, and I'm sure before you go open the club,"

"So, what's on the agenda for this morning?" she asked.

"I thought we might go ahead and move Devin into my place, or rather our place."

"Do you need any help?"

"No, I really don't have that much yet to move. You just relax and enjoy your last morning of peace and quiet."

"Well, there goes the quiet," Devin teased as Lucia pulled into the drive.

"Wave her in for coffee and breakfast."

"Good morning everyone." Lucia took a seat beside Devin.

"Were your ears burning? We were just talking about you," Kaitlin told her.

"Whatever it is, I did not do it," Lucia teased.

"Actually, I think you might be interested," Devin replied. "I'm moving in with Tia, so my apartment will be vacant, if you want."

Lucia looked at Kaitlin, who nodded her head.

"Heck yeah, how much is the rent?"

"How about a hundred a week, plus some occasional sweat equity when we need painting or other chores?"

"Sign me up. Just give me time to talk to my landlord, but I'm on a month to month with him already, and I'll let you know when I can move in."

"I bet we could get George to help us with his truck," Devin told her.

291

"Welcome to the family then." Kaitlin lifted her mug.

"Awesome," Lucia replied with a huge grin. "Do you have anything you need done today?"

"Devin and I are going to get her stuff moved and then we have a meeting later," Tia said.

"You want some help?"

"Actually, we do. Moving won't take long, but we could get back on your "honey-do" lists while we wait for Damien."

"Let's just spend a relaxing day. There will be time for those later," Kaitlin replied. "You gals have already done enough this week."

"Maybe a quick spin around town on our bikes then," Lucia suggested.

"Only if I can ride too," Kaitlin teased.

"You can ride with me anytime."

"Let's finish up these beignets and get to work then," Devin smirked as she bit into another pastry.

✝

Tia left first to make room in her closet for Devin's clothes. Devin and Lucia went up to her apartment to start carrying stuff downstairs. "Yeah, I could get into living here," Lucia said, looking around. "I take it the bonding chat went well last night. I saw an auspicious looking mark on Tia's neck this morning."

"It went beautifully." Devin grinned. "I would have never dreamed it could feel so good."

"Congratulations then, my friend, I pray it is a long and healthy bonding."

"Thanks Lucia. I really look forward to having you move in here too."

"We will have a blast together." She took a pile of clothes from Devin and started to the door.

It took barely an hour to move Devin's belongings and the group was ready to ride. "Is there anywhere special we want to go?" Lucia asked as Kaitlin climbed on back of her bike.

"The Garden District is always beautiful," Kaitlin suggested.

"Great idea," Devin said. *That will give us an opportunity to locate Lord Jordan's place for the meeting tonight* she projected to Tia.

I had almost forgotten about that, she answered.

"You two take the lead," Devin told Lucia and they rolled down the driveway.

They could not have asked for a better day to ride. The sun was shining brightly and the air had coolness to it, so uncommon for this time of year. They rode through the Quarter, speaking and waving to shop owners who were busily preparing to reopen for business. The sun peeking through the branches of the large oaks in the Garden District make the ride almost surreal as they passed one beautiful home after another.

Tia felt a strong tingling sensation several times as they rode, but when they reached a humongous house, the sensation grew to nearly a hum. *Let me guess, Lord Jordan's place* she projected to Devin.

You would be correct, Devin answered, slowing the bike to get a good look at the house.

"Beautiful isn't it? I would love to see the inside," Kaitlin commented.

Not if she really knew what was on the inside, Devin projected to Tia.

Don't make me any more nervous than I already am, Tia pleaded as she nuzzled Devin's neck.

"Sorry, my love, I wasn't thinking."

"I will forgive you," Tia replied, squeezing her tightly.

They rode past the zoo that had a few cars in the parking lot. "How about we take a ride up to Lake Ponchartrain and back?" Devin suggested.

"Great idea," Lucia answered as they pulled back onto the road.

†

When they had made the circuit around the lake and stopped off for shrimp po'boys it was time for Damien to be arriving. They had pulled back into the drive, and barely dismounted from the bikes when he pulled up in his truck.

"That was great timing." Devin hugged her brother and made the round of introductions.

"It is a pleasure to meet you both," he said to Kaitlin and Lucia. "I have heard so much about you I feel like I know you already."

"It was only the good stuff, I promise. Did Miss Anna come with you?"

"Surprisingly she did. I just dropped her off at Marie's place."

"Excellent. Well come on in," Tia told him.

"I'll catch you guys later at the club." Kaitlin walked back into the house.

"Me too," Lucia responded. "It was nice to meet you, Damien. Call me if you need me," she told Devin.

"Later, my friend," Devin replied as they began walking to their apartment.

Damien hugged Tia and whirled her around once they got inside. "Welcome to the family." He leaned down to place a kiss on her cheek.

"Thank you, Damien, for all you have done for me and allowing me to be with Devin."

"You are very good for her, and I hope you will cherish the love you have for one another for eternity."

"I'm parched, would anyone else like a bottle of water?" Devin asked.

"Yes please," Tia and Damien replied in unison.

"May I see the note, Lord Jordan sent to you?"

Tia walked into the bedroom and picked up the note.

"Have you ever met him?" Devin asked.

"No, I haven't. I had occasion to meet up with a General of his years ago, but I've never met the Lord."

"Any ideas on how this will go tonight?" she asked her brother.

"I hope that once he sees that Tia is bonded, he'll have a change of heart and things will move swiftly." He turned to look at Tia directly. "Are you willing to offer your services in an emergency?"

"If you think I should, then yes," she answered. "I honestly do not know enough about my abilities yet to determine what I can and can't do yet."

"That would be of great advantage to Lord Jordan and he could offer you knowledge of the vampire world that may be useful to you in your magic."

"I hadn't even thought of that angle," Devin confessed. "Would she be safe?"

"I don't trust any vampire to be alone with Tia, even when she is under the protection of Lord Jordan. I would insist that either you or Lucia, if she is willing, be there as well at all times. He will not like the presence of a wolf, but he has no choice."

"Do you think this is wise to deal with any vampire?" Devin asked.

"Lord Jordan rules over New Orleans and can be a powerful ally or a powerful enemy. If you and Tia will live here until she graduates, I would prefer he be your ally."

"That makes good sense," Tia said. "Can you tell me what to expect? I never believed vampires even existed until recently."

"Lord Jordan is the oldest that we know of in this area, yet he may not look any older than I. I do not expect him to be dressed in a Count Dracula tuxedo and cape, but more the modern GQ look." He saw Tia crack a smile at his attempt at humor. "The biggest difference in us is that we are hot-blooded creatures, where vampires are almost frigid to the touch. When he touches you, and he most assuredly will take your hand to see if he can enter your mind, do not flinch or show any signs of weakness."

"He will try to enter my mind?"

"One of the greatest strengths of one that ancient is mind control and he will try to tap into yours to read what he can about you."

"Can I block him?" she asked.

"I am working on that, but I need something from Devin."

"What do you need?"

Damien pulled out a talisman on a leather necklace, not unlike the one Devin wore as protection from Cedra. When she saw it, her hand immediately went around her neck to check to see if hers was still there.

"It is very similar to yours, Devin, and you should continue to wear it as, since Cedra's death, Tia's power now protects you. Miss Anna has made this for Tia, but she did not have two ingredients. It requires a sample of your blood and of your wolf's coat to protect Tia from other supernatural creatures."

"Get some scissors, please, Tia." Devin's canines appeared and she opened a small wound on her wrist. Damien held the talisman under her hand to collect several droplets of her blood.

Without hesitation, she then shifted into wolf form and sat in front of Damien. Tia returned with the scissors and watched as he cut a small patch of fur from her coat and in a blur of motion Devin shifted back to human form.

"Will I ever be able to witness that transformation?" she asked in awe of her lover's ability.

"Unfortunately, your human eyes cannot capture the speed of a wolf's transformation. It will always seem as if time blurs for a few seconds and then a wolf or human will be there in front of you." Damien placed the hair inside the talisman. "This should do it." He tied the leather around Tia's neck. "Never, and I mean never, take this off. As long as you wear it, you will have protection from the bond you and Devin have forged."

"Will anyone else be able to remove it?"

"No one but you," Damien said. "That will prevent Lord Jordan from entering your mind and, as a backup, when he takes your hand, think only of the love you two share. There is no way he can see through that."

"Is there anything else you can think of that I might need to be prepared for tonight?"

"I cannot anticipate what will occur in the meeting, but stay strong and do not allow his position to intimidate you. You are a powerful being in your own right and even more so with the protection of the Baton Rouge pack."

He turned to look at Devin. "And you, baby sister, need to remain calm and cool, no matter what is said. Tia has a good head on her shoulders and can handle whatever comes her way. Adding tension to the situation will only delay the outcome."

Devin nodded her head in understanding.

"Now, that business is done, where can I buy my two favorite sisters dinner?"

"I'm sure we can find a spot," Tia said.

The trio ended up at a local oyster house and ate their fill of the Gulf delicacies. Tia and Devin chatted nervously and Damien did his best to keep their anxiety under control. "Maybe we should have the next round with some heavy garlic butter," he teased.

"Like that would really help." Devin shook her head. "We would be better off stocking up on toothpicks."

"You two are crazy," Tia muttered, but she did appear more relaxed. "Will you stay the night with us tonight?"

"I wish I could, but I'll need to get Miss Anna home. I'll be back though," he promised.

Damien paid the check and the sun was beginning to dip toward the horizon when they walked outside. "Let's do this." They climbed into the truck. "Who has the address?"

"I do, but we scouted it out today while were out riding," Tia said. "The place is huge."

"Point the way." Damien pulled out of the parking lot.

†

They drove in silence other than the occasional instructions on directions as each of them contemplated the meeting ahead of them. Damien had talked with Simon, who described Lord Jordan with respect and one whom he deemed a fair leader, which made Damien feel much more comfortable.

"This is it, on the right," Tia said.

"You weren't kidding when you said this place was huge. It takes up a whole city block." He pulled into the driveway.

Devin did not see any signs of security guards posted on the grounds. However, her acute senses alerted her that there was no doubt that their approach was monitored. She could hear the whir of cameras as they approached the house. A place this size would probably cost a fortune to secure with all the high-tech equipment, which Devin found ludicrous given the superhuman powers of the home's occupants.

✝

They found the bodyguards when they entered. Two very large men frisked them, rather professionally, to check for any weapons. When the older of the two nodded to the other, they were ushered down a brightly lit hallway to a set of large double doors. The man knocked on the door and a very powerful male voice said, "Enter."

He opened then closed the door behind them as they passed through into a large formal living room, elegantly furnished with heavy leather furniture. "Good evening, and welcome to my home," a very tall handsome man said as he rose from his chair. "I am Lord Jordan, Master of the New Orleans Clan, but then again I'm certain you know that or you would not be here."

Damien led them over to the area where Jordan was standing. "I am Damien Benoit, Alpha of the Baton Rouge pack. I present Devin, my sister, and Tia, her bonded mate, who I assume, by your invitation, that you are already aware of her powers."

"I am indeed. Please, would you care to join me for a drink?" He gestured toward seats next to his. "I am enjoying a very fine brandy, if that would suit your tastes."

"That would be delightful." Tia surprised them by answering.

Jordan poured them each a glass of the darkly rich liquid and handed it to them. Devin could feel his gaze lock with hers as his fingers brushed lightly over her skin as he handed her the glass. The contrast of his cold touch against her fevered skin made them both smile, Devin even more so when Jordan could not penetrate her mind.

"My watchers told me of your presence yesterday and I couldn't wait to meet you," he said to Tia. "Now, here you are." He offered her a glass.

Tia did not hesitate to reach forward and take the glass from him, which made Devin swell with pride.

"Thank you," she said.

"I was not informed of your bonding." He returned to his seat.

"It occurred only recently," she answered as she proudly took Devin's hand.

He cocked an eyebrow at them and studied them for several long seconds. "A very curious bonding it is. I don't know that I have ever heard of two females successfully bonding, much less across two very different species."

"They are a very unique pair," Damien responded.

"Yes, I can see that, Quite a lovely couple." He smiled. "I have to be completely honest with you, my dear. I had hopes of seducing you and bringing you into the Clan," he added with a tone of disappointment.

"I sincerely appreciate your interest, Lord Jordan, but would rather like to suggest a mutually profitable proposition to you."

"Oh, you do have my interest, young lady." He sipped his brandy. "Please proceed."

"The Baton Rouge Pack has my allegiance as well as my heart, but I would be in favor of learning about your kind from one of your wise elders and assisting you if the need arises in ways that would not violate my bonding."

Well said, Devin projected to her.

Jordan sat back in his chair and chuckled. "Tell me this. How did one so young become so diplomatic at such an early age?"

"I told you they were very unique," Damien said.

"You are a fortunate Alpha, my friend Damien, to have two such beautiful and talented creatures within your pack."

"That I am, Lord Jordan," he answered and took a drink of the fiery liquid.

"So you would propose to learn about my kind?" He cocked his head to study her curiously.

"That would interest me very much," she answered.

"Jonathon," he called loudly to the man in the hall. "Ask Marcus to join us please."

"Yes, Lord Jordan."

"Marcus is my second in command, only a few centuries younger than I, and is the most educated of our clan. He would make a most excellent teacher for you."

"Yes, My Lord?" A slightly smaller but no less handsome man entered the room.

"A proposition has been made that I would like your opinion on, my friend."

"Certainly, My Lord, what is it?"

Lord Jordan introduced him to Damien, Devin, and then Tia. "She is the young power wielder we discussed last night. She has entered a bond with young Devin here, but has proposed learning from you, or one of our kind, to aid in any future assistance she may afford us."

"What a clever suggestion. Quite an unusual bonding." Marcus studied the two women closely.

"As I have also remarked," Lord Jordan said.

"I would be delighted to assist you in any manner possible," he said to Tia. "Perhaps there is much to be learned by both of us. When would you like to begin?"

"I will be returning to college full-time in a few weeks. Would it be possible for me to check my schedule to see when we can meet?"

"What are you studying?" he asked.

"I wish to be a nurse, and when graduated I will return to Baton Rouge to serve my pack," she answered.

"Such a waste of good talents, but if that is where your heart leads you then it must be right," he answered a bit dryly. He reached into his breast pocket and pulled out a business card. "Just let me know when you are available." He stood to leave the room.

"I will, thank you," Tia answered.

"It was a pleasure meeting you all." He bowed to his Lord before departing.

"So how long will you grace our fair city?"

"I hope to graduate in two years."

"That should give us ample time to forge a bond of our own then." He smiled.

Sensing the meeting was over Damien rose, followed quickly by Devin and Tia. "I will be in touch," she said and they walked out of the room.

✝

Once they were safely inside the truck, Damien turned to Tia. "You did quite well, very impressive in fact."

"You did us proud," Devin added.

"Thank you both. I would have never been able to face him without you there."

"You will never be alone," Devin reminded her. "A part of me will always be with you."

"When did my baby sister become such a hopeless romantic?" he teased.

"Oh, about a month ago," she said. "Tia brings out the best in me."

"That she does." Damien gave her a warm smile. "Where to now?"

"We don't need to be at the club for another couple of hours. I would like to see Miss Anna and Marie."

"That's not a problem." Damien pulled onto Canal Street.

✝

Later that evening, after a visit with Marie and a promise to return soon, Damien helped Miss Anna into his truck for the drive home. "Can I drop you at the club?" he asked.

"Thanks Damien, but I think we are just going to walk," Devin said. "Give our love to all and we will see you soon."

Tia looped her arm through Devin's and they waved together as Damien drove away. When his taillights disappeared, Devin turned to Tia. "Would you care to take a stroll down by the river with me, my love?"

"I would love that," Tia answered.

The moon had risen and was close to a full phase as it shone down on the two young lovers as they strolled down the River Walk to begin their lives as bonded mates.

Bound

Hunter Series
Book Two

Chapter One

Rain from Tropical Storm Jacob pounded the Miami streets as the residents rushed for last-minute supplies. The storm-darkened skies allowed the nightly predators an early reprieve from their daily slumber. The hunters woke ravenous and emerged from their lairs in search of prey and fresh human blood.

A lone figure stood on a hotel balcony using thermal scanning goggles to search the bustling crowds on the sidewalks below for bodies devoid of normal heat signatures. She knew from nights of surveillance that the streets of this section of Miami were home to at least a dozen of the frigid-bodied, blood seekers. She expected that tonight she would find the prey she sought. The horrid weather had no effect on their bodies, or their abilities to hunt the living. Nor did it hamper her skills. Her eyes found what they were looking for—a body registering fifty degrees, "Hmmph, found ya."

†

Winona "Win" Weston fished a pack of Marlboro Lights from the pocket of her knee-length all weather coat and flipped open the top to tap out a cigarette. The snap of her Zippo lighter broke the silence on the balcony as she lit the cigarette and took in a lungful of smoke.

"You know that shit is going to kill you one day," a deep voice said from inside the bedroom.

Win smiled. "Only if I live long enough." She waved away the plume of exhaled smoke as she turned to peer inside the room.

From the shadows of the darkened room, a large figure approached the balcony. Dressed identically to Win, the dark-clad watcher, a woman with piercing amber eyes, stepped out onto the balcony. Alix's size dwarfed the smaller watcher who turned at her approach.

The rain pelted off Alix Augustus, a steam cloud forming an aura around her figure. Her Werecat metabolism, which raised her body temperature at least ten degrees above a normal human level, would prevent her from becoming chilled on a night like tonight. She smiled, thinking that her partner Win may, too, benefit from the added heat, if her smaller, human form required rapid warming.

"Damn, you're smoking hot," Win said as the woman's figure, glowed bright red in the goggles.

"I bet you say that to all the girls." She peered out across the balcony. "A great night for a hunt," she added.

A feisty human with exceptional fighting skills, Win trained as a bounty hunter along with Alix, a Werecat with

306

tremendous strength and hunting abilities. Together, they had become an excellent team. Their skills and years of experience made them perfect hunters for all manner of supernatural creatures. Partners and lovers for five years, they had learned quickly that once they bonded it enhanced their ability to hunt together, each knowing what the other's reaction during combat would be. Their reputation as an efficient killing team had spread throughout the supernatural world, and they rapidly became the most sought after team of elite assassins in the United States.

✝

Such was their mission in Miami. King Renaldo, the eldest of the Miami vampires, had contacted them to dispose of two undisciplined rogue vamps whose careless hunting habits were drawing unwanted attention, and threatened exposure of Renaldo's clan. The Vampire Laws prevented vamps from killing one another unless it was in an all-out war. The two rogues plaguing Miami were merely a tiresome distraction, so Renaldo contracted the bounty hunters to exterminate them.

✝

Alix and Win had no problems killing rogues, whether vampires or any other type of supernatural being, as long as there was a bounty on their head. They were both born to hunt and relished the adrenaline rush they got from the danger of tracking and exterminating dangerous supernatural beings. Alix especially despised rogue vampires as one of them had destroyed her family, leaving her orphaned as a toddler.

Alix and Win had tracked the feeding patterns of Jimmy Juice and Ricardo for three nights. In hindsight, the two young vampires should never have been allowed to turn. They lacked the discipline to keep themselves, and the clan, safe from exposure. Renaldo was paying handsomely for their services, and after tonight, the two rogues would no longer be a threat to him or his clan.

Alix growled as her keen sense of smell alerted her to their approach. She despised the reeking scent of the undead. "Smells worse than a boatful of long dead fish," she snarled.

Win, crushed out the butt of her cigarette and glanced at her watch. "Right on time," she grinned. "At least they're predictable."

They knew from previous surveillance that the two vamps would turn left at the next block and wait in a small park for unsuspecting victims to rush toward a parked car, or to catch a nearby bus to escape the weather.

"Are you ready?" Alix asked.

Win double-checked her weapons and nodded. "Let's do this then go someplace where it's not raining." She grinned and a shiver from the dampness began seeping into her bones. "I get the bigger one again, right?"

"You always get the big ones," Alix said.

"That's because they always underestimate my size. They see you and know you'll be a brute to kill," she teased.

"All right, Win, you can have the big one just this once more." Alix winked. "You really need to work on picking on someone more your size though."

Win chuckled as they left the room. Their bags were packed and left on the bed. Once the job was complete, they would retrieve their belongings, drive to South Beach to collect their fees from Renaldo, and then make a beeline north to escape the approaching storm.

Bypassing the elevator, they made for the stairwell, the four flights of stairs warming up their muscles for the impending battle. Win kicked open the heavy metal exterior door and they stepped out into the pouring rain. Still wearing the unusual goggles, she watched as their prey turned ahead of them to approach the park, and then separated to hunt.

"You get the right side of the park," Win said.

Alix grinned and they went in separate directions. The right side was darker, and had landscaping that would allow her to undress and shift undetected into the form of a sleek black panther.

Win stalked the larger of the pair, her heart beat steady and strong as she slipped her right hand into a compartment of her cargo pants to grasp the handle of a specially equipped revolver. Instead of bullets, the chambers held six sharpened wooden bolts. That would be her weapon of first choice, but if necessary, she would draw the silver bladed sword strapped across her back, concealed by her dark coat. She looked to her right to see that Alix had completed her shift, and was silently stalking the vamp. She would need no manmade weapons, just her razor sharp teeth and claws to tear the vamp to pieces, removing his head from his body if necessary.

Win's prey sensed her approach, and spun on his heels to face her with a hiss, baring his pointed canines when he saw the revolver loaded with bolts.

"I can hear your heart pounding," he sneered.

She released the first bolt from her revolver, but the vamp known as Jimmy Juice easily dodged its flight.

"You have to do better than that, hunter," he hissed and began running toward her in a blur of movement.

"I'm just getting warmed up," she growled back at him.

Win released three more bolts in a pattern she knew would cover his approach, and then drew her sword. The third bolt caught him in the left shoulder as he dodged the first two, and he howled in pain as he reached for it. A fierce cry of pain from off to his right froze his movement briefly, when he realized his partner was also under attack, and the hesitation allowed her to swing the shining blade and separate his head from his shoulders. She watched his body collapse to the ground and burst into flames, leaving only the wooden bolt untouched. A smile of victory crossed her face.

She had learned early in her career to soak the bolts in holy water for the extra pain effect, and to protect them from incineration when the vamps body disintegrated into ash. She stopped long enough to retrieve the bolt then rushed to Alix's aid.

She aimed the revolver, and without hesitation, released a shot sending a bolt into Ricardo's heart. Win waited for his body to complete his unholy cremation before collecting the bolt, which she tucked into a pocket inside her jacket.

Turning to Alix, she saw the big cat wiping the fresh blood from her face with large paws, and waited until she shifted back into her human form.

"I think we're done here. I'll get the car and meet you at the back door if you'll collect our bags," Win said.

Alix stood and stretched, willing away the discomfort she felt while waiting for her remaining muscles to shift back into place then nodded her agreement. She walked back to collect her clothing and returned to Win.

As Alix dressed, Win admired the beautiful naked form of the woman she loved. Alix saw her watching and the desire smoldering in her lover's eyes. "See something you like?"

"Oh most definitely," Win answered.

✝

They swiftly jogged back through the rain-soaked darkness to the hotel to finish their work. They were both fully aware one of Renaldo's generals followed them and would report to him the rogues' destruction. Win would also present him with the two bolts, which would still hold the scent of the recently deceased vamps as further proof when they arrived to receive their payment.

They caught a glimpse of him as he disappeared in the shadows when they reached the hotel.

✝

Alix took the stairs, two steps at a time, as she raced up to their room. She opened the doorway from the stairwell and the hackles on the back of her neck rose in full alert as she sensed another supernatural being in the hallway ahead. She determined by the scent that another vampire was present and stepped out of the stairwell with caution. She could shift more quickly than most of her kind, but if the vamp were close, and aggressive, she would have to rely on her power and agility to ward off an attack.

There was no one in sight so she rushed to the room to gather their bags. When she opened the door to step back into the hallway, a small female vamp lunged at her. The dark circles around the woman's eyes betrayed her hunger and her weakened reflexes. Alix thrust out her right hand, catching the vamp by the neck and lifting her off the floor, then slamming her into the wall of the hallway before moving quickly to the stairwell. Still carrying the stunned

311

vamp like a rag doll, Alix rushed down the stairs, kicked open the exit door and stepped into the darkness.

†

Win retrieved the black Yukon from the parking lot and drove to the back door to wait for Alix. She put the heavy SUV in park and emerged to run around to the passenger side. Her partner had much better eyesight at night, especially in this weather, so Win would concede her dominance to allow Alix to drive. She had removed her sword as she reentered the vehicle and placed it safely in the backseat.

The door slammed open, and when Win looked up she saw what Alix was carrying. Jumping out of the passenger seat, she drew her revolver in a smooth motion. She pulled the trigger as Alix held the vamp, who was struggling for release, at an arm's length away.

Alix dropped the vamp as the bolt struck true, and she began smoldering then burst into flame.

"That was a nasty little surprise." Alix bent down to retrieve the bolt from the pile of scorched clothing.

"Let's get going before anyone else shows themselves." Win tucked the third bolt in her coat.

"You'll get no argument from me." She tossed the bags in the backseat and slipped in behind the wheel.

"Let's go to South Beach to collect, and then drive up the west coast so we can hopefully bypass this rain."

"Can we find a drive-through somewhere along the way afterward? I'm starving."

Win smiled at her lover. "Yes, we will find a spot to feed that beast of yours."

Alix growled her pleasure as she put the SUV in gear and followed the GPS directions to Renaldo's South Beach home.

✝

The streets of south Florida were beginning to look like a ghost town. Business owners were closing up shop, and heading for higher ground as the storm intensified. Hurricane Andrew had taught them all a brutal lesson when it devastated nearby areas in 1992, causing billions in damages and claiming sixty-seven lives.

✝

When they reached Renaldo's home, they pulled into the large circular drive and parked. Two huge men greeted Alix and Win at the front door and ushered them inside.

"King Renaldo is waiting for you in the parlor," one of the men stated as he pointed to large double doors.

Win did not expect an ambush from someone as well respected as King Renaldo, but she had re-loaded her revolver out of habit. The weight of it on her thigh gave her a sense of security, and her hand remained close until they stepped inside to find Renaldo waiting for them alone.

"Welcome back, ladies." They walked across the room. "My sources have informed me your contract was completed tonight," he said with a charming smile. "May I offer you something to drink?"

Win asked, "Do you have bourbon?"

"But of course." Renaldo drifted more than walked to an elegant bar. "For two?" he asked, looking at Alix.

"That would be fine," Alix answered.

313

"I brought the bolts if you need further proof," Win offered.

"Not necessary. Rafael witnessed the execution of the two rogues, and then the third waiting for you at the hotel," he answered. He poured two glasses halfway full with caramel-colored bourbon and handed one to each of the women.

"Thanks," Win said and Alix nodded her appreciation.

Renaldo returned to the bar and picked up a large envelope, which he handed to Win.

She took a sip of the bourbon before handing Alix the envelope.

"You won't even check it?" he asked.

"No need. I checked my account on the drive here and saw that fifty thousand had been deposited into the account as we agreed. Besides, I know where you live," Win added with a deadly look.

Renaldo smiled. "The envelope holds the receipt for the transfer, the ten thousand in cash to cover your travel expenses and a small bonus of appreciation for your excellent work."

"That's always a nice surprise," Win said.

"So where are you off to next?" he asked.

"We've been requested to visit New Orleans, to help Lord Jordan out with a minor problem," Win told him.

Renaldo grinned. "Please give my regards to my friend and remind him to come visit me, if you will."

"Consider it done." Win slammed back the rest of the bourbon.

"One more for the road?" he asked.

"Thanks, but no, we have a long road ahead of us tonight."

"Be safe then, and as always, it was a pleasure doing business with you," He extended a cold hand to Win.

She didn't hesitate to reach out to shake his hand. "You know how to reach us should you have future problems."

"I have you on speed dial." He chuckled, revealing his unsheathed canines.

They handed him the crystal glasses and turned to leave.

"Ready to go?" Alix, asked as they reached the foyer.

†

They stepped out into rain and a howling wind as they dashed to the SUV. "West across to Alligator Alley and then we'll run up the coast to Clearwater. Hopefully we can find a room," Win answered. "If not, we crash in the back."

Alix handed her the envelope and started the SUV. "I think I would rather drive all night than try to sleep in this vehicle."

Win smiled at her lover. "Find someplace still open for food if you can, before we leave town. I can hear your stomach grumbling."

"I'm all in for that." Alix said as Win programmed the GPS.

When Win opened the envelope, she whistled in surprise to find another five thousand on top of the ten agreed upon for travel expenses. "Too bad there isn't a decent steak house open, or I'd buy you the biggest steak I could."

"There's always tomorrow."

They finally found a fast food restaurant that was the last open business in the area and drove away with a bag of twenty double cheeseburgers, French fries, and supersized drinks.

"This should hold you for an hour or two." Win removed a cheeseburger from the paper wrapping and handed it to her lover. "Don't forget to chew this one," she teased and took a burger for herself.

Two hours later, they were deep in the heart of the Everglades and heading north. The rain had begun to lessen with each passing mile and when a deer beside the road was illuminated by the SUV's headlights, Win heard Alix growl.

"Would you like to stop for a run?"

"That would be great," Alix said.

Win glanced at the GPS. "There should be a turnoff ahead a few miles. Take it and find a safe spot to park."

"Thanks." Her amber eyes aglow with excitement.

†

Win reclined in her seat while Alix undressed before she shifted and went for a run. She hoped her lover would scare up some wildlife to hunt and kill. Her cat needed a fresh kill to remain happy and there was no more promising area than the Florida Everglades to satisfy that hunger.

As her eyes closed, Win reflected back on her life. Delivered to a Memphis orphanage as an infant, she never knew or cared about her biological parents or questioned why they had abandoned her...

Her petite size had made her an easy target for larger children at the orphanage and daily bullying became a part of her young life. As she began junior high, and her size remained smaller than her peers, Win realized she needed to learn ways to protect herself. She was a fast runner but knew some of the boys were faster and she feared for her safety. After her school day, she worked odd jobs whenever she could to earn money. When she had the required funds, she entered a martial arts program on the campus of Memphis State.

Her instructors found her to be a motivated student and challenged her development at every potential level until she had reached the highest level of black belt possible for her age and training. When she entered high school, other students found out quickly, and for some painfully, that she was not one to be harassed or intimidated.

As soon as she turned eighteen and graduated, Win left the orphanage that had been her home and traveled south. It did not matter where she ended up, as long as it was out of Memphis.

Her first major stop landed her in Jackson, and on a stormy night similar to tonight she was wandering the rain-slicked streets, munching on a burger, when she met Harley. She had stopped under the front stoop of a closed business to escape the rain for a few moments while she ate. It was the first food she had consumed all day and even though it had probably sat under a heat lamp for hours, it tasted like a gourmet meal to a starving teen.

The darkness had concealed her on the stoop and movement to her left caught her attention. A park took up the entire city block and Win strained her eyes to detect the movement. A sliver of light flashed, followed by a burst of flames, and then the most horrific smell assaulted her nose. Curious, she ate the last bite of her burger and slipped into the night to investigate.

In the center of the park she saw a dark man standing over what appeared to be a burning body. She watched with amazement as he bent down and withdrew something from the fire. She froze when the man turned and their eyes locked.

"Approach if you are a friend," he spoke.

Win, drawn to the sound of the man's voice, found her feet moving forward.

His steel-gray eyes followed her as she approached. He sheathed the sword across his back, beneath a black leather coat, and Win realized that it was the moonlight flashing off his blade that she had witnessed. "Who are you?" she asked.

"My name is Harley. Who are you?"

"Win," She eyed the burning body warily. "What happened here?"

"Something too dangerous to be discussed out in the open, follow me." His eyes searched the surrounding area.

Win was amazed at how easily she followed Harley, but her instincts told her he was to be trusted. She followed him down the sidewalk, almost running to keep up with his long strides, until they reached an all-night diner, allowing him to hold the door for her as she entered the building. As she walked past him, she felt a buzz of electricity radiating from his body and she shivered with excitement.

†

Harley led her to a secluded corner booth and handed her a menu. "You look like it's been a while since you had a decent hot meal. Order what you want, and lots of it."

The server brought them both strong coffee and Harley gave her his order, "Two eggs over easy, bacon, and dry toast."

"And for you, young lady?" she asked.

"I'll take that and an order of pancakes. Some apple juice too, if you have it," Win said. She waited for the server to leave. "You realize I don't have the money to pay for this, right?"

"Did I ask you if you had money?" he asked.

"No, you didn't."

"With the money I just made, I can afford to buy you breakfast," he told her as he leaned across the table.

She wiggled in her seat. "What are you?" she asked, "Some kind of bounty hunter?"

"You're very clever." He chuckled.

"I saw enough to know you used a sword. I presume to decapitate them based on the arc of your swing." She had a worried frown on her face as she contemplated her next sentence. "What I didn't see was how the body was set on fire."

She studied the weathered face of the man sitting across from her and judged him to be in his late forties. Win noticed he had a quick smile when she made a comment, but his eyes were what drew her the most. His steel-gray eyes appeared to look deep inside her soul as he gazed at her.

Harley started to speak, but after a quick glance beyond her, he realized the server was approaching. He waited until she placed the plates of food in front of them and returned to the counter. He began mashing up his eggs as he spoke. "Do you believe in vampires?" he asked, not looking at her.

"I've never seen one, but I guess anything is possible in this crazy world," she answered and took a bite of pancake.

"You are correct in assuming I'm a bounty hunter, but my prey is not human. I only hunt vampires, Were creatures, and witches that have caused havoc in the supernatural world by their actions," he said as simply as if he were describing a banking job.

Win stopped mid-chew to look into his eyes. "You're serious, aren't you?"

"Deadly serious," he answered, dredging a triangle of toast through the egg yolk. "What you witnessed tonight was the execution of a rogue vampire who has been feasting on small children in the area, causing the authorities to ask some uncomfortable questions about what is going on in Jackson."

"But how did you do that?" she asked.

"I shot him first with a wooden bolt, but just missed his heart, so I had to use my sword to take his head. Once relieved of that, his body burst into flame, sending him to hell where he belongs. That Win, is what you saw."

Win did not appear shocked by his answer, which brought another of his mischievous grins to his face.

"Are you from around here?" he asked.

"Nope, just passing through," Win said between bites.

Harley cocked his head to the side. "Headed where?"

Win stopped chewing and swallowed. "I don't really know," she admitted. "I just aged out of an orphanage in Memphis that has been my home for eighteen years."

"Have you ever been to Monroe, Louisiana?" he asked, already knowing the answer.

She chuckled as she looked up at him. "Who are you kidding? Until yesterday, I had never left the Memphis city limits."

Harley resumed sopping up the egg yolks with his toast.

Anxious to learn more about the mysterious man, she asked, "Is that where you're from?"

"I travel all over for business, but yes, that's where I call home," he said. "What are your plans for the future?"

Win placed the coffee mug back on the table. "I thought I would travel around a bit until I find someplace I like, and where I can find a job."

"What job training have you had?"

"I've done some odd jobs, painting, cleaning, and have limited fast-food experience," she answered. Even to her ears, she felt she had little work experience to offer a potential employer.

"So what are you good at?" he asked.

Win chuckled. "Surviving," she answered. "I had to learn to fight to protect myself at the orphanage and in public school. I worked after school to pay for martial arts lessons and I can hold my own in a fight." She continued eating as she weighed her options. She had little money, very few clothes, and no means of transportation. Her instincts, which generally were spot-on, made her think she could trust Harley.

Harley liked the grit in her voice, and though she was small, he bet larger opponents frequently underestimated her. He could also imagine many left in shock by her ferocity and skills as she took them down. He decided to go for broke and come right out with an offer.

"I have an old barn that needs a fresh coat of paint and an extra room that you could stay in," he said. "Nothing fancy, but it would get you out of the weather and fed regularly."

Harley could see that she was considering his offer and decided to sweeten the pot. "We would love to have you stay for as long as you wish," he added.

"Who is we?" she asked, curious.

"Alix, my daughter. She's also an orphan who has lived with me since she was a toddler," he said. "Maybe a year or two older than you, but still close to your age."

Harley saw a spark of interest when she looked up at him.

"How do I know you aren't an ax murderer or someone who will do me harm?" she asked.

He found himself chuckling as he formed his answer. "I use a sword as you've already seen, but I will not harm a human."

She thought about his answer a few more minutes as she ate, then looked up at him. "Tell me about Alix and how she came to live with you."

Harley pushed his empty plate away and began his story. "I was contracted for a job near Jonesboro and had been tracking a rogue vamp for two days. He was killing off every Were being he encountered. His last targets were Alix's parents. When I crashed into her home, I was too late to save her parents, but I did kill the vamp before he could rip out her throat." He smiled at the memory. "She lifted her arms for me to pick her up and I couldn't resist her charms. Her parents were the last of their clan. She had no relatives to leave her with, so I brought her home with me."

"Were, as in werewolf?" she asked in disbelief.

He shook his head no. "There are plenty of werewolves around, but no, Alix is a Werecat. When she grew into her teens, her first shift was into a sleek black panther."

First vampires, and now werewolves and werecats, this night was growing stranger by the minute. She studied him. There was no sign of humor or dishonesty in his face.

"What other types of Were creatures are there?" she asked with genuine curiosity.

He was pleased that she was showing an interest in the supernatural. "Wolves are the most *predominant*. Cats like Alix used to be more common, but the breed is dying out. Hunted almost to extinction for their pelts, mating pairs are rare these days. Birds, primarily large raptors, are rare, although I've heard stories about overly large eagles spotted out west. Foxes are also talked about on occasion."

"What does Alix do for work?"

"She runs our small farm, and is in training to become my future partner."

That piqued her interest more than anything he had said. "Would you train me?" she asked.

"I would consider it," he answered. "After you finish painting the barn," he said with a grin…

✝

The sleek black panther slipped deeper into the night as she found a game trail leading away from the parked vehicle. She scented the fear of a small animal as her feet glided silently down the trail, and her ears picked up the distant sound of a wild pig rutting through the underbrush looking for food. *Perfect.* She began silently stalking the pig. When it came into sight, she circled slowly to remain downwind of him. Alix felt a brief pang of guilt for hunting the smaller prey and decided it would be no challenge if she attacked him while he fed, so she intentionally stepped on a branch to make a crunching sound.

The pig's keen hearing picked up the sound and his wild eyes were frantic when he turned to see the black panther twenty feet away from him. He immediately fled the underbrush in an attempt to save his life, running as quickly as his short legs would carry him. The cat continued to walk slowly, giving the pig a head start to make the hunt as fair to the pig as possible.

As her pace increased, she opened her senses to track the animal. The scent of his terror made it easy to follow his trail, even though the light rain had begun to fall once more. She loped through the forest following his trail. When he was only several feet ahead of her, she pounced. Her sharp teeth sank into his neck as her powerful legs tripped him, her grip on his neck snapping his spine and killing the pig instantly. Her teeth ached for the taste of a fresh kill, a low growl escaping her as she ripped the first mouthful of flesh from his body.

She feasted on the pig until her hunger was sated, and then located a small creek to drink the fresh cool, water and cleanse the blood from her face and paws.

Alix turned away from the creek to run back to the SUV and for a moment, she thought Win was asleep. The big cat planted her large paws on the door and placed her face against the window glass, her heated breath fogging up the window.

†

A loud purr rattled against the window and Win turned to find large amber eyes staring at her. She rolled down the window, buried her fingers in the silky coat of the cat, scratching behind her ears. "Welcome back, my love. I hope you had a good hunt." She softly stroked the cat. Win watched as the body of the cat blurred as her shift began, then watched as Alix stood from a crouch, the light rain trickling down her bare skin.

She reached into the backseat for a towel. "You better wipe down and get dressed in something dry before the clouds decide to open up again."

Alix took the offered towel. "Thanks." She quickly wiped her body down and slipped back into a new set of clothes.

"How was your hunt?"

Alix's damp black hair fell into her eyes as she looked up from lacing her boots. "It was just what I needed. I killed a nice little pig that has me stuffed for now."

"Do you want me to drive for a while to let your meal settle?"

She brushed the hair out of her face. "Yeah, that would be great."

Win stepped out of the vehicle and walked around to the driver's side to slip in behind the wheel, as Alix pulled a shirt over her head and took the vacant passenger seat.

She drove back to the highway and as she turned north, the sky opened and torrential rains began to fall. Alix looked over at Win. "You good to drive in this mess?" she asked.

"Yeah, go ahead and crash for a while. If it gets too dangerous, I'll find a safe spot to pull over until it breaks," Win said.

Alix nodded and curled her lithe body up in the seat. It wasn't the most comfortable position for her but until her body metabolized the pig, she would rest the best way she could. She placed her right hand on Win's thigh and closed her eyes.

The warmth of the hand was very comforting and helped her to relax tense nerves. The SUV cut through the dark night as Win raced to get ahead of the storm. It didn't take long for Alix to fall asleep, and start purring softly while she slept, bringing a smile to Win's face.

About the Author

Ali Spooner

Ali Spooner, a native of Florida, currently lives and works in Memphis, TN. As an "Indie" author, Ali has been writing for many years as a hobby, and with the assistance of the Affinity team has taken her love of storytelling to a new level.

Ali's characters range from cowgirls and psychics, to a healthy dose of supernatural beings. She has written stand-alone titles and series. Ali is an avid reader and her other hobbies include photography, outdoor activities, and watching college sports.

Other Books from Affinity eBook Press

The Case of the Beggars' Coppice by Erica Lawson Edda Case is a woman in crisis who discovers that things are not as they seem. Is it truly a message for her from beyond the grave or is something more sinister taking place? Can Edda solve the mystery of The Beggars' Coppice?

Locked Inside by Annette Mori How much does the power of love matter to someone who must overcome obstacles far greater than most people face in a lifetime.

Line of Sight by Ali Spooner Sasha and her lover Kara are back. Continue the thrilling adventures of this couple from the Sasha Thibodaux series.

Requiem for Vukovar by Angela Koenig Requiem for Vukovar continues the Refraction series and the exploits of Jeri O'Donnell and her partner, Kelly Corcoran. In an epic siege largely ignored by the wider world, Kelly, who was prepared to give up comforts and certainties when she became part of Jeri's nomadic life, encounters more than physical danger. Her ability to maintain her core integrity is assaulted by the inevitable ugliness of war. For Jeri, the true battle is confronting her attraction to violence as she struggles against losing herself in the exhilaration of combat.

Against All Odds by JM Dragon From award winning and bestselling author JM Dragon, with significant updates by, Erin O'Reilly comes an original tale of romance where everything seems to be stacked against two women whose destinies bring them together. Life however takes a twisted path setting both Steph and Louise in directions they never thought possible. Will love win out against all odds or will love be forever lost?

The Settlement by Ali Spooner The outpouring of love and friendship toward Cadin helps her on her path to healing and learning to trust her heart to love once again. Join bestselling author Ali Spooner on this sensational journey that ends with a heartwarming romance.

Once Upon a Time by Alane Hotchkin Raven only wanted to escape the blows that life had dealt her. She longed to be on the open sea and free. When she came upon a beautiful young girl sitting alone in the middle of a meadow, little did she know that her destiny would be changed forever. Will they become the pawns of the ancient vision or will both paths lead to the same port of destiny? Find out it in this exciting high seas adventure that will capture your imagination.

Asset Management by Annette Mori Follow the twists and turns to the explosive conclusion. Not everything is black and white. There are many shades of gray and sometimes it's difficult to decipher who is good and who is evil. No one is all virtue or all malevolence, but sometimes love helps us rise above.

Do Dreams Come True? by JM Dragon How do two people who really shouldn't get on end up in a relationship? Find out in this deliciously ordinary romance.

Return to Me by Erin O'Reilly Will Salvation bring just that to Ellie, allowing her to find peace and happiness again, or will it have her questioning all that she believes in? A wonderful romance cloaked within an intriguing mystery.

Arc Over Time by Jen Silver This wonderful romantic continuation with the characters from Starting Over ties up loose ends. But the question is—does everyone have a happy ending? A must read.

The Presence by Charlene Neal Can Rebecca and Kayleigh overcome ghosts from the past and their own insecurities, or will a presence from the past tear them apart?

A Walk Away by Lacey Schmidt Sometimes chance brings you to the right person to help you resolve some of your baggage, and you learn to like yourself a little more. Kat and Rand are smart enough to recognize this chance in each other, but they also find that there is a catch to every opportunity—walking toward something is always walking away from something else.

Possessing Morgan by Erica Lawson The investigation has barely begun when Andrea becomes the target of a nearly fatal hit-and-run. But was it really aimed at her? Can she and Morgan find the common ground they need to solve the case and stop the attacks, or are the gaps just too wide to bridge?

Twenty-three Miles by Renee MacKenzie This is a story about community, and how it comes together in dangerous and devastating times. When you don't know who to trust, you better have friends who will rally around you. Will Talia and Shay find the answers they need to the mystery of the murders on the parkway, or will justice be elusive? Will they survive their quest for the truth?

Reece's Star by TJ Vertigo Under Faith's guiding, loving hand, will Reece successfully traverse the rocky road of emotion and embrace the positive changes in her life? Or will she panic and be unable to control that Animal part of herself? Will she take that next step to declare herself fully capable of love and devotion? This third installment in the popular series that began with Private Dancer continues the passionate and often hilarious romance of Reece and Faith as they both grow in love and in trust.

Confined Spaces by Renee MacKenzie Corporate politics, complicated romance, and long distances conspire to keep Andie and Kara all boxed in. Can love triumph despite the Confined Spaces?

Cowgirl Up by Ali Spooner Ride along with the MC2, for boot scootin', butt kickin', dirt eatin', rodeo adventures, with a love story thrown into the mix.

If I Were a Boy by Erin O'Reilly Will Katie and Helen be able to make a life together work or succumb to doubts and the pressures of family? This story will fill you with the thrill of passion and the tenderness of love.

The Chronicles of Ratha: Book 2 A Lion Among the Lambs by Erica Lawson Can Jordana believe in herself like her Noorthi sisters do? Only then can she fulfill her destiny as The Chosen One. Follow the colorful cast of characters in this action-packed adventure sequel as they traverse the galaxy. Of course, nothing ever goes smoothly when Jordana is involved.

Terminal Event by Ali Spooner Will the killer be caught or continue to evade authorities? Can Tally and Blair's budding romance survive the possibility? Read this intense murder mystery romance and find out.

Love Forever, Live Forever by Annette Mori Fate intervenes and puts Nicky directly back into the path of her first love, Sara, and the corresponding events send her into a tailspin. Now she must decide—who will be the person she ends up living with and loving forever?

The One by JM Dragon 2015 GCLS Winner for Romance, Intrigue, and Adventure. The One is a romance with everything, love, intrigue, misunderstandings with a happy conclusion—the only question—who gets the girl?

Reflected Passion by Erica Lawson Through a mirror, Françoise embraces life anew, while for Dale it is a powerful awakening, forcing her to discover not only her sensual nature, but the inner strength she possesses.

Flight by Renee Mackenzie Some lives will be lost and others changed forever when the sisters' lives intersect. Will they be consumed by the wreckage, or will they be able to pick themselves up and take flight?

E-Books, Print, Free e-books

Visit our website for more publications available online.

www.affinityebooks.com

Published by Affinity E-Book Press NZ LTD
Canterbury, New Zealand

Registered Company 2517228

www.ingramcontent.com/pod-product-compliance
Lightning Source LLC
Chambersburg PA
CBHW051231260626
47162CB00002B/381